MW01472410

The Land Between Two Rivers

R.A. Wilson

authorHOUSE

AuthorHouse™
1663 Liberty Drive
Bloomington, IN 47403
www.authorhouse.com
Phone: 1-800-839-8640

© 2012 R.A. Wilson. All rights reserved.

No part of this book may be reproduced, stored in a retrieval system, or transmitted by any means without the written permission of the author.

Published by AuthorHouse   1/4/13

ISBN: 978-1-4772-8379-0 (sc)
ISBN: 978-1-4772-8377-6 (dj)
ISBN: 978-1-4772-8378-3 (e)

Library of Congress Control Number: 2012919884

Any people depicted in stock imagery provided by Thinkstock are models, and such images are being used for illustrative purposes only.
Certain stock imagery © Thinkstock.

This book is printed on acid-free paper.

Because of the dynamic nature of the Internet, any web addresses or links contained in this book may have changed since publication and may no longer be valid. The views expressed in this work are solely those of the author and do not necessarily reflect the views of the publisher, and the publisher hereby disclaims any responsibility for them.

Dedication

To D. and the R-IV crew, who give me courage, and those who believe *I don't know* is an excuse, not an answer.

Introduction

The war in Iraq is not as simple as two armed forces fighting each other; it is not as simple as one guerrilla insurgent force fighting the Americans. It is complicated with many factors, most of which are unseen. In this book, I took the views of some of those roles that figure into the war in Iraq to create a story. There are several more roles out there that have not been seen or explored. This book was created from hundreds of true stories that have been fictionalized to make this story. I hope it creates an understanding of the complexity of the war that we are fighting.

This book is set in the third-largest city in Iraq, Mosul, which is located in the north and has approximately 2 million inhabitants. Mosul is a hub between the southern cities, such as Baghdad and Basra, to the cities of the north and the surrounding areas.

The story takes place during the months of August to December 2004, leading up to the first Iraqi elections in January 2005, and is about the ups and downs of security in Mosul as it got closer to the elections. The elections themselves are not depicted in this book. This story entangles the lives of many men who are in some aspect caught up in the war by circumstance and believe they are doing what is right. They are far removed from the political decisions that led them to this point and have no choice but to survive.

1. The Soldier

The parking lot was full of tears and quiet talk and was considerably busy for three o'clock in the morning. The rest of Fort Lewis was tranquil, with no people in sight, but here, at these buildings soldiers were entering and exiting buildings in what seemed like chaos to the untrained eye. Nearly five hundred soldiers and their families swarmed the battalion area in the crisp, moonlit night. The base, a remnant of the Vietnam era, still echoed the wars of the past, even in 2004. The fluorescent lights from inside the buildings backlit the poorly painted pale yellow bricks that made up the homes of the young men who were considered the protectors of the country. The soldiers were drawing the weapons they would cling to for the next year of their lives, for the protection of not only themselves but also of their fellow soldier, while conducting the final checks on all the things they would need in Iraq. This created a hive of excitement understood only by the people inhabiting the building.

In reality, the soldiers did not know what they really needed. Instead they packed everything, just to make sure they were not forgetting anything. "Do we really need this extreme-cold-weather suit? I thought we were going to a place that is really hot!" No one had an answer to the question. This was going to be Operation Iraqi Freedom Three, but there were still not many people in leadership who could provide the soldiers with the answers they needed to be ready for war. Instead they prepared for the worst and expected the ugliest.

In between waiting in lines and finding each other, soldiers were visiting with their families and introducing them to the people that they would eat with, sleep near, and trust for the unknown year that lay ahead. All the soldiers were well trained and by army standards "ready" for a war that had never faced this army before, but the soldiers still did not know what to expect. When they thought of this deployment, they thought *hot, desert, sand, danger, and very poor living conditions, perhaps just tents in the middle of nowhere.* As they stood there in their desert combat uniforms, watching the slowly solidifying mass of chaos, they knew that not all of these people would come back and that that some would come back missing a leg, an arm, an ear. They were still soldiers and still proud to serve their country, even though not all would say so aloud, too pompous to admit that they liked being an American soldier. Still they stood there, despite that the odds that faced them.

"Babe, you seen my family?" Sergeant Jeremiah Bernard asked his new fiancée, Mckayla.

"I haven't seen them yet. Oh, wait. I think I see your mom."

Jeremiah looked over into the parking lot and saw his mom with her arms crossed, peering into the pandemonium. She was wrapped up in a jacket that was much too thin for the frosty air. Jeremiah set down his protective vest and helmet and wandered over to retrieve her. As he approached her, he could see the fear in her eyes. Although Jeremiah stood six inches taller than his mother at five feet ten inches tall and had the build of a triathlete, his mother still did not believe her little boy could take care of himself. His mother was always supportive, but she was still very protective of him. In high school, when Jeremiah went out for the wrestling team, she went to every match. Even though she was there, she almost never watched him, as she cringed at his every movement on the mat, sure he had broken something.

"Hey, Mom, we're over here," Jeremiah called across the parking lot. "Where is Dad?"

"You know your father; he refused to come, but you know he sends his love," Jeremiah's mother replied in her constantly reassuring voice.

Jeremiah's father was very liberal and did not hide it. He had always been against the war in Iraq; he was convinced it was a war about oil, and the reasons for invasion were all propaganda to support Bush's ridiculous war. Because of this, Jeremiah was not surprised his father did not show up. When his father found out Jeremiah had joined the army, he drove down to Jeremiah's college dorm fuming and nearly got into a fistfight with him.

"I have to finish getting my stuff together; let's go over here by Mckayla," Jeremiah asked his mother when he turned back toward his bags. As they weaved back over to the bags, Jeremiah wondered if his father went through the same thing when he went to Vietnam. His father was drafted in the later years of the Vietnam War and thought the army was a joke. He didn't want his son to experience the scarring section of his life, which he had pushed out of his memory, and therefore never discussed with his family.

A voice hollered from behind Jeremiah, his mother, and Mckayla,

"Sergeant Bernard." Jeremiah turned around to find Private First Class Wynn, who was one of two new soldiers among his four.

"Got all your stuff over here?" Jeremiah asked him.

"Yes, Sergeant."

"Good, now go find your twin, and I will check over it," Jeremiah replied. He had just earned the rank of sergeant two months ago and had four soldiers under him, the youngest and newest being Specialist Duncan and Wynn. The pair had entered the military on the buddy program, meaning they trained together and went to the same duty station. They were college buds when they decided to join, after Duncan had graduated and Wynn flunked out of his classes; they couldn't find jobs. Duncan had lost his uncle on September 11; he was at the Pentagon at the time of the attacks. They thought the army would be the next big step for them.

Duncan and Wynn approached, dragging their large duffel bags behind them. "How you guys doing? Are you ready to go?" Jeremiah asked them as he checked to make sure they had their weapon and other important equipment like their protective mask.

"Good, our families already left last night. My mom said it would be too sad to watch us pack up and get on the buses," Duncan replied.

"Yeah, she said that she would just imagine we were still at Fort Lewis and not think that we are in Iraq," Wynn added.

"This is my mom, Pam," Jeremiah said.

"Nice to meet you, ma'am," Wynn said,

"Take care of my boy, please; I know you boys will always be together."

"No problem," When said.

"Mom, please," Jeremiah said, rolling his eyes. "You two go over by Greene and Crow," he said, indicating Jeremiah's other soldiers who had been in the unit almost as long as he had.

Just then, the First Sergeant called out, "All the duffel bags need to be stacked by the trucks, and formation will be in fifteen minutes. Pass it around."

"Does that mean we have to say good-bye now?" Mckayla asked in a panicky voice. She had not said much; she did not want to believe that the man of her dreams was going to a foreign country for a year.

"Don't worry, baby. They will give us time for that," Jeremiah said.

The bags were stacked, and everyone lined up in the company formation, with their families standing to the sides, looking on. The squad leaders made sure all the soldiers were present and none had run off. The chaplain then stepped to the front and led them all in a prayer.

Sniffles echoed through the crowd as he asked for the protection of the fathers, sons, men who stood in uniform in front of them.

"Alright, now that we know that you all showed up, I'm going to give you twenty minutes to say your last goodbyes, and then we are getting on the buses," First Sergeant announced at last and let them get out of formation. When Jeremiah left formation, he noticed that Mckayla was sobbing, and he immediately put his arms around her. Meanwhile, Jeremiah's mother was trying to be strong, but he could see the anxiety in her movements and the way she held her arms around herself. He turned to his mother and held her, and she broke down crying. Jeremiah pulled both of his girls into his arms.

"Baby, take care of my mom. I'll be fine. I will call both of you as soon as I get a chance."

They stood there in silence, unresponsive to his attempts at comforting words. There was a stir in the crowd, as people began to pick up their gear and line up near the buses. He kissed his mother and his fiancée and disappeared into the organized chaos he called the 2/38 Infantry Battalion.

2. The Iraqi Policeman

Ali shoved his identification into the depths of the bag that held his uniform, pistol, and the other things he would need for the next few days. He tried to make sure everything was hidden to the outside eye, in case someone looked in the bag. Ali was proud to be a policeman, but he was not stupid; he knew if people found out, word would get around to the terrorists. This would put not only his life in danger but also the lives of his family. He zipped up his bag and looked around the room to make sure he was not missing anything. Ali found his wife, Fatima, in the kitchen, making his breakfast. He looked at her, amazed at her beauty, as her black hair cascaded down to the shoulders of her thin frame. As he watched her work, he heard a knock at the door. He couldn't peel his eyes away from her; two months ago, he had married her, his uncle's daughter, and he had been extremely happy since. He felt his life was coming together. Until his marriage, he had been living with his older brother, in the house that used to belong to his father, but his brother moved out just before the wedding. He had the fairly small house just for him and his wife.

Ali went to the door to find his best friend, Yassin. "Welcome, brother. How is your family?" Ali asked.

"They are well, and how is your wife?"

"She is well; would you like to come in for some tea? I believe we have enough time."

"Of course."

Ali and Yassin had joined the police force at the same time, eight months ago. They decided they wanted to help their country and fight terrorism. Alone they were afraid to join, but once they discovered each other's feelings, they agreed that they could do anything together.

The two sat down in the reception room, and Fatima brought them tea. "I think it is getting much worse out there," Yassin said with a worried look.

"I agree, there seems to be more attacks on a daily basis. I heard that Yarmook Police Station gets hit nearly every day with anything they can hit them with."

"That is not the worst. The Iraqi National Guard that is working on the west side has lost almost twenty men in the last month. The Americans have even asked commanders to increase security at each government building."

"People say that Mosul is becoming the next Fallujah, the way things are going," Ali said. "I'm worried that there will be so many terrorists that the Americans have to come through and bomb, like they did in Fallujah. If that happens, many innocent people will die."

"We are police; we will have warning, and we can get our families out of the city. Besides, I don't think the terrorists will ever be able to take over Mosul. It is too big, and there are many forces here."

"You're right; I always imagine the worst of things. We must get going."

The pair finished their tea, grabbed their bags, and left the house. They walked down the small road near their house and found their way to the nearest main road, where they found a taxi to get to police headquarters in downtown Mosul. They had the taxi drop them off near the police station, but not right at it, not wanting anyone to know they were policemen. They wound their way through the market and up to the police station. Right after they arrived, they changed into their uniforms.

The supervisor then told them they would be conducting a checkpoint just outside the city, on the road to Tall Afar, for the next three days. Tall Afar was a larger city approximately one hour west of Mosul. The next three days seemed to drag on as they worked uneventfully, tediously, and repetitively in the blistering heat for twelve hours and then went back to headquarters each night to pull short shifts of guard duty. The situation in Mosul did not permit the policemen to go home. If they were to head home each day, they would be easy targets for terrorists. So instead they worked for three days straight and then went home for two days. This was the kind of work they had been doing since they joined, and after these three days, they were tired and ready to go home. Yassin and Ali changed into their civilian clothes and headed out the door.

"It's been a long few days. I am so glad to go home and see my family," Yassin told Ali as the two of them exited the gate of the police station. They were still ever so cautious of their surroundings as they left.

"Well, thanks are to Allah that nothing has happened these past few days and we are all well."

"We all give thanks to Allah for this," Yassin said with a smile.

"Even though sometimes I wish the terrorists would come out, so we can rid the city of them. If you think about it, we did not find anything at the checkpoint, but that does not mean the weapons or the terrorists are still not coming into the city. It just means that they found a different way into the city," Ali said in dismay.

"You cannot stop everything, Ali. We changed our location several times, and we were bound to find something. We can look on the bright side: maybe they did not come to Mosul during these days. Maybe the terrorists don't have any more weapons to bring into the city."

"Maybe they are afraid of us?"

Ali and Yassin laughed as they wandered through the market to the taxi stand. They passed countless shops in the downtown market that had everything imaginable, from food to blankets to electronics and hardware. The market was always busy and packed with countless people from in and out of the city. There were hundreds of cars packed around the taxi stand, with people begging for passengers. Ali and Yassin hopped into a car that could make it out the market without any problems.

"Look, we have time to make it mosque before the noon prayer," Ali said. "Would you care to join me?"

"The Al Mahmoud Adeen Mosque?"

"Of course. I love hearing from Mullah Abdullah about his thoughts on the current situation," Ali said.

"He never really talks about the current situation. I guess he is just trying to play it safe. You know, stay off both the good and bad people's radars. Talk bad, the Americans arrest you; but if you talk good, the terrorists threaten you. It is just a lose-lose situation for these guys."

"The shame really lies in the fact that they are leaders and should be able to say what they want," Ali chimed in.

"Actually give us guidance in times of need," said Yassin with disgust. The two sat in silence for the rest of the ride to the edge of their neighborhood. They walked down to the mosque and headed in for prayer.

Mullah Abdullah chose to speak of theft and how it is wrong. Just as Yassin predicted: no real advice.

"In the neighborhood, there have been a few cars stolen. They were cars belonging to members of the community that were poor and very much need the cars, and now they have nothing. One of these cars belonged to my cousin." Mullah Abdullah continued to speak about the subject and made sure to add in verses from the Koran about how stealing is wrong. He also asked people to donate to the families who lost cars.

After his speech concluded, Mullah Abdullah wished everyone well before they headed for the door. After the prayer, Ali stood up and started for the door. He talked to his neighbors that he saw in the crowd. "Abu Khadija, how is your family?" Ali asked an old man who lived next door to him.

"Good, thanks be to Allah, and how is yours?" Abu Khadija echoed the greeting as they both found their shoes.

"They are good, thanks be to Allah."

As the two approached the door, the crowd started to jam up, and no one was moving. Ali's attention began to focus ahead as he tried to see over the heads in front of him. Ali was short and was unable to see much of anything. He could vaguely hear Abu Khadija talk to him as he tried to see what was going on. Ali could hear arguing in the street. He walked out the door of the mosque, and it became clear what was going on. There were two men wearing ski masks, passing out some sort of flyer by the door. As Ali made his way down the sidewalk, one of the men shoved a flyer into Ali's chest. Ali grabbed it and started to read the leaflet that was causing such commotion. He slowed his walk as he stepped into the street and then looked up to see where he was going and saw Yassin. Yassin's face was gray with fear, and he looked nauseated. Yassin usually had pale skin, highlighted by his light reddish-brown hair and dark eyes, but the gray was definitely a change. Yassin and Ali were nearly twins, except Ali's hair was curly. The two stood eye to eye at about five feet six inches tall, and Ali gazed into Yassin's eyes, wondering what had happened. Ali looked back down at the handout; he had not read enough to know what was going on.

"Are you okay?" Ali asked as his voice trailed off as the words of the flyer floated into his brain.

> *In the name of Allah the most merciful and compassionate*
>
> *We are the assassination battalion and we warn those traitors that work with the infidel forces, the Police, the Iraqi National guards, and most of all the people that work with the Americans on their bases as interpreters or contractors, we warn you, you must quit your job and ask forgiveness. You are traitors. A resignation letter must be posted on a mosque admitting to your sins as a traitor. You must say that you quit your job, and you will not go back to working with*

the traitors. You must do this if you wish not to die. If a letter is not received then we will, in the name of Allah, rid the country of traitors by ridding the traitors of their heads.

In the name of Allah the most merciful and compassionate

The Assassination Battalion

"Do you think they know?" Yassin whispered in Ali's ear as he put his arm around him and directed him to walk away from the mosque toward their homes.

"There is no way that they know. We are not high-ranking, and they will not waste their time on us."

"I think they know, and that is why they came to our mosque."

"Don't be silly; they go to all the mosques. This week it was just our mosque's turn. When Mullah Abdullah finds out this happened, he will not ever let it happen again."

"You're probably right; we are low-ranking."

"Besides, how do they expect us to quit? We have to support our family. They don't know."

The two went their separate ways and headed for home, wondering what their fate was.

3. The Cousins

"It's time to go; it's nearly seven thirty," said Mustafa to his younger brother, Juma, as he stepped outside to see his father surrounded by the older men in the village. Mustafa and Juma's father, Ahmed Agoub, was an old man and well-respected as the *muktar*—the mayor—of Aski Mosul village. The sun started its ascent into the blue sky and gave a nice, cool glow in the morning of what was going to be a fairly warm day, as the men of the village sat around drinking tea and discussing the good farming season they were having.

"Abu Mustafa," the name others used to refer to Mustafa's father, "your son has grown to be a good man and must make you proud. When are you to arrange his marriage?" one of the villagers asked as Mustafa walked out the door. Everyone chuckled, knowing he was already engaged to Abu Mustafa's niece, Marwa. Mustafa stepped up to the men; he seemed to fit in, considering his mature age.

Mustafa was a stout man, standing around five feet seven inches tall, with a heavier build; his eyes were soft brown, accented by his light-brown hair. He was the oldest offspring in his family and took care of the family because of his father's advancing age.

"Good morning. How is everyone?" Mustafa said with a smile as he thumbed his brown prayer beads.

"Thanks are to Allah, we are all well," said one of the older men in the group..

Juma rushed out the door saying, "Good morning." He rushed by and headed for the red—more accurately, *rusted*—pickup truck. Mustafa followed closely behind him, annoyed by his brother's rude behavior. They got in the truck and drove down the dusty main road that ran through their village to the house of their cousin, Mahmoud, Marwa's brother.

Mahmoud was waiting in front of his house, as always, eager to start

The Land Between Two Rivers

work every morning, because he had not only his wife and three young children to care for but also three sisters and a brother to provide for. One night, when Mahmoud was fourteen years old, Iraqi Intelligence surrounded the house and broke down the door. They rushed in with weapons and took his father without explanation. There was nowhere for his family to turn. No one could answer any questions about why he was arrested, or if they knew the reason, they did not give it. One month later, they returned to the house with a death certificate. On the grim notice, it stated that his father had incited revolution. Mahmoud's father's only crime was never joining the Ba'ath Party.

Ever since then, Mahmoud had been in charge of his family. He dropped out of school and did everything that he could to provide them with food and money.

Mahmoud stood with a smile as the dust kicked up into his pitch-black eyes, which seemed to glisten with knowledge only held by men who have seen a thousand lifetimes. To look at his bald patch, highlighted by his graying hair, and how tired he always looked, one would think he was reaching his fifties, when he was actually only twenty-four years old. The pickup parked in front of him, and Mahmoud climbed into the back and waved good-bye to his children.

They drove to the middle of Aski Mosul, a growing town of nearly three hundred houses, to the local market, to purchase the vegetables that they would take to Mosul to sell. Forty kilometers northwest of the city of Mosul, Aski Mosul sat to the west of the Tigris River, offset with small farms cresting the hill next to the river and protected with the greenery of a hundred groves of olives and other trees to the north. To the south, it seemed unusually drab, with its few trees and sprawling swell of unplanted hills of weeds and gravel pits. As they made their way into the market, it was hard for them to get things done, as so many people would stop and talk to Mustafa. Juma and Mahmoud resorted to having Mustafa talk to the people as the two of them loaded the truck.

"He is more like your father every day," Mahmoud said as they loaded the goods onto the truck.

"I don't know where he gets it. People just seem to love him. I imagine he acts as my father did at a younger age. I only wish that I was blessed with Mustafa's charisma."

"You are your own person, Juma."

"I suppose."

"On a more important note, are there any women that you have looked at for marriage?"

Juma blushed at the question; he did not discuss such topics out loud. "Is there someone that you have in mind?"

"I was just asking about your prospects. I see the way women look at you, like they are in love."

"I am a good man, and I would never discuss such a thing," Juma said embarrassed of the topic.

Mahmoud and Juma began to laugh, and Mahmoud pushed Juma. "Go and get your big brother, and let us get to work."

They loaded back into the truck and headed into to Mosul, to the vegetable market, which was nestled on the far west side of the city. They arrived around nine in the morning, set up their stand, and began to sell their produce.

As the morning continued, the temperature rose, and one could not help but notice the similarities between Juma and Mustafa. Juma imitated Mustafa in his actions, to the point that they were both wearing gray *dishdashas*. Juma looked up to Mustafa ever since he could remember but could never quite match him. Juma was shorter and weighed more, but their round faces were identical, surrounded with the same light-brown hair. When they were young, Mustafa was the captain on the soccer team, and Juma wanted to be a captain also, but he just was not in shape to be a soccer player. It didn't matter how hard he tried. Juma tried to do everything that Mustafa did and always wanted to be around him. In turn, Mustafa took Juma under his wing and tried to teach him what he knew. They seemed more like twins than brothers a few years apart.

As the noon prayer sounded over the speakers, a slow-moving American patrol rolled into the market.

"Look, the Americans are coming," Mustafa said observantly to no one in particular.

"Look, Mahmoud, here comes the Americans," Juma repeated, as if it needed repeating. The big machines the Americans were driving were taking up most of the road, and people had to scramble to get out of their way. Just as the last of the four American vehicles rolled around the corner onto the busy street, a large explosion rattled the market. Glass shattered and sent a bustling avenue into chaos. The road was jammed full of people who, two seconds before, had found it hard to move, and within a matter of seconds, the crowd dissipated into stores and buildings that lined the boulevard, leaving countless wounded scattered about the street, begging for help as gunfire cracked through the air, accented with smaller explosions.

Juma and Mahmoud sought refuge in a nearby cigarette shop and huddled with strangers on the floor near the back of the shop. The firecrackers and the undecipherable yelling thundered the streets, and dust filled the air.

As Juma felt the sweat pour down the front of his face, he searched the store for his brother. "Mustafa ... where's Mustafa?" Juma asked Mahmoud in a desperate search for an answer. The two made eye contact and rose to their feet, peering in the direction of the war zone that lay only a few feet from them.

Juma felt a spike of pain shoot up his spine. In the confusion and the chaos, and in the interest of self-preservation, Juma had run for the cigarette shop and had not checked for his brother.

"Oh, Allah, please say he is in a store," Mahmoud said to Juma, who was in shock and did not register the words that came out of Mahmoud's mouth.

Juma crept up to the store window with the sounds of Mahmoud's prayers echoing in his head and peered out of the corner of the window, desperately searching the smoky street for his brother. He saw a ball of gray with a reaching hand on the ground in the street, and without regard and in fear that the ball was his brother, Juma staggered toward the door. Mahmoud frantically tried to hold Juma back.

"Don't go, Juma! Stay, we must wait until it is safe," Mahmoud begged of the man he considered his brother. "Please stop; you must wait until the fire has stopped." Juma slowly pulled away from Mahmoud's clutches.

As the door opened, a rumbling roared into Juma's ears, but nothing made sense.

"This is a dream," Juma said out loud. "Wake up, wake up." As he approached the ball, he could hear someone yelling at him. "It's him," Juma whispered to himself as he collapsed to his knees next to the mess that was once his brother.

"Come back, take cover!" Mahmoud yelled from the store.

Juma looked up toward the Americans, who had their weapons pointed in his direction. Then, as swiftly as it began, the world seemed to become silent. Juma picked up his brother and cradled him in his arms.

"Is that Mustafa?" Mahmoud yelled as he ran to Juma's side. "No, no, it can't be."

In the sea of deep-red blood that surrounded Mustafa, it was unclear what had happened to him. "I think he was shot," Mahmoud said as they begged for help from the people who were trickling out of the stores. Juma reached down and touched the blood that had seeped deep into the cloth wrapping Mustafa's soft body. He looked up in the direction of the American soldiers and the large weapons that were pointed their way, as they drove away in a hurry.

"Juma," a whimper softly exited Mustafa's lips. Juma snapped back to his dying brother. Then there was silence as a pool of red soaked into the dirt that lay around them.

4. The Media

Mohammad clicked on his TV to see the latest reports, and on came the blaring noise of the American news; undoubtedly left on by his father, who was using the news to brush up on his English. "The war rages on in Iraq. Nearly one thousand soldiers have lost their lives since the 'the end' of the war in Iraq. Today in Mosul, a city in northern Iraq, where experts are saying insurgents are creating a new stronghold, a suicide bomber tore through a busy downtown market. The target was an American convoy. The attack occurred when a vehicle suicide bomber ran into an American Stryker during the morning rush in the crowded Mosul vegetable market. After the attack, there was a gunfight lasting nearly ten minutes, and the results were dire. The combination of the bombing and the firefight caused the death of one American soldier and the wounding of several other soldiers. In addition roughly fifteen Iraqi citizens were killed and more than thirty wounded. We go now to Rob Jansen, our associate in Baghdad, to see what he has to say about this situation."

"Thanks, Susan. I have spoken with several people, and they say the initial blast did not cause the greatest number of casualties, but rather the firefight after the blast is when most of the injuries occurred. I have heard from witnesses who say there were no insurgents even seen in the area. Several witnesses say the American soldiers were just firing in every direction. Essentially, it is just trigger-happy soldiers harming these innocent ..." He clicked the TV off.

Mohammad Sultan Mohammad, a student at the technical institute in Alapo, Syria, was sick of hearing about Iraq and could not stand to listen to the news any longer. Everywhere he went, everyone was concentrating on it. Even down at the mosque, the Friday speaker often talked about Iraq and the Americans being in Iraq.

Mohammad stood up and looked around his room; he couldn't

stand being indoors any longer. He wanted to get out and see his friends. He walked down the stairs, through his house, and toward the front door. As he got near the door, his father, Sultan Mohammad, walked in the door. Mohammad's father looked nothing like Mohammad, who was tall and slender. His skin was light, soft, and delicate. His father, on the other hand, was of medium height but was getting increasingly overweight with age. His skin was dark, and his hair was gray. Their looks never hinted at their being related. They didn't even have the same ambitions. Mohammad's father was an up-and-coming Ba'ath Party member and was supposed to reach the rank of division member any day now. Mohammad, on the other hand, just wanted a simple life, maybe opening an electronics shop someday.

"Did you hear what happened in Mosul?" Sultan asked his son.

"I heard, Father," Mohammad said with conviction as he turned away from his father and proceeded to walk. Under his breath, he muttered, "I'm so sick of these Americans thinking they can do whatever they want." He proceeded out the gate, letting it slam behind him as he walked out into his neighborhood. His neighborhood was different from others; each house had its own personality. In most neighborhoods, the houses had the same concrete walls, but in Mohammad's neighborhood, each wall had a fresh coat of paint. Each house had a nice, new car—most of the time a Mercedes—parked out front. The neighborhood was also very clean.

Mohammad proceeded to the edge of his neighborhood along the main road to get to the neighborhood café. It was a small café that only had a few chairs inside; most of the seating was out on the sidewalk. The usual patrons were cooling off inside the shop. The old, retired men of the neighborhood smoked cigarettes and discussed their sons and their occupations out on the sidewalk. There was also a small number of high school students.

Mohammad's friend Arab was sitting inside, with his hand propping up his head, his elbow on the table, watching TV while sipping some tea. Without looking away from the TV, he greeted Mohammad as he stumbled into the shop. "Hello, friend, what brings you here? What have you been doing?"

"Well, I was taking a break from my homework, and I turned on the news." Mohammad trailed off; Arab had heard the story many times before.

"Let me guess," Arab said, anticipating the comments that Mohammad often liked to throw in, "you are sick."

Mohammad cut him off. "I am sick of this. Did you hear about what is going on now?"

"I can only be so concerned with another country's problems." Arab dropped his hand and turned his head toward Mohammad, who was finally sitting down. "You need to understand that these things happen every day around the world. You should be aware of these things, but there is nothing you can do."

"Arab, how can you be okay with these things? Look what happened at Abu Ghraib. Americans have no sense of human beings and certainly no respect for Islamic culture."

"I'm tired of this subject, Mohammad."

"Allah is all-knowing, and he will make a plan for the infidels."

"Allah willing," Arab said, knowing that was a signal that Mohammad might drop the subject. "Relax, Mohammad, have some tea, and let us talk about something else."

"You are right; I need to get my mind off of this."

"Well, I hear that your father will soon be promoted."

"Yes."

The two continued to discuss Mohammad's father as they watched the sunset and observed the hustle and bustle of people walking by the café.

5. The Raid

Jeremiah sat in the dusty trailer called the phone center, which was covered in trash and graffiti. Phones lined both walls, eight on each side, and every phone was occupied; the room echoed with voices, making the noise deafening. It did not help that the connection was horrible and delayed, and Jeremiah had to strain to hear what was being said on the other end of the line. Somewhere in the room, a soldier was crying; another person was obviously having a hard time hearing, as he repeated over and over, "*What?* Say that again." The person next to Jeremiah started to yell about money and credit cards. Jeremiah knew that he should get off the phone anyway.

"I'm fine, Mom." Jeremiah said into the phone for the fifth time, trying to signal to her that he needed to get off the phone. "Listen, Mom, it's not bad over here. Everything that you thought is not true. I'm not in a tent, I'm in a trailer. I'm not on a cot, but on a bed with a mattress. The food is good too, Mom."

"I know, but I just worry," his mom said faintly. "Your father sends his love."

"I know, Mom, I understand. I have to get going, okay?" Jeremiah said to his mother, trying not to seem too anxious and upset his mom.

Jeremiah hung up the phone and picked up his M-4, brushed off the dust, and slung it over his shoulder. He stepped out of the trailer and past the line of people waiting to call their families. At the end of the line, he stopped to look around. As he pulled out a cigarette, he looked off to the west, away from the city. As the midnight-blue monster of night engulfed the sunfire orange that danced on the horizon, Jeremiah was overcome with an urge to chase the sunset. As the silhouettes of buildings disappeared into the darkness, Jeremiah hesitated before turning away from the west, in awe of the falling daylight. When he finally turned, a gust of wind dusted his face with razor-sharp sand. Jeremiah was reminded of the nightmares that kept him awake at night when he was a child. He had not been this frightened in a long time. He turned back to the fading yellow and wanted to run, wanted to chase the sunset, to keep the light where he was. In the night, the people were kept in their houses by curfew, making the roads safer, but Jeremiah couldn't help but be afraid, but he didn't want to show it. He knew that in time, the pitch-black calm of the night would soon be his friend. For now, he would have to be brave; he had soldiers who looked up to him.

Jeremiah turned again to head off to the trailers, the place he would soon call his home but other people would call shipping containers. He paused and puffed on his cigarette before he continued on his walk. So far, Iraq was not what he expected. Mosul was surprisingly green; sure, it was warm in the daytime, but as night fell, it became cool. The people he replaced warned him of the rain and the huge puddles that were unavoidable all over the base. The nearby Tigris River created an unexpected humidity.

Before stopping at his trailer, Jeremiah paused to check on the twins, Duncan and Wynn. He found them sitting on the bricks outside their room, smoking cigarettes, throwing rocks, and joking with a group of guys from the platoon. "Formation is in one hour; make sure you have all your gear. This is our first solo mission, without the guys we replaced, and I don't want to fuck it up!"

"Roger, Sergeant," echoed through the group. This satisfied Jeremiah for the moment, but he knew he would have to check on them again before formation. Jeremiah then continued to his room.

Jeremiah climbed the bricks in front of his trailer and entered the small area generously called a room. The rooms were more than expected, yet still small. Jeremiah shared his room with another sergeant from his squad. They each had their own small bed, which were just as wide as the men themselves, as well as a small wall locker for their gear. He couldn't complain, though; it was better than cots in tents. At least they had electricity, air conditioning, and a heater. Jeremiah had purchased a TV and DVD player from a soldier who was leaving at the time he got there. He put his favorite CD in the player, Johnny Cash, and listened to it as he checked and rechecked his gear. Jeremiah was surprised at how nervous he was, and he stopped to say a prayer. He sat down on his bed and bowed his head, still holding his helmet.

"God, I know we don't talk much, but I have a good feeling that we will become good friends over this year ..." Jeremiah continued on, asking for strength and clarity until he had calmed down.

The mission briefing was not at all like the ones they had received before, with the unit they replaced; there was not as many details. Before they headed to the Stryker, Jeremiah pulled his team aside, to make sure they were good to go. "Okay, guys, keep your eyes open. It is supposed to be an insurgent meeting, so things can get really ugly. Don't think, just react. We have been through this training a million times over, and we know what to do. Don't be stupid. You got it?"

"Yes, Sergeant," they said after taking a glance at each other.

"Let's mount up," Jeremiah said while taking one last look at their gear and then heading over to the Stryker. As they waited inside the Stryker, time seemed to slow down; it felt like eternity before they rolled out. They were headed out to a village about fifteen minutes outside of Mosul, one they had not been to before. The unfamiliar road was nerve-wracking at best, and potentially deadly at worst. As the Stryker drove down the dirt road that twisted its way through the fields, a small cluster of houses appeared.

As they neared the village, Jeremiah's heart began to race. *This is it,* he thought to himself. He had been on the raids in the last two weeks, but this was the first time there wouldn't be experienced soldiers with them. "I'm ready for this," he said to himself to build confidence. He knew he had enough training, and this wouldn't be difficult. As the adrenaline kicked in, he was excited to finally do what he had trained to do.

The Stryker came to a stop, and almost instantly, the ramp dropped; Jeremiah and his soldiers poured out the back and around toward the gate. There were already three soldiers by the gate, setting up a blast to bring down the locked gates. Jeremiah took cover by leaning up against the wall, making sure to pull security, by keeping an eye on their surroundings. He scanned the area, looking for anything suspicious. The area seemed serene; it was quiet except for the hum of the Stryker's engines. The sky was clear, and the moon illuminated the houses.

The blast made Jeremiah jolt immediately into action. Soldiers ran toward the gate, trusting the gunners mounted on the Strykers to pull all the security they would need. The front door was only a few steps from the gates, and by the time Jeremiah got there, the first team had already made it inside. Jeremiah's team was second and close on their heels. Upon entering the house, there was a hallway and not much to see. The first door was kicked open, and inside was a large group of men.

Everything seemed to come to a halt; hesitation was not an option. "Get down, get down," Jeremiah began to yell, motioning with his M-4. It was not their language, but it seemed they understood what he wanted. They began to lie on the ground. He did not see any weapons. As he searched the men, he noticed sweat dripping from his brow and that his heart was pounding. There was no time to worry about that.

He started to flexi-cuff each of the men and put them on their knees next to the wall. After searching two men, Jeremiah noticed something wrapped in white cloth. He paused and looked at the cloth more closely, and as he knelt down, he realized that he was near a dead body. *What the hell is going on?* Jeremiah thought to himself. He continued to help handcuff the rest of the individuals in the room.

As things calmed down, the Platoon Leader started questioning everyone. The owner of the house turned out to be the mayor of the village. The body was of his son, who was killed in the suicide bombing in the vegetable market in Mosul.

"This is not an insurgent meeting," Jeremiah commented to Duncan as they pulled security on the men, "just a funeral. Everyone here is relative of the dead guy."

After questioning everyone and making a thorough search of the house, Jeremiah and the others mounted up and headed back to base.

6. The Recruitment

Juma couldn't sleep all night; in fact, he hadn't been able to close his eyes since Mustafa's death. The last time Juma tried to sleep, he was jolted by a terrible dream.

During the dream, he saw a blinding light, accompanied by an undeterminable noise that deafened him. Juma started to feel dizzy and his stomach turned over. Off in the distance, a whispered cry tickled his ears: *"Juma."* The light faded as the soft cries from his brother's breath grew louder and left an eerie feeling in Juma's heart. Juma found himself spinning, looking to find his brother, but saw only an empty road. As things moved in unbearably slow motion, Juma looked down and found a dark, brownish-red blood on his hands. He then started to cry; confusion set in, and fear overcame his body as the nausea built a lump in his throat. Juma then looked down to find himself standing on the edge of a puddle of blood that came from the street. A clattered noise deafened him. He knelt down on the edge of the puddle and followed the origins of the blood and the growing cries. In the middle of the seemingly empty road, Juma found Mustafa, and the racket ceased.

"Juma, help me," Mustafa called.

Juma started crying profusely and crawled toward his brother, feeling like a helpless sheep. As he reached the body of his brother, lifelong companion, and best friend, Juma placed his hand on the chest, holding his brother's hand. Mustafa then opened his eyes and looked directly at Juma but said nothing.

The world started its agonizing whirling, and when it stopped, all Juma saw was the rifle of an American soldier sitting on top of an armored vehicle, pointed directly at him. The soldier pulled the trigger, and bullets moved in slow motion in a straight line for Juma. He tried to lie down but realized he was not himself but Mustafa. Up ahead, he looked at what seemed to be himself running into a building. Juma felt an explosion hit his back, and he jolted awake. He sat up, and a cold sweat ran down his brow; his entire body was in pain. Tears poured down his face. "Why did this happen, Allah?" Juma called out. "What in your plans made you choose my brother? Mustafa was my brother, my best friend. How will my mother, my father go on without my brother? How will they survive? How will I survive?"

Juma calmed down and looked down at the ground. He was exhausted. He whispered to the rug, "My mother has not stopped weeping; my father is near heart attack." Juma's cries grew quieter still as he sat talking to himself. "My brother was supposed to be the next *muktar*, not me. How can I fill those shoes? They belong to Mustafa."

Juma could not close his eyes from that point on. The dream was too real, too painful, too much. He looked at his watch; it was almost time for morning prayer. He gave up on the tossing and turning, got up, and went to prepare for prayer. He slowly washed himself. While washing, he prepared himself for the long day ahead; it was time to put his brother into the ground.

The last two days had been excruciating for him, waiting to get his brother from the city morgue. Then, after finally getting him, the Americans had burst into this house, disrespecting his father and his family.

As Juma washed his face, his father joined him in cleansing, not saying a word to Juma. The two then prayed together, Juma to the right of his father. After the prayer, Juma caught a glimpse of the pain on his father's face, causing him to weep.

Juma went to his room and found a *dishdasha* that his mother had washed and laid out for him to wear on this day. He slowly dressed, dreading that he would soon have to face his brother's burial and the people who would attend the funeral. After dressing, he poured a cup of tea that his father had made, and he slowly began to drink. Juma found himself in a daze. When he heard a knock on the door, he was confused, and it took him awhile to realize what the sound was.

At the door was Mahmoud; they held a long embrace. Juma pulled back and saw the wounds that were deeply cut into his eyes. As long as Juma could remember, Mahmoud and Mustafa had been attached at the hip, brothers. Mahmoud was accompanied by his wife, who brought breakfast for the family. Juma was not hungry and could not eat.

As the time for mid-morning prayer drew near, Juma gathered his father, and they walked with Mahmoud down to the mosque. The call to prayer seemed to echo in Juma's heart, and it became difficult for Juma to stand with the weight of a thousand sheep on his chest. As the prayer started, Juma felt weak, and when he knelt down, his heart broke for his brother. As his forehead touched the ground, it felt like the earth grabbed his head and would not let go. A river began to pour from his eyes. His back hunched, and it became difficult to move. He found the strength to stand, but it took all of his energy. His movements were slow and deliberate, as he concentrated on every movement and every word of prayer. As Mahmoud heard the sobs coming from Juma, his heart shattered. As the prayer ended, Juma's knees collapsed.

Abu Mustafa looked at his son in a sad state and immediately turned and walked away.

Mahmoud grabbed his hand and whispered, "Allah is with us," in Juma's ear. He went to help him stand. "Come with me, brother; we must finish this."

They carried the body, softly placed in a cradle, toward the cemetery. As the walk continued, Juma started to gain his strength. He softly whispered sections of the Koran, and he could feel strength growing inside of him.

As he neared the cemetery, Juma noticed the sheer amount of people who had come to attend the funeral. The sheik of the tribe, Faris Abdul-Kareem Al Hadiddi, was there. *Muktars* from all the surrounding villages and distant relatives from Mosul.

After Mustafa's burial, Juma started to walk home. He was stopped by Jasim Hussein Ahmed, a branch member in the Ba'ath party during the old regime. He was recently released from Camp Bucca Jail, known as Um Qasr. He had been held by the Americans after the collapse of the regime. Jasim's house was in a nearby village.

Juma was not fond of Jasim, but he did not feel like being curt. As Jasim placed his arm around Juma, he said, "What happened to your brother is terrible. You know who is at fault," Jasim stated as a matter of fact. "The infidels—you may call them Americans—but Muslims would not let this happen. If the infidels were not here, then your brother would still be alive."

Juma stopped dead in his tracks, and Jasim circled in front of him, crouching down to look him right in the eyes. "As if your brother's death was not enough, they had the nerve to come to your house and disrespect your whole family."

Juma stared passed Jasim into the blazing sunlight, contemplating what Jasim had said but felt very confused. Jasim turned and walked away from Juma as Mahmoud approached.

"What did that pimp want?" Mahmoud said. Mahmoud believed that Jasim was the cause of his own father's death many years ago. He could not prove it, but he felt it whenever he saw the man.

"He just gave condolences," Juma said, not really acknowledging Mahmoud's presence. He was still mulling over what Jasim had said.

"Let's go, brother; there are guests to attend to," Mahmoud said, pulling on Juma's shoulder.

By the end of the day, Juma was drained. Countless relatives, some of whom he didn't know existed, tribesmen, and friends had all come by to show their respect. The whole time, he chewed over Jasim's words a million times. As the day finished, he felt surer of what he should do.

"Father, I must clear my head," Juma said as he grabbed the keys to the pickup and headed out the door. He walked outside and stopped to stare at the setting sun. He pulled the keys to the truck out of his pocket and turned to get into the pickup. Juma stopped and looked at the keys in his hand and spun them around a few times. He looked back up at the setting sun and pulled open the door to the truck. The bloodstained seat stared back at him. They used the truck to transport his brother to the hospital, hoping he still had a chance. Anger overcame him, and he quickly sat down and started the engine. He sped off down the dusty road.

Arriving at Jasim's house, he turned off the truck. The anger had subsided slightly, and confusion settled into the foreground. Juma felt lost. *Why am I here? What am I doing?* Before he could turn the truck back on, Jasim greeted Juma at the front gate.

"I've been waiting for you, Juma," Jasim said as he waved him toward the house. "What brings you in such a hurry?"

Juma stared out the front of his truck, and without thinking replied, "My brother was young; he had much life to live and many children ahead of him." Juma paused and turned to Jasim. "These infidels did this."

Jasim nodded understandingly. "Come inside; let us drink tea."

Juma got out of the truck and walked through the gate. Jasim put his arm around Juma's shoulder and escorted him to the inner courtyard of the house. There was already tea sitting out on the table. Juma sat uncomfortably, not sure of what he was doing.

"How is your father?" Jasim inquired.

"He is near heart attack; my mother is the same," Juma said as Jasim poured some tea into a small teacup that looked to be worth a lot of money. Juma stirred in several spoonfuls of sugar and began to sip.

"Tell me, are you a religious man?"

Juma stopped for a second while he fiddled with the teacup. Then the words started to slowly creep out of his mouth. "I left school in the sixth grade, in order to help the family. I was working while I went to school before that, but I kept failing. After one of the times I failed, I decided not to go back. I can't read the Koran, but I try to pray five times a day."

"You are still a good Muslim, Juma. First the Koran tells us to declare your faith, which you have done. Then you must pray five times a day, and that you do. I know that your family has given much to those who need, which is what the Koran has told us to. I also know that you fast during Ramadan, which is also good. I'm sure that one day, if you have the money, you will make your Hajj, but there is one more section that I have brought you here to talk about."

Juma paused for a second and turned toward Jasim.

"One section of the Koran people in these days are afraid to talk about is the necessity of jihad. The Americans have made jihad sound like a very bad thing. A jihad starts with oneself, the inner struggle. You must perform self-discipline, praying five times a day and resisting temptation, right?"

"I know this, but I'm sure ..."

Jasim cut him off. "Then we must take care of our families, provide for them, and build relationships with them, is this not true?" Jasim said as he leaned into Juma.

"I'm sure this is not the part you want to tell me about," Juma stated, half-knowing what would be said next, yet not knowing how it would be said.

"We must also take care of your neighbors and your fellow Muslims. In 1979, when Russia invaded the Muslim state of Afghanistan, Muslims from around the world joined together to fight the infidels. The infidels tried to rid the country of Muslims, and because Muslims came together, they were able to defeat the infidels. They fought for Allah on a sacred jihad. Each fighter went home a hero because they fought to protect the lives of fellow Muslims." Jasim paused, sipped some tea, and gave Juma time to digest the information that he had set forth.

"The infidels who have landed in our country are no different. They say they are here for our rights, but what rights do we have when they take the lives of innocents? Your own brother was taken by these people, who wish to rid the Muslims from the state of Iraq for their oil. Your brother was an innocent Muslim. As his brother, it is your duty to seek revenge; as a Muslim, it is your duty to seek revenge for all other Muslims who have lost their lives due to the Americans being in this country. Tell me, Juma: say someone from another tribe killed your brother. What would you do?"

Without hesitation, Juma replied, "Simple, I would go to seek revenge for his death. I would kill the man who killed him. I would also take the life of another person from his tribe."

"Mustafa had many generations in front of him, true?"

"True."

"If you wish to feel your revenge, I can help you feel it. If you wish to be a true, good Muslim, I can help you feel it."

"How do you mean?"

"You must think and make a decision. If you decide you want to be a good brother and a good Muslim, I will take you to a man that will make you feel your revenge."

Juma turned away from Jasim and looked up into the dark sky, where the stars glittered above him. He turned back to Jasim; his face had disappeared in the fading light, and he could only see the outline of his head with the white fluorescent light behind him. Juma looked down at his empty cup of tea. "I'm ready to be a good man. I am ready."

"If you are sure, meet me at the Baghdad Garage in Mosul on Wednesday, around two in the afternoon. You are making the right decision. If you feel it inside, it is Allah telling you this is the right thing to do," Jasim said as he leaned forward and touched Juma's leg, trying to catch his eye. "You must go, attend to your family. They have had a long day, and they need their son."

The two of them stood and walked out toward the gate. Jasim stopped at the truck. "Go with Allah."

"Thank you for your hospitality, and you go with Allah," Juma said as he climbed back into his truck and started the engine. Juma felt better already. He could feel he was doing the right thing. He drove slowly back to the village, contemplating what Jasim had said. As he pulled up to the edge of the village, he saw Mahmoud standing out in front of his house. Juma sat up straight in his vehicle. He had not thought of what others would think. Surely Mahmoud would not understand him.

Mahmoud waved, indicating for Juma to stop, And Juma stopped. Mahmoud leaned in the passenger window. "Where did you go?"

Juma could sense the discontentment in Mahmoud's voice. "For a drive to clear my head."

Mahmoud took a good, hard look at Juma and turned in the direction he saw Juma approach the village. Mahmoud's heart sank. "What was your business with Jasim?"

"No business," Juma said, looking straight ahead toward his house.

"It has been a long day. I know that your mother must be worried," Mahmoud said, standing up straight and moving away from the truck.

Mahmoud watched Juma drive home, turned to stumble back into his gate, and sat down outside his door. He wondered what was brokered with the man he hated so much. Just then Mahmoud's two-year-old son Hassan ran up, yelling, "Bappa, Bappa," carrying a soccer ball that seemed to be half his size. Mahmoud reached down, picked up his son, and gave him a hug. After setting him down, he took the ball from Hassan, put it on the ground, and softly kicked it away. Hassan chased after the ball and struggled to pick it up. He gave up and walked over to a big, red bucket used to wash clothes that was sitting on the ground and tried to climb in. Mahmoud smiled at his son.

"This is not the answer," he said aloud to himself as he watched his son. "This anger will ruin the honor of his family. He will come to his senses tomorrow."

7. Eerie Feeling

Ali opened his eyes and sat up slightly so he was leaning on his elbows. He squinted as the sunlight crept through the blinds into his eyes. "What was that noise?" Ali asked his wife, who was asleep and did not seem to hear him. Ali looked down at his clock. "Oh no, Yassin is supposed to be here any minute."

Ali jumped up and started to get ready. He got dressed and shoved his work gear into a bag in a rush. As he finished, he realized that Yassin had not knocked on the door yet. Ali woke up past the time Yassin usually showed up at his house. He stopped in confusion and thought to himself, *Where is he? I guess he slept in too. I'll go get him.*

Before leaving the house, Ali crept back into his room to look at his wife one last time before he left for work. He was amazed with her beauty and wished he had more time to spend with her.

Ali made his way quietly out the front door. The morning was fresh, and it felt like the day would not be too hot. He walked out his gate and turned toward Yassin's house. As Ali started getting closer to Yassin's house, he noticed that something was not right. An eerie feeling crept up from his stomach. Something was missing. Fear built up inside of him, telling him to run. He started walking faster, and the hair on the back of his neck stood up straight. Ali could not fight the urge to run any longer. He took off running straight for Yassin's house, dropping his bag in the process. As he got near, he noticed it was the only house that had the gate open. He could hear the shrill cries of a woman.

Oh, Allah, please say no one has died. Ali started running at full speed. As he rounded the corner into the gate of Yassin's house, he saw Yassin's mother beating herself in the driveway. She was in tears. Ali desperately searched the yard, looking for signs of what was driving this woman to act in such a manner. Yassin's little brother was trying to calm her down and tell her it would be okay.

"What ... what?" Ali half-shrieked, half-commanded. "Tell me, what has happened?"

Yassin's mother looked up at Ali and scooted across the ground on her knees. She grabbed at Ali's legs. Mascara that streaked from her eyes down her cheeks made her tears look black. She desperately looked up at Ali, begging, "Please, Ali, please ... please!" She trailed off as she shrank down on the concrete. Her sobs overcame her, and her mumblings did not make sense.

Ali looked down at her, wondering what was going on. The fear that had caused him to run built up behind his eyes. He could feel the tears on the verge of pouring down his face. His knees started to buckle. *Yassin must be dead*, he thought to himself. His lifelong friend, his brother. The two of them had been through everything together.

Ali heard the door open; he looked up and saw Yassin's father, who stopped at the door and looked down at his wife. He slowly crept down the stairs. "Son, help your mother into the house." He sat down at the bottom of the steps. Yassin's brother pulled his mother up the stairs, and they squeezed by Yassin's father. Ali joined him on the stairs. A tear slunk down his face; he was confused and wished he knew what was going on, but he knew something had happened to Yassin.

Yassin's father stared toward the street, and it didn't seem he really acknowledged Ali's presence. They sat for a few moments, moments that seemed like eternity for Ali. He could see his friend. "If only I ..."

Yassin's father cut him off. "We had just finished breakfast. I went to the guest room to read the Koran. Yassin got ready to leave for work. He stopped by the guest room to say he was leaving for three days. I said good-bye, and I didn't look all the way up at him. He walked out the door. Just then I remembered seeing his ID card in the guest room. I picked it up and went after him. When I opened the door, he was opening the gate. I called down to him. Maybe if I didn't, he wouldn't have turned away from the street."

"Please, tell me. Whatever happened it is not your fault. Tell me what happened next," Ali said in desperation.

"He turned back to look at me. His eyes were so beautiful; he looked right at me. We were fixed in each other's gaze, and time seemed to stop. It must have only been a split second. Then there was a screeching of tires coming up the street. Yassin whipped back around. The cars, they were dark Volkswagens or BMWs. Maybe one or two was an Opel, the other was a blue Volkswagen or BMW. There were three cars." Yassin's father stopped, and the hand that cupped his knees started to shake. "The three cars came and stopped at our gate. Two men got out, from the middle car. I could not move fast enough, like in a bad dream. They got out of the car with guns, AK-47s. You could hear the neighbors were out, but a couple rounds shot into the air scared them away like doves. They had on masks; I don't know who they were. Then another man got out of a different vehicle. They went toward my son; they went for him. Yassin pushed on the gate to shut it, but before it could lock, they kicked it open. I wished it was me, not my son. I was frozen; I couldn't act, didn't know what to do. They came in and threw Yassin on the cement, and he hit the ground hard. I knew they were coming to kill him, and I wasn't going to let it happen. Then a surge came over me, and I rushed toward them. One of them used the butt of his weapon to knock me to the ground. I couldn't see. I couldn't help my son." He reached up and touched the fresh bruise on his head. The shakes got worse, and the tears started to fall onto his sunken cheeks. "First they asked his name; then they tied him and threw him in the trunk. They took him away."

"If Allah wills it, he will be fine," Ali said without hesitation. He wanted to comfort Yassin's father, but he knew deep down that his best friend would not be okay. These sorts of kidnappings had happened all over Mosul, and no one was ever fine. "I will find him. We will find him," Ali said, hoping that his police force was ready to get these people. "He is my brother; I will find him."

"I called the police, but because of the danger right now, they will not come here. They only took my statement over the phone," Yassin's father said, shaking his head in disgust.

"I will go to work, and we will find him, alive," Ali said as he wiped the tears from his face and rose to his feet. He turned and hugged Yassin's father.

Ali took off in a full sprint for the main road, picking up his bag along the way, and caught the first taxi that drove near him. As Ali sat in the taxi in traffic, he noticed all the black cars. He couldn't help but wonder if Yassin was in the trunk of one of those cars.

As Ali looked at his surroundings, he couldn't help but hear the words of Yassin echo in his head: *Do you think they know?* "There is no way that they know ... they will not waste their time on us," Ali had said confidently to Yassin. Ali could not help but feel responsible. They should've been more careful.

Then Ali remembered while walking out of the mosque, the man was standing to the side calmly handing out flyers, as if it was normal to hand out flyers that threaten someone's life. As Ali got near the man, he had pushed into the crowd and forced a flyer into Ali's hand. The details of that incident became clear; he could see the man make eye contact with him through his ski mask. He had stepped out in front of an old man, almost knocking him over. He had pushed a flyer onto Ali's chest, holding it there until Ali took it. Thinking about it now, it seemed so clear, but he had not thought of it before.

The Land Between Two Rivers

Terror rushed into Ali's heart for the second time that day. He had just started to cool after the first rush, and now he was afraid. "Maybe they are following me now," he said under his breath as he checked every car, every person who was around the car, looking for suspicious people. Ali hurriedly pulled out money for the taxi driver and handed it to him before they got downtown. Ali noticed that traffic was horrible getting downtown, and when he could not take any more, he hopped out of the car. He walked at a fast pace toward the police station. He tried to not stand out, and it took all of his will to keep from running. After Ali made it through the checkpoint into the police station, he ran up the stairs and through the door. As he opened the door and passed through, he ran squarely into the chief of police, Colonel Ilyas Khuthaiyr. His bodyguard grabbed Ali and awaited the command of the chief.

Colonel Ilyas barked at Ali, "Why did you come through that door so fast, and why do you look as if Saddam has just regained power?"

Ali stepped back from the bodyguard and tried to regain composure. "Sir ..." Ali stopped for a second to catch his breath. "Sir, my apologies." Ali knew he was in trouble.

The bodyguard pushed him against the wall. "Answer the question."

Ali stuttered to get the words out. "Sir, they ... they kidnapped Sergeant Yassin about one hour ago, and I think they know where I live ..."

Colonel Ilyas cut him off. "Not another. That is the tenth in two days. This is getting out of control." Colonel Ilyas turned around and barked at Major Saleh, "Time to get a taskforce together that only deals with kidnappings of our police."

Colonel Ilyas turned to one of his bodyguards. "Call the Americans. Set up a meeting."

"Corporal Ali, go with Lieutenant Salem, and he will debrief you," Colonel Ilyas said as he handed out more orders. "This is top priority; everyone get to work."

Ali went with Lieutenant Salem into his office. He was much calmer with Ali. He handed him some tea, and they sat and talked over all the details. Ali told him about the black Opel and the Volkswagens or BMWs that took him away. Ali told him about the mosque and the man who handed out the flyers.

"Unfortunately, this stuff is happening all over Mosul. I myself can no longer go to market. My wife, I send her, even though it is dangerous. Sometimes I will send my son, when he is not at school," Salem said to Ali, trying to comfort him. "Some other officers have chosen to move or live with relatives. Others are just moving around the city. I heard many people are going back to their tribal villages, where kidnappings would be near impossible. The road there is a different story."

"I don't know what I am going to do. My wife, I hope she is safe."

"They are not after your wife; they are after you. If you just change your schedule and take different routes, you should be okay."

"If Allah wills it," Ali said, placing his hand on his heart and looking up.

8. The Amir

Juma met with Jasim, as instructed, at the Baghdad Garage in Mosul. Jasim pulled up in a white 1992 Chevy Malibu, reminiscent of all the cars that Saddam Hussein gave to his highest Ba'ath Party members.

"Get in the back seat," Jasim said as he leaned toward the passenger window to talk to Juma.

Juma got in. "Lay down. Do not put your head up, and do not look around. Do you understand?" Jasim demanded.

"Why?" Juma said, confused, as he lay down in the back seat.

"Just do it, and don't let me catch you looking," Jasim said as he drove off. He drove around the city for fifteen minutes before stopping in the driveway of a house. Jasim got out of the car and motioned for Juma to follow him. He walked around the front of the car and up the steps and knocked on the door of the middle-class, two-story house. No one answered. Jasim turned around and sat down at the bottom of the stairs. Juma looked at him inquisitively, and Jasim motioned for him to sit next to him.

"We may be here awhile," Jasim said. "I have to wait for him to come back. That could be any minute or in a couple hours."

Juma took a seat next to Jasim. He was feeling nervous and wasn't quite sure what was going to happen. He looked at the sparse garden in front of the house. The dirt looked too dry to grow anything, yet there was a tomato plant sitting next to the wall. Juma could tell that no one had attended to the garden in a long time. He was surprised that there was even a garden there in the first place.

Jasim pulled a cigarette out of a broken-down Miami cigarette box and began to smoke.

Juma, fixated on the tomato plant, imagined the garden at his house. He wondered who lived at this house. "Who are we waiting for?"

"Abu-Zah'ara," Jasim said, as if Juma should already know the answer to the question.

"And he is ...?" Juma said as he grabbed a cigarette out of the box that sat next to Jasim.

"Don't act as if you have never heard of him!" Jasim said as he turned to Juma with a condescending look. "You have a lot to learn. Where do I start?

"Well, Abu-Zah'ara is a great Muslim man, a man of jihad. He is a man that every Muslim should look to, every Muslim that wants to fight jihad. He took his name from his sister, who died at the hands of the infidels, shortly after the invasion of Iraq. You must have heard of him; maybe the name Abdul-Jahliel Hassan Sulayman rings a bell. Everyone talks about him," Jasim said as he peered at Juma. "This is pointless. I guess I will have to start from the beginning.

"As I said, he is great Muslim man. His face is that of an Egyptian prince; his eyes are deep brown, and to peer into them, one could get lost in his sorrow. He has hands of an average working man, rough and torn. He is a true soldier of Allah. He is fighting a true fight.

"Way before the invasion of the infidels, Abu-Zah'ara was exiled from Iraq by Saddam's army. Abu-Zah'ara went to the north to live with the Kurds, where Saddam could not get to him. Before that, he used to smuggle blankets and clothes from the Kurds to Mosul. Three of the people he worked with got caught by Saddam's customs agents, and Abu-Zah'ara, at the age of twenty-two was forced to leave his family. Friends of his in the smuggling business provided him with a place to stay in Irbil.

"His smuggling business continued for two years, until the Peschmerga started to hunt him. Abu-Zah'ara quit that business and went to live in Sulaymania with other refugees. These refugees were warriors for Allah. Thanks be to Allah that they went to Afghanistan to win the war against the Russians. When the Americans went to Afghanistan, these heroes were pushed through Iran into northern Iraq. Thanks be to Allah that Abu-Zah'ara met these people.

"While Abu-Zah'ara lived with these people, he went and found odd jobs in order to make money. He started to take jobs in construction, any type. He kept to himself; he was just trying to make enough money to make it back to see his family.

"Then one day, he met Salahadeen, a warrior from Afghanistan, at a local restaurant. They talked of the situation in Afghanistan and how the Americans went to Afghanistan illegally, just like the Russians. They talked of situations where there was suffering of Muslims, like that of Afghanistan and that of the Palestinians, and how this is a reason for one to fight jihad. The two of them met several times over the next five months, discussing the politics and the Koran. They became good friends. Salahadeen was intrigued with Abu-Zah'ara. He was a good Muslim man that kept to himself and did not ask too many questions of anyone. He never once asked why Salahadeen talked so much of jihad. Salahadeen once asked him why he did not ask questions, and Abu-Zah'ara said that Allah will give me the answer to my question if I am supposed to have the answer to such questions.

"Finally, one day, Salahadeen asked Abu-Zah'ara to ride with him. Abu-Zah'ara got in the car and did not even ask about where they were going. They drove out of the city and into a small village. They parked the car and continued on foot out of the village. They went up into the mountains. They continued their talk of religion and the Koran, as they always did, as they walked up the winding trail.

"After a short climb, they were stopped by a young kid that looked of high school age, holding an AK-47. When the young man noticed Salahadeen, he moved off the trail and greeted them. Salahadeen and Abu-Zah'ara continued into a small encampment. As they approached, Abu-Zah'ara noticed a clearing where a man stood on a small platform surrounded by young men. The man in the middle was teaching the men around him about moving during an attack and was teaching from the Koran. He moved fluidly through his speech. Abu-Zah'ara was intrigued; he felt at home. This is what he had been waiting for, and he not realized that this is what he was meant for. He listened to the man teach the young men.

"After the lesson was complete, Salahadeen took Abu-Zah'ara on a walk toward the edge of the encampment and asked, 'What do you think?'

"'You have done well here,' he said with a smile on his face, 'Thanks be to Allah.'

"The two of them laughed. A few weeks later, Abu-Zah'ara started at the camp. From the beginning of the camp, the other men were impressed with Abu-Zah'ara's knowledge of the Koran. He was also an eager learner of all the training had to offer. Abu-Zah'ara became an instant leader among the other students. He was catching on quickly and was able to help teach the other students.

"After three months at the camp, Abu-Zah'ara was finished with training and was leaving the camp when he ran into Salahadeen. Salahadeen asked Abu-Zah'ara what his plans were, and Abu-Zah'ara replied with, 'They are always looking for day laborers, and should my fellow Muslims need me, I will be there for them.'

"Salahadeen shook his head and told him to go with Allah, and they parted their ways. A few months later, the infidels landed in Iraq. Abu-Zah'ara did not fight initially, because he believed the eviction of Saddam would be good for his fellow Muslims. He took the opportunity to go and see his family that he had not seen for four years.

"When he got home he found that his sister was nearby an area with his father, and that area was bombed by the Americans. They both died. Zah'ara was only ten years old. This is when he took the name of his sister.

"The following day, he went to Mahmoud Adeen mosque and asked Mullah Abdullah Rasheed for advice. They spoke of his sister. The Imam told Abu-Zah'ara that the *mujahideen* needs to develop, in case the Americans decide to become occupiers.

"That is when Abu-Zah'ara made contact with three of his friends, and they began the process of making an army. Soon they attacked American military vehicles with RPGs, and the attack was successful and aired on international news."

"You make me bigger than I am," Abu-Zah'ara said, leaning against the front gate. "I am just a man. Where did you hear such tales?"

Juma turned quickly and stood up to meet the man he had just heard so much about.

"How are you, brother? We have been waiting for you," Jasim said to Abu-Zah'ara.

"Good, brother, and this is the one you told me about?" Abu-Zah'ara said as he shook hands with Juma. "Let us go inside and talk."

9. The Village School

The drive out to the village of Aski Mosul was long and hot in the baking sun. Even though Jeremiah was wearing gloves, the black weapon he was holding on to was burning his hands. He squinted through his sunglasses for signs of danger ahead. Jeremiah thought to himself, *It is time that we do something good for the people.* On this day, they were going out with the Civil Affairs team to go and fix a school and equip it with air conditioners and heaters. They were also going to get to know the local villagers.

As they got close to the village, Jeremiah thought about his first raid and what the village looked like at night. The area was lifeless at night, but as he rolled into to the town, children were all over the streets, women and men were in the fields working, and older men were sitting by their houses, drinking tea. The children surrounded the vehicles, smiling and waving. The vehicles made a perimeter for security, and the soldiers began to dismount. They were greeted by the *muktar,* Ahmed Agoub Yassir, of the Hadidi tribe. He asked the soldiers to call him Abu Mustafa. Jeremiah wondered if he had met the man before.

Kids swarmed the soldiers, holding out their hands, asking for candy. Wynn and Duncan were prepared for this; they were told that the kids would do it. They looked at each other and reached into their cargo pockets and started to hand out candy. As the Civil Affairs met with the *muktar,* they took pictures of the kids.

The group moved toward the school, which was made of cement, rather than mud like most of the villages. It was in pretty good condition and only had minimal damage. The soldiers took the heaters and air conditioners off the trucks and loaded them into the school. Some of the kids hugged the commander, "Thank you, mista," they said in broken English.

Civil Affairs had also prepared backpacks, complete with notebooks, pens, and pencils for all the students. They were handed out of the back of the truck. The older kids pushed the younger kids out of the way, trying to get one. In the end, all of the children had a backpack, and the extras were given to the schoolteacher to give to students who may not have been there to receive one.

After that, the *muktar* invited the commander into his house for lunch and tea. That was when Jeremiah noticed that this was the house they had raided before. Jeremiah was glad the *muktar* was still friendly to them.

As they walked toward the house, a young man exited and walked off. He did not say a word to the soldiers who were entering his house.

"That's odd," Duncan said to Jeremiah.

"Sir, did you see that?" Jeremiah said to the commander.

"Leave it alone, Bernard," he replied as he talked to the *muktar*.

Once the commander got inside the house, Jeremiah stayed outside to pull security. Many of the villagers swarmed the area, trying to see inside the house.

Jeremiah noticed a toddler walking toward them, carrying a soccer ball that was almost as big as he was. His father was following close behind him. Jeremiah reached in his pocket and found another piece of candy. He reached out and handed it to the little boy. The little boy walked up and tried to hand his soccer ball to Jeremiah. He didn't pay attention to the candy. As he lifted up the ball, it dropped out of his hands. Jeremiah kicked the ball gently back to the boy. He started to laugh, and tried to kick it back but wasn't successful and fell backward. Jeremiah rushed over, picked him up, and handed him the candy he had offered him before. Before the tears could well up in the boy's eyes, he took the candy and smiled. Jeremiah set him down. The little boy ran over to his father, showing him what he had just gotten from the soldier. His father picked him up and opened the candy for him. Jeremiah picked up the soccer ball and handed it back to the father. "Thank you," said the father. Jeremiah took a look around and went back to the edge of the house.

A little while later, the commander emerged from the house and told everyone to mount up. Jeremiah checked around to make sure nothing was wrong. The kids swarmed the soldiers again, asking for candy. "I'm sorry, I don't have any," he said, hoping they would understand.

As everyone finished loading up the vehicles, Jeremiah waved goodbye, and they drove away from the village, careful not to use the same roads they had used before. Jeremiah sat inside the Stryker, thinking about the events of the day. As they approached the city of Mosul, the roads were paved, and the ride smoothed out.

Just as Jeremiah was settling into the ride, now that the road was free of bumps, Jeremiah felt a large jolt and saw the black-and-red cloud engulf the gunner before Jeremiah lost sight of him. Gunfire erupted.

The gunner's knees collapsed. "I'm hit. Oh shit, I'm hit," he said with an eerie, soft breath as he slinked into the Stryker.

Jeremiah pushed by the gunner, poked his head out of the hatch, and took his place as gunner. He was unsure of what he would see. Over the headset, Jeremiah heard "Small arms, three o'clock." Jeremiah grabbed the .50-cal and swung it into position.

Jeremiah then noticed that the Stryker in front of theirs was hit by an IED. Jeremiah could not see who was firing or where they were.

"Move, move, we gotta go!" Jeremiah heard over the radio. He looked at the stores that flanked at their position. He could not see down the alleyways, which is where he thought the gunfire was coming from.

"They are in the alleyway to my two o'clock. I can't hit them. We got to move forward," Jeremiah hollered to his driver. The Stryker that was hit was taking heavy gunfire, and they were just out of Jeremiah's sight.

"RPG, RPG, nine o'clock," Jeremiah heard over the radio. Jeremiah turned to look and saw the rocket aimed at him. Jeremiah struggled to swing the .50-cal around. The guy fired, and Jeremiah fired back. Jeremiah ducked down, in fear of being hit. The RPG grazed the top of the Stryker and slammed into the stores behind him. Jeremiah popped back up to find the RPG gunner lying on the ground. He felt the Stryker move forward.

"Thank you, God," he said. He remembered the gunners who were down in the alley next to the other Stryker and swung the weapon to the other side of the vehicle, hoping he could pick off a few as they went by. As they passed the alley, it was empty. Jeremiah searched the area, looking for any other dangers.

The Strykers crept forward slowly, compared to the pace they were going before. The Stryker hit by the IED could only move so fast. They went straight for the base, and once they were through the gate, the commander ordered them to go straight to the CaSH—the Corps Support Hospital.

10. Juma's First Mission

"This is your day, your chance. I have a mission for you," Abu-Zah'ara whispered to Juma as he leaned over the table in a coffee shop in the middle of downtown Mosul. The air conditioner on the wall blew cool air, but it all it was doing for Juma was annoying him, as it did not diminish the heat that left his brow dripping sweat. Juma sat awkwardly in his black pants and brown button-up shirt, his red-and-white head wrap draped across his shoulders.

Juma smiled back at Abu-Zah'ara, wondering what was in store for him. Finally, the day was coming on which to get his revenge.

Abu-Zah'ara winked back as he stood up in his pristine white *dishdasha*. Juma put down his teacup and followed suit to Abu-Zah'ara's actions. Abu-Zah'ara handed some money to the server and thanked him for the tea.

The two of them stepped out into the blistering sun and into the bustling marketplace. The two turned and walked through the market as if on a stroll. They walked toward Juma's truck, which was parked in the nearby neighborhood.

They rounded a corner to head into the neighborhood. A few steps in, Abu-Zah'ara stopped and pulled some keys out of his pocket.
"This is the car you will drive today," he said as he pointed to a sky-blue Opel Vectra. He handed the keys over to Juma and sat in the passenger seat.

It took Juma a second to figure out what was happening, and then he hurriedly ran around the front of the car and hopped in the driver's seat.

As Juma pulled his door shut, Abu-Zah'ara turned to him. "This is what you do. Go down to Hajj Ali village. Do you know where that is?"

Juma nodded. "The village to the south of Mosul, about thirty minutes on Baghdad Road."

"I don't care how you get down there, but listen carefully to what else I have to tell you."

"Okay."

"Take the road that heads toward the Tigris River. About two kilometers out of the city, the road dips down into a small valley. In that valley, there will be a black Opel Omega. Park next to that car." Abu-Zah'ara waved his hands in the air to indicate the end of his instructions.

"What next?" Juma asked.

"They tell you what to do; just listen to them."

"When?"

"Now. It is time."

Juma looked around and checked his watch. He felt confused.

"Don't worry, Allah will be with you. This will be an easy mission for you, and it will be good for you. Allah will smile on you for conducting missions in his name. Allah is with you."

Abu-Zah'ara pushed the passenger door open and stepped out, "I'll tell them you are on your way."

"Do you need my truck?" Juma asked as he fumbled through his pockets.

"No, you will come and get your truck later," Abu-Zah'ara said as he shut the door and waved good-bye.

Juma pushed the keys into the ignition and took a deep breath. "Hajj Ali, go toward Tigris River, stop in valley next to Opel," he said, recounting what Abu-Zah'ara had just told him. He didn't want to mess it up. This was his chance to prove that he was serious about this business.

Juma turned the car around and drove through the neighborhood, to prevent being held up in the crowded streets of downtown Mosul. He headed to the Baghdad Highway and started on his thirty-minute journey to the south of Mosul.

Juma thought back to the last time he went south of Mosul. It must have been over a year ago. His distant relative had passed away, and he had gone to pay respects with his father, who had known the relative quite well. Juma could not remember his relative's name. Thinking of the funeral reminded Juma of why he was driving the car on that day. His brother had died an unrighteous death at the hands of infidels. No apologies, nothing. It was time for him to fight, not only for his brother but also for all his fellow Muslims who suffered similar deaths every day since the invasion of the infidel forces. Juma could feel the rush of the drive. It felt very right. For the first time, he felt like he was doing something greater than himself.

The last few weeks had been confusing to Juma; everything felt like it happened very fast, and he felt numb—until today, when he knew this was the time he was finally doing something for himself. He put a tape in the player and listened to an imam from Saudi Arabia.

Juma turned off the main road and headed into the village. His heart started to race, and he turned down the volume on the player to concentrate. He took in his surroundings, very cautious of who was watching and how well they would see him. He knew that if a stranger came into *his* village, everyone would notice and would watch to see what that person was doing in the area. Hajj Ali is a hub to several smaller villages in the area, and Juma took comfort. No one would notice if he drove straight through.

He headed east out of the village, toward the Tigris River. Juma felt like he was entering a dreamland. As he crested the hill, he saw the car down in the valley. He became nervous. *What if they kill me?* Juma took a deep breath and parked behind the car.

Two men in the car in front of him exited. Juma got out of the car and walked up to them. "Peace be unto you?"

"And you," one of the men said back to him, with his hand on his heart. "Open your trunk."

Juma immediately thought *weapons transfer*. He ran over to the car and fumbled to find the trunk-release button. He was not used to the car.

He finally got it open and noticed the two men pulling masks over their faces. Juma pulled his head wrap around his face. He did not understand what was going on.

The two men opened their trunk and pulled a man out. His arms were tied behind his back, and he had a gag in his mouth. Juma noticed that the man must have been in his early twenties. The man smelled of piss, and his brown pants were dirtied with blood. His light-blue, collared shirt was torn, and the buttons seemed to be ripped out of place. The blindfold, made of a torn cloth, was falling down off of his face. The two men dragged the man backward, as he kicked and twisted and turned. As they reached the back of Juma's car, they picked up his feet and shoved the man inside. They gave him a final shove and shut the trunk. Juma could hear him kick.

After slamming the trunk, one of the men pulled off his mask. "Brother, go back toward Hajj Ali. Take the road headed to the north. When the road splits, take it to the right. Whatever you do, don't go down the main road. Follow this road until you get to a small village. Then head toward Hamam Alil village. Once you hit the main road in Hamam Alil, take it until you find the road that goes to Highway 1, Baghdad Road. Head over to Baghdad Road and head back up into Mosul. Go straight to the Yarmook Traffic Circle. Park in the middle of the circle."

"Why? What is going to happen?"

"Do this, and Allah will be proud of you. This is your mission, and you need not worry about the missions of others. I hope that at another time we will meet each other, and we can speak. Today is not that day."

"If Allah wills it," said Juma. He hugged the two men and got back into his car.

Abu-Zah'ara sat on the curb with Abu Ahmed at the gas station near the Yarmook Traffic Circle. Abu Ahmed had been with Abu-Zah'ara since the beginning of this war, and they were also the closest of friends.

"How are you today?" Abu Ahmed asked.

"Well, thanks be to Allah. Today we will be doing good work."

"If Allah wills it," Abu Ahmed said as Abu-Zah'ara's phone rang.

Abu-Zah'ara picked up his phone. The sun beat down on them as they sat near their cars, which were in line to get gasoline. Abu-Zah'ara put down the phone without saying a word. He looked into the heavy traffic that moved about the area. This happened two more times. Abu-Zah'ara seemed to be concentrating on something. Abu Ahmed got up and moved the cars forward with the line, making sure to allow enough room to pull out of line at anytime. After the last call, Abu-Zah'ara said, "Twenty minutes."

Abu Ahmed nodded and got on his phone. Abu-Zah'ara checked the area to see who was coming and going. Abu Ahmed and Abu-Zah'ara did not really talk, so much as pay attention to who was around and who was coming and going along the roads. After fifteen minutes, the two got up and went to sit in their cars. Abu Ahmed looked around and made sure he could see the five other cars that were in the area. He held up his hand, signaling five minutes. After he got a nod from everyone, he looked at Abu-Zah'ara and nodded. Abu-Zah'ara carefully watched the traffic circle, waiting to see Juma pull into the circle.

As Juma approached the circle, Abu-Zah'ara cut his car into traffic, going straight for the center of the traffic circle. At the same time, the other five cars pulled out into the circle. Cars honked and screeched to a halt in the busy circle. Drivers started to yell at Abu-Zah'ara's erratic driving. Before stopping their cars, everyone pulled a black ski mask over his face. The five cars stopped traffic from entering the circle and brought the circle to a halt. People started honking immediately. Two more cars pulled into the circle with Abu-Zah'ara and Juma. Everyone exited the cars, weapons in hand. This calmed the honking from the other cars. People ducked back into their cars, and people on the streets ran to the nearby shops.

The busy traffic circle dipped into a quiet serenity. Juma opened the trunk, and Abu-Zah'ara pulled the young man out. Abu-Zah'ara controlled the man with one arm, as he moved him into the middle of the circle. For a man of only five feet eight inches with a skinny build, Abu-Zah'ara was incredibly strong. Two more men were pulled out of the other two trunks and escorted to the center of the circle. The men were on their knees.

Juma could hear the sobs from the young man who came from his trunk, echoing in the normally busy area of Mosul.

Abu-Zah'ara looked around at the cars, to make sure the area was still secure. He then pulled a large knife from his belt, as did two of the other men.

"In the name of Allah, the most merciful and gracious. These men are the supporters of infidels that infect this country. Sergeant Mohammad Yassin works with the ING, Lieutenant Bakr Ahmed of the Iraqi Police, and Sergeant Yassin of the Iraqi Police. These men are fighting the true protectors of Islam. They were warned to quit their jobs. These men are being put to death in the name of jihad." Abu-Zah'ara's word echoed and caused the young man from Juma's car, Sergeant Yassin, to vomit through his gag. Abu-Zah'ara looked down at the sight as Sergeant Yassin crumpled over on the ground, crying. Abu-Zah'ara picked him up, in unison with the two other men.

Abu-Zah'ara grabbed his hair and pulled his head back. He sliced into Yassin's neck in a sawing motion. Abu-Zah'ara was familiar with the squirting blood and the gurgling noise that crept out of the throat. The blood poured down the front of the man. Abu-Zah'ara continued to saw. He soon dropped the knife and allowed the body to fall onto its stomach. Abu-Zah'ara grabbed under Yassin's chin and twisted it back. The neck snapped, and the head was left dangling in Abu-Zah'ara's hands. In a matter of seconds, he had pulled off Yassin's head. He held it up and then placed it on Yassin's back.

Gasps came from the nearby area; muffled screams were felt in the air.

Abu-Zah'ara knew that this was necessary to show the people of Mosul they were serious. It brought them support and kept the non-supporters from reporting on their activities. Abu-Zah'ara turned to Juma and said, "Let's go," as he grabbed Juma's arm. He picked up his knife, and they hurried over to the Opel. Another man got into the car that Abu-Zah'ara was driving.

"Take that road," Abu-Zah'ara said as he pointed to the road, to the bridges up ahead. All the other cars split in separate directions.

Abu-Zah'ara smiled at Juma, who was terrified by what he just saw. He directed Juma to return to where his car was parked.

"Juma, you must understand, this is what we must do. People do not listen, and we must make examples for the people to see. I sure you will understand, and I will have to explain it to you later. Don't worry; you are with us now. You did a good job."

Juma could not respond.

Abu-Zah'ara climbed out of the car, walked around to the driver's side, and opened the door. "I'll contact you later," he said, motioning for Juma to get out of the car. He sat down inside and adjusted the seats. He looked at Juma, who stood right next to the car and then slowly walked around to his truck. Abu-Zah'ara knew Juma had potential.

He drove off to the parking garage, where his 1993 Toyota Supra was parked. He cleaned out the car. "It's a shame, this was a nice car," he said to himself, knowing that the car might be gone next time he came back for it.

He took his Supra to the Mahmoud Adeen Mosque to meet up with Mullah Abdullah, parking down the street from the mosque. Abu-Zah'ara's cousin used to live in the area, and as children, they played on these streets. He relished the walk to the mosque. Filled with pride, he strode down the road, remembering the times when they used to play soccer in the street. As he approached the mosque, he was greeted by Abu Ahmed, who had just arrived before him.

They washed together and went and sat in the mosque. Abu-Zah'ara sat in the back and leaned up against a wall. There was still time before prayer. He felt drained; he had not rested much in the last few days. Things were busy, as new fighters who were fleeing American surges in different parts of the country were arriving in the city every day. New groups wanted to join forces. He was busy making sure they were taken care of, in addition to his usual business. The new fighters were a strain on the limited funding, but he knew they had to find a way to make it work.

He watched as Mullah Abdullah greeted Abu Ahmed and they sat in down near the middle of the room. As he watched, he thought about the road they had traveled over the last year and a half. He had gone from nothing to becoming a true defender of Islam and in the process surrounded himself with respectable religious men. As he sat and pondered the past, he watched as Abu Sayf, Abu Zakiriyah, and Abu Aiya filed in and took seats. All of these men worked shoulder to shoulder with him to get the resistance up to its current strength. Abu Ahmed and Abu Zakiriyah had been his good friends for as long as he could remember, but Abu Aiya and Abu Sayf were friends with Abu

Ahmed in college. Regardless of how their paths initially crossed, they were all proven fighters.

Their first mission together occurred four months after the first attack that Abu-Zah'ara, Abu Ahmad, and Abu Zakiriyah had conducted. He often thought back to the attack with all five of them, which left them in high spirits.

Abu Zakiryah had contrived a bomb from some leftover artillery rounds from Saddam's army that he had smarts enough to steal and store away after the regime collapsed. All he had to do was pull a wire to make the bomb go off. He hid the bomb in with some garbage along a busy roadside. Abu-Zah'ara had orchestrated the attack from what he learned at camp. The bomb was dropped off at night, and the wire ran into a small nearby valley, near a small abandoned pump house building. Abu-Zah'ara then hid behind a wall one hundred meters before the bomb location along the road; he could see the street, but the wall provided protection. He sat at the location with Abu Sayf, and Abu Ahmad was another hundred meters up the road, behind a wall with a PKC automatic rifle. Abu Aiya was in charge of the getaway car and parked in an alley behind the ambush site and walked up closer to the site with his AK-47 to be backup. Then there was the waiting game.

They waited for an American convoy and were aiming to set the bomb off on the first or second vehicle. This would stop the convoy in the ambush zone. They had been sitting in the heat since 10:00 a.m., when the locals were out in force and provided them easy cover. They knew Americans traveled down the road quite regularly. They had been waiting two hours when Abu Ahmad called Abu Zakiriyah as he saw Americans turn onto the road. Abu-Zah'ara kept an eye out for the convoy. As the first vehicle passed, he went behind the wall, and as the second vehicle passed, there was a loud explosion.

It was his signal, like the gun at the start of a race. He then swung out from behind the wall, dropping to his knee and steadying the RPG on his shoulder to aim at the fourth vehicle in the convoy. Simultaneously, Abu Sayf dropped down next to him and aimed at the vehicle right in front of them. They both pulled the triggers, letting the rockets loose, which slammed into their targets. Gunfire erupted as they started their escape. Abu Ahmad started to fire at them, shifting the direction of fire, ensuring their escape. Abu Aiya then let loose with his AK-47 and allowed the other two to make a dash for the car. Abu Aiya ducked behind a building and ran up a side street. By the time the three of them reached the car, Abu Zakiriyah was already seated in the back middle seat with an ear-to-ear grin. Abu Aiya started the car and drove a few blocks as Abu Ahmad emerged from an alley and jumped in. Abu Aiya drove down the alleyways and back streets of the neighborhood to ensure their getaway. Abu Zakiriyah couldn't stop gloating over how well his new bomb had worked out.

Abu-Zah'ara snapped back to reality with the sound of the call to prayer. He stood up and smiled at his partners as he walked over to join them on the rug. "We've done well!" Abu-Zah'ara stated as he sat down.

Abu Aiya chimed in, "That was a good way to show them we are no joke."

Abu-Zah'ara sat puzzled for a second and said, "Yes, but I mean we have come a long way from where we started." They all nodded in agreement.

11. Rage and Salvation

"A tip was received on the location of two-day-old dead bodies that have been laying in the Yarmook Traffic Circle," Lieutenant Salem said as he walked up to Ali in the hallway.

"Who are they?" he asked as he followed Salem into his office.

"Don't know. Call the hospital and have them send some ambulances to meet at the location; we are leaving in ten minutes." Ali didn't like the idea of going to the Yarmook Circle; it was notoriously dangerous.

As they pulled up to the scene, Ali was immediately dispatched to ask the local store owners what had happened. He tried to talk to the gas station attendants and some black-market gasoline salesmen and it seemed no one was interested in cooperating with the police. He was then approached by a large, slow-talking man at the pump, who claimed he saw it all happen and was very eager to share his story, as if he had no one to talk to. Ali took his statement, knowing that it was better than the cold shoulder he was getting from the rest of the people.

"Well, first a car pulled right into the island of the circle, and out of nowhere, all the traffic going into the circle was blocked by other cars—it was like ten or eight cars. Then more of the terrorist cars parked on the island. There was like fifty terrorists there. Then they pulled those three out of the trunks of the cars." He made a motion to the ambulances and police cars that were not sitting in the circle, surrounding the scene of the crime, and then continued on with his story. "Then one of the guys started to yell something about jihad, and before I knew it, all their heads were cut off." The man stopped and stared off into space for a second. "I saw it with my own eyes, and I still can't eat because of it."

"Is there anything else you want to add?" Ali waited for a reply and noticed the man start to tear up, so Ali turned to walk away.

"Their names ..." Ali turned back around. "They said their names. I think they were national guard and one was police."

Ali thanked him for his statement and reported to Salem, who stopped him before he reached the bodies. Ali gave a brief synopsis of the man's story and pushed by him to take a look at the bodies. Ali didn't recognize anything about the bodies; they looked so foreign, the way they were posed. He couldn't believe that what he was looking at was real. He leaned in closer to get a better look, and then he saw him—Yassin. His head was posed on his chest, and his identification was shoved in his teeth. Ali stumbled back into Salem.

"I tried to warn you ..." Salem trailed off, and Ali began to puke. Salem held him up and walked him over to sit down in the car.

Ali sat there, thinking about the situation. He mumbled half to himself, half to whoever would listen, "That could be me, could be anyone." The thoughts pushed up his throat, and his body lurched; he leaned out the door and puked again.

Thoughts started racing through his head. *How am I going to tell his family? If I woke up on time, I would be lying next to him. They didn't ask for ransom. Yassin had so much ahead of him. I don't know if I can do this anymore. Is it worth it?* Ali leaned his head back on the headrest. All the doubts in his head began to fade, as rage and salvation for those wrongfully harmed coursed through his blood. He stood up and walked back over to look at the dead bodies. He stared down on them, and his strength grew. He watched as the body bags were rolled out next to the bodies, and he leaned down to pick them up. Even with his newfound strength, it was hard, but at the moment he watched the bag zip closed over what was left of these noble guardsmen, he made a vow to take down the cowardly criminals who fight in the name of Allah, disgracing his name. They were merely killers, terrorists, not real *mujahideen*, and he would not let this happen again.

"I hate these bastards," he muttered as he lifted the bodies onto the gurney and helped push them over to the ambulance.

They escorted the ambulances to the Republican Hospital and then drove back to headquarters. They left calls to the families regarding the fate of their loved ones to the hospital morgue staff. The disgust of what they saw was easily read on all the faces. Ali was eager to take a shower and take a break. As the policemen began to unload out of the truck, Salem stopped them.

"We have just received information about a possible location of one of the vehicles that was involved in the beheadings. It is in the northern parking garage."

"Should we call the Americans for backup?" one of the police officers asked Salem.

"We can handle this. Americans won't be here forever," Salem barked back.

They added a few more police trucks to their convoy and headed out to the garage. A perimeter was set up around the garage. Ali, along with several other policemen, was instructed to clear the garage and mark the locations of blue Opel Vectras. As soon as they entered the garage, they decided the best course of action was to check all the vehicles, just in case the description of the vehicle was off. They found four vehicles that matched the description in the garage, but they didn't find any evidence in any of them.

As Ali was looking through one of the vehicles, he heard a call from across the garage. "I found weapons!"

They all rushed over to find out what he saw. In the car were RPGs, AK-47s, PKCs, grenades, and lots of ammunition. It was a red Mercedes; it wasn't what they were looking for, but it was good find nonetheless. All the weapons were loaded into the trunk of the car, and one of the police officers hotwired the car. A policeman was told to drive it in the middle of the convoy back to headquarters. The police fanned out and started to ask the garage attendants what they knew about the weapons.

"We don't know anything," an attendant answered.

"Don't you search cars before they come in here?" Salem asked them.

"Yes ... I mean most of the time ... I mean when we can."

"Well, who owns this car?"

"I swear to Allah we don't know."

Salem was very displeased with this answer but knew that these guards probably didn't pay attention to who was going or coming into the garage at the sight of a few thousand dinars. "Who owns this place?"

One of the attendants motioned to a small office nestled in the guard shack.

"Someone come and arrest this guy," Salem said as he started to walk toward the guard shack. "So, you support terrorists," Salem called out as he kicked open the door to find a startled man on his cell phone. Salem then clocked him over the head with the butt of his weapon. Ali and another man placed cuffs on the unconscious man and dragged him over to the truck and put him in the back. Ali was pissed that this man was supporting the destroyers of his country. The man was taken back to headquarters for interrogation.

At the end of questioning, the interrogator stuck his head in Salem's office, where Salem and Ali were filing papers. "The garage is a weapons transfer point. There is a person that drives a car full of weapons in, leaves the keys with the garage attendant, and another fighter comes to pick up the keys and drives the cars to the terrorists. The car came from Irbil. The garage owner was paid to keep his mouth shut, the attendants as well. They didn't know about the Opel Vectra or the beheadings."

12. Bad Mutha Fucka

Jeremiah rushed out of the chow hall. He knew if he hurried, he could write his fiancée an e-mail before he had to head out that night. He went straight to the Internet café. He missed McKayla and wanted very badly to start his life with her. They had met in college, both majoring in business. Jeremiah hated college; he wanted adventure and a change of pace. He watched the war in Afghanistan and felt a strange desire to help out. He chose infantry because he wanted to be a true-green soldier. He went to basic training in Fort Leonard Wood—Fort Lost-in-the-Woods, as the soldiers called it. Jeremiah loved the physical demands and the mentality of the army. He spent his first year in Korea, away from McKayla, away from the fighting in Iraq and Afghanistan. Of course, McKayla preferred Korea, where he was safe. They only saw each other twice while he was in Korea. When Jeremiah got back to the States, he knew he couldn't go any longer without McKayla, and he asked her for her hand. He was then put in a unit that was leaving for Iraq six short months later.

Jeremiah was torn between his love for McKayla and his love of the army. He couldn't wait to see some real action and do real "soldier stuff." Now that he was in Iraq, he missed McKayla terribly; missed her laugh and her horrible jokes. He clicked on the Internet Explorer icon to find out the Internet connection was down. Typical for the makeshift café they had made for the soldiers.

He hustled back to his room to write a letter, to take the place of his dependence on the unreliable Internet for a connection between each other. When he was done, he gathered up his gear and went to check on his soldiers.

"You guys get your shit together and don't forget your … ah … you know, that thing that shoots stuff." He motioned toward their M-4 rifles. They all laughed. Jeremiah knew they were annoyed with the number of times he checked up on them to make sure they had their gear, but he wasn't about to let a little annoyance to them lead to complacency. When he went out, he wanted a full team, not part of a team because someone forgot their night-vision goggles. His team pulled together their gear and wandered over to formation.

After everyone arrived, Captain Wylie began to spout of the operation brief. "The target for the brief is a dude that was big during Saddam's regime, Jasim Hussein Ahmed. Apparently he recruits for the muj. The main thing we are told is to expect resistance; he just got released from Camp Bucca four months ago and is already up to no good. Don't expect him to go down easy."

Captain Wylie provided all the details of the operation and everything they would need to know while they were out of the wire. At the end, he added, "By the way, Lieutenant Colonel DeLuca is going to be with us today so keep your shit sharp today, just like every day."

Jeremiah love to hear when DeLuca was going out. DeLuca was their Battalion Commander. Intel claimed that terrorist groups put a bounty on his head because he was breaking apart the terrorist organizations; he was aggressive and very successful. He didn't want to leave time for the groups to recover from the blows he delivered. The soldiers loved him; he was inspirational and would go out on a mission almost every day. He seemed not to fear anything and loathed the hit-and-run tactics of the cowardly terrorists. He demonstrated to all of them the true qualities of a soldier. All the soldiers in their unit looked up to him. They were then released to do final checks before going out.

"Stay alert, stay alive," Jeremiah reiterated to his soldiers; he depended on them, and they depended on him. They all climbed into the vehicle for the ride out to what appeared to be a small palace, compared to other houses in the area, surrounded by trees in the farmland.

Raids still raised Jeremiah's heart rate, but they were an adrenaline rush that he thrived on. The more they did, the more he knew what to do at every step, and he worked hard at his team perfecting every move. They hit the house hard and fast. As they raced through the house, they pulled all the women and children into one room, and the men were brought out to the courtyard.

They found two men, three teenagers, one of whom could have been in his early twenties. It was hard to judge the age of an Iraqi. Jeremiah was pulling guard duty on them as they were questioned by Captain Wylie. The two men claimed they were brothers of the guy they were looking for, and the other three claimed to be his kids. None of them claimed to be him. They continued to ask them for the current location of their targets, but their attempts were fruitless. At one point, one of the younger ones was about to talk, but after a quick glimpse at the older ones, he closed his mouth. One of the men claiming to be a brother looked just like the picture of the man they were looking for, and they had no real way of telling if he was lying about being a brother. They decided to arrest him and have the interrogators sort it out. There was nothing in the house of interest, no weapons and no interesting documents. They then left the house with one detainee and headed back to base.

Jeremiah's team was picked to guard the detainee as they processed him into the facility and headed out for questioning. A few hours later, Jeremiah overhead the interrogators talking. "He claims he is not him, and he claims Jasim was never in the Ba'ath Party. He claims to not know about terrorists or anything of interest. I don't think we are going to get anywhere with this guy tonight."

Jeremiah and his team were allowed to leave a few hours later. As they walked back, Wynn said to Jeremiah, "I hope they get something from that guy."

"I think they will; they are the ones that get us all the info that gets us out there in the first place."

Duncan chimed in, "I hear they're the best, but of course that was from them, and that was kind of a biased opinion."

"I just want to get that guy," Wynn said as he lit his cigarette. "Something about what they said about him and his family just rubs me wrong and gives me a bad feeling. I just know he is a bad mutha fucka."

As they reached their trailer of homes, the sun started to turn the dark sky into a yellowish haze, and they all parted ways and headed for bed.

13. The Land between Two Rivers

It was around noon, and the temperature just reached over one hundred degrees, and the heat was only beginning for the day. The streets of Alapo were at a near standstill due to a large traffic accident that was blocking most of downtown, close to city hall in the city center. Mohammad and Arab sat at the corner coffee shop, smoking cigarettes, drinking tea, and watching the chaos of the jam-packed streets unfold. In front of them was a man laying on his horn and yelling at young teenager who had not yet mastered the clutch of his pickup truck, compounded by his inexperience of driving under the pressures of traffic.

"I heard about your dad. Tell him congratulations for me," Arab said to break the silence in their traffic voyeurism.

"Yeah, he finally got his division membership a few days ago. He has been looking forward to it for quite some time." Mohammad continued to stare at the spectacle of the young kid grinding the gears of his truck and getting stuck in the intersection, making traffic worse that it already was. "He got so nervous, he didn't think that he would get it and was trying to brush it off. He has been working for it for the last few years, and even though he was becoming powerful as a politician, he just didn't think they would give it to him. I told him he would, but he wouldn't listen. Then when it did happen, it took him awhile to believe it."

"My father sends his congratulations too, but you know him; he'll stop by to say it in person." Arab paused and looked over at Mohammad. "I hope we can still be friends."

"Funny." They both laughed as the call to prayer sounded. Simultaneously they both finished up their tea and started walking toward the mosque. Mohammad had been looking forward to hearing the guest speaker from Damascus who was going to be at the mosque today. The man had made many appearances on TV and had a large following.

The mosque sat on a major road and overshadowed the surrounding small businesses and apartments. It had a large dome painted gold and a minaret that could be seen from several blocks away. The mosque was finished last year and was large enough to fit five hundred people comfortably. Today, the mosque was packed. Water spigots ran along the inner wall and dumped water into a trough, paralleled by benches where men could conduct their ritual washings.

After dropping off their shoes in cubbies, Mohammad and Arab pressed their way over to get cleaned before finding a place in the large room complete with beautiful rugs. Just as they squeezed into the back of the main room, the prayer was ready to begin. Their imam led the prayer before handing the podium over to the guest speaker. He spoke loudly and elegantly, flowing in and out of verses from the Koran, speaking a classical form of Arabic mastered by a man who clearly had committed every line of the Koran to heart and had a vibrant passion for his religion. His speech flowed out into the neighborhood over the loudspeaker, for those who could not fit into the mosque and for all those who did not attend to hear. He was focusing on the importance of helping out one's neighbor.

"... and as much as you should worry about the man next door, you should worry about the community that is next door to yours, each city next to it, each province next to it. Islam is not bound by the borders of a country; our neighbors next door are no less important than our neighbors in the next country over, and those who are in Far East Asia, Europe, or the Americas. Today, we have a country very much in need of our help. Not a country that is an island of the Philippines, one that is very much a part of our everyday life, as we are to it. This country was the birthplace of civilization and lies in the land between two rivers. Our borders touch, and trade flows from there to here and from here to it as we speak. This country, my fellow Muslims, has been occupied by infidels. These infidels have promised much, but we see through their veiled lies to the truth: they only seek personal gain. The people they enforce this tyrannical rule upon are Muslims, and as such should not be ruled by these Jews and Christians. This shakes the core of our religion. Our brothers in this country have been demoralized by infidels. Their country has been crushed, and the rights and culture of Islam have been abandoned from the very streets of Iraq. These Muslims cry for our help, and we have not answered. We ask our country to assist, and they fear these infidels of the Judeo-Christian alliance. We cannot wait for the politics of our nation or those around us to rise up against these forces; it is time for us to take it into our own hands. I ask you, brothers of the Iraqi people, to join me and set forth on a journey to free the land between two rivers, and return it the hands of Muslims ..."

The imam continued, and the words of this articulate orator coursed through Mohammad's veins. He felt a strong connection to the speaker and ached for the Iraqi people. He had felt this way before when he watched the news, but this time he could feel it in every inch of his body. The Iraqi people had been through so much in the last thirty years, but he knew that the pains they endured under the Americans were far worse than all that happened to them under Saddam.

As the speech concluded, chatter about Iraq ran rampant through the crowds. Mohammad and Arab waded out of the crowd and started down the road home. Arab had frequently mentioned the indecencies brought upon Iraqis, and this provided him another opening.

"I heard if you go to a mosque more than once a week, you're arrested and sent to that awful prison, Abu-Ghraib," Arab said with as much enthusiasm as if he had just heard about it, and as if he had not repeated this fact to Mohammad more than a hundred times.

Mohammad wallowed in the words of the speaker as he listened to Arab continue to tell the woes of the Iraqi people. Mohammad wanted to help Iraq but felt helpless. He was just finishing school this year, and with his father's help, he would get a good assignment in the government.

As they reached their neighborhood, Arab and Mohammad went their separate ways. Mohammad walked through the gate of his house and took a seat out on the front steps. He contemplated the issue in his head several times and then stood up and walked inside. He pushed it into the back of his head and sat down to eat lunch. His father came into the room and turned on the TV.

"You got to see this," he said as he flipped the TV straight to the news.

"Early this morning, an American convoy traveling through Baghdad got into a firefight in the vicinity of a mosque. Americans, in their haste to return fire, shot at the surrounding neighborhood and shot two tank rounds into a mosque. We turn to our correspondent in Baghdad."

"What I am hearing from our reporters on the ground is that at 10:00 this morning, an American patrol made up of tanks was driving by a mosque in the Yarmook District of Baghdad when there was a large explosion, after which a firefight erupted between the insurgents and Americans. The tanks turned their guns and fired two rounds into the mosque, after which the firefight came to an abrupt end, just as it had started. The mosque sustained heavy damage. There is no count on casualties, but what we do know is that no Americans were hurt."

"Please, turn that down or change the channel," Mohammad asked his father, who turned it down. Mohammad had decided to take a break from thinking about Iraq, and his father had placed it right back in the forefront of his mind.

"Arab and his father send their congratulations and said they would be by later," Mohammad interjected. He then began to tell his father about the speaker at the mosque.

14. I Fear I Must Leave

Jasim sat in the front room, smoking cigarettes and watching TV. He wanted to go out, but he wasn't quite sure about his situation. A few days ago, the Americans went to his house, and he didn't know what the Americans found out from his brother. Jasim took a second to look around the barely furnished house. He went into the kitchen, but there wasn't much to eat. He had heard about this house, where they kept the foreign fighters hidden from the world. Abu Zah'ara had put him there until they could figure out what to do with him next. The house was in a bad section of town, but not so bad that the Americans had gone through all of the houses. The neighbors were too afraid to say anything and were paid off by the insurgents leaving them alone.

It was a nice day outside, and Jasim wished he could be out and about, but he knew better. It wasn't worth risking accidentally running into Americans or a checkpoint and then being arrested. He had already been in jail and wasn't going to let it happen again. After he got out the last time, he started to make contact with his friends in the Ba'ath Party in Syria. They had already offered him a place to stay; he just had to get there first. He had been racking his brain for ways of getting there. He knew a passport, fake or real, would be very risky.

The front door handle turned. Jasim got up and walked over to the kitchen to see who was coming in. He saw Abu-Zah'ara's strong, confident face appear in the light. Jasim exhaled.

Abu-Zah'ara walked in the door with his phone pressed to his ear. "Scared you, didn't I?" Abu-Zah'ara joked.

Jasim didn't find it amusing.

"Are you well? Have they been taking care of you?" He asked, still attentive to what was being said over the phone.

Jasim knew he was talking about the two men who were in charge of taking care of people at the safe house, but he had only seen each of them once since he had been in hiding. "All is well, but I fear I must leave Mosul."

"I know," Abu-Zah'ara said as he finally hung up the phone. "I don't think you should stay in Iraq, and your service to us can still be performed from another country."

"I have contacts in Syria. I just need to get to Syria."

"Jasim, you should have more faith in me. I can offer you much help in that division. After all, I used to be a smuggler, and I have many friends; the same friends that supply us with fighters, money, and weapons. I'm sure they can take you as far as Kamishly."

Kamishly is the largest city in eastern Syria and sits on the border with Turkey in Syria's northeast panhandle. It is a major trading post between Turkey, Syria, and Iraq. "From there, you should be able to find transportation to wherever you need to go."

Jasim was hoping Abu-Zah'ara would have a way out for him, but he wasn't sure that he had set up such a system.

"I have sent Juma to your house to pick up your bag, some money, and anything else your wife finds necessary."

"I should know by now you always have everything planned out." As Jasim finished his sentence, they heard a knock at the door.

Abu-Zah'ara peered out the window and caught a glimpse of the rear end of a faded red pickup. "There's Juma now," he said as he walked over to open the door.

Juma came in carrying two large bags. "Your wife insisted. I took them and thought you could just go through them and take what you wanted." He set the bags down in front of Jasim.

Abu-Zah'ara produced some money and sent Juma back out for some food for the three of them. After he left, Jasim and Abu-Zah'ara sat down side by side to discuss what would happen.

Abu Zah'ara leaned back on the pillows and rested his head against a wall. "I'll keep this simple, so you don't have to write anything down. Abu Sa'ad is going to come pick you up. Take one bag with you and listen to what he says; it's that simple. Make sure you keep contact with the person that drops you at your final destination. He'll be the one that gets stuff back into the country. Anything you need to send back here, you'll go through him."

"That is pretty simple. Will I be going through any checkpoints? Do I need my ID?" Jasim leaned toward Abu-Zah'ara, begging for more than the little information he was given.

Abu-Zah'ara lifted his head up and turned to look Jasim in the eyes. "Look, I have to keep it simple for more than not writing it down. We will make the trip as easy for you as possible. Just be ready when he comes."

"When's that?" Jasim asked, fiddling with a cigarette butt in the ashtray.

"That, my friend, is dictated by situations outside our control." Abu-Zah'ara leaned his head back again, this time closing his eyes.

"Can I at least get an idea?"

"It could be today; it could be next week. I'm exhausted. I haven't had a second to rest since Friday," Abu-Zah'ara said in an attempt to change the subject. Just then Juma pushed the door open. "And I guess I still don't," Abu-Zah'ara said as he sat back up.

Juma placed the food between them, and they all sat down to eat. He then began to give the details of what happened at Jasim's house, according to Jasim's wife and son. "They ended up only taking your brother, because they thought he was you."

"Everyone does say we look alike, and Americans have a hard time telling Iraqis apart."

"Here," Juma said as he produced a letter from his pocket, "your wife asked me to give this to you." They ate the rest of the meal in silence.

Juma ate quickly, because he could see he was causing the awkward silence. He made up an excuse to leave and showed himself out the door.

"Okay, later today, Abu Sa'ad will stop by for some food for the house," Abu-Zah'ara explained. "When he gets here, he will tell you when he expects the next delivery. It could be anytime, so get ready to go. This is it; you won't be coming back for a while."

"Will I see you before I go?" Jasim asked.

"Allah willing. I have to go; missions have not stopped." Abu-Zah'ara got up, and they both said their good-byes.

Jasim sat and watched TV, and a few hours later, Abu Sa'ad showed up at the house. "I have no food, but I am about to receive a delivery. It's a few days earlier than expected."

"Already, how much time ..." Jasim said as he started to open the two bags his wife packed for him.

"We got to go," Abu Sa'ad said, looking down at Jasim fumbling through his bags.

"Give me two seconds," Jasim said as he dug through the first bag. "I'll do this in the car." He stood up as he zipped up the first bag. Abu Sa'ad bent down and zipped closed the other bag and picked it up.

They both scuttled out the door and into Abu Sa'ad's car. They drove over to the Tall Afar Garage near the Yarmook Traffic Circle. When they pulled into the garage, they parked next to an occupied Opel

Omega. Jasim looked up and noticed that the passengers were definitely not Iraqis. Abu Sa'ad got out and walked over to the car. Jasim listened to them exchange greetings, after which Jasim was sure they were not Iraqis. They had a Saudi Arabian accent.

Jasim pressed the rest of what he wanted into one suitcase and got out of the car. So did the Saudis from the other car. They exchanged hellos, with strange looks on their faces.

Abu Sa'ad leaned in the window of the Omega and explained to the driver that Jasim was headed to Syria and that he was to take him with him. Jasim got in the passenger seat of the Omega, and the Saudis joined Abu Sa'ad in his car.

Jasim sat down next to the man who was clearly aggravated with his presence. They drove west and then north toward Rubiyah, a Syrian border town. To Jasim's surprise, they did not come across one checkpoint. The driver must have known where they were and had managed to avoid all of them. Jasim tried to explain his situation to the driver, but the driver seemed annoyed to have a passenger and was only mildly courteous toward his small talk.

When they pulled up to Rubiyah four hours later, just as the sun was going down, the driver cut off the road and went down a canal road to a house that was set back from the rest of the village. The driver pulled up by the gate and told Jasim to stay put, disappearing into the house. Jasim turned and watched the sunlight fade and nearby farmland dim in the dark of night. The driver appeared twenty minutes later with a man who must have been in his fifties but in considerably good shape. Jasim stepped out of the car with his suitcase in tow and was greeted with a smile.

"Welcome to my house. How are you? How was your trip?" The man began to pepper Jasim with questions, and Jasim felt much more welcome than he during the ride up. Just as Jasim began to answer questions, the driver jumped in his car and sped off, leaving a cloud of dust.

"My name is Jabar. Don't mind Mukhles, the driver; he is perpetually in a bad mood. You didn't do anything. I understand you are looking to get out of the country."

"Yes, Abu-Zah'ara said you could help."

"Abu-Zah'ara?" Jabar stopped and stared at Jasim like a bewildered child. "Do you mean Abdul-Jahliel?"

"Yes."

"That young man has helped me very much in the past. I met him as a child, maybe nineteen or twenty years old. He was such a bright young man. He started out as a checkpoint scout for me and quickly commanded respect and was proven to be a leader in my operations. Easy to trust, hard worker, and above all, very intelligent." Jabar started to lead Jasim into his front room. He turned his body toward Jasim as he walked slowly sideways into the building. "We were smuggling cigarettes back then, between Mosul and the Kurds. He could smooth-talk his way through any checkpoint, and he kept our bribes at a minimum. It was a shame to lose him when Saddam was after him. I am always glad to hear he is still out there doing well. Please have a seat." Jabar and Jasim sat down on rugs covering a dirt floor of the mud house Jabar called home.

"He is the one that receives your shipments of fighters and puts them to work."

"I know. He enlisted me when they got the border patrol back, but he doesn't maintain contact with me." Jabar stopped, stared into the rug, and started to rub his prayer beads in his hands. "It's too dangerous."

"I will say he is doing a wonderful job with the resistance." Jabar looked up and gave Jasim a knowing smile.

"We must sleep, and tomorrow night we will make the journey." Jabar lay down on a pillow.

"Can you get me all the way to Alapo?" Jasim was tired but was anxious to find out his faith. He also wondered if he would make it out of the country or if he would somehow be caught.

"It'll be arranged." Jabar sat up, anticipating that the one answer would not satiate Jasim's curiosity. The two discussed late into the night about the future contact and the activities Jasim could conduct in Syria with Jabar's assistance. Then, as the sun was ready to break the horizon, they fell asleep, which was fine; they would be up late the next night.

Jasim didn't wake up until well after lunch. The small room he was in looked more depressing in the light; it had been a long time since Jasim had slept in a concrete house. He wiped his eyes and took a quick look around to find Jabar was not in the room. He slipped on his sandals and walked out into the blistering sunlight. Jabar was outside, near a couple of cars, talking to some men. Jasim could feel that his presence was not wanted near the cars and kept his distance. He leaned up against a wall and lit a cigarette. After a few minutes, Jabar finished talking to the men, and they drove away.

Jabar made his way back over to Jasim. "Would you like something to eat? My wife fixed some lunch earlier. We should eat. We need to leave soon."

Jasim returned to the small room he slept in, and Jabar brought a plate of vegetables and bread for him to eat. Jabar handed him the plate and looked down at the bag Jasim was carrying. "You might want to get rid of some of that."

Jasim pulled some clothes out of his bag and handed them to Jabar.

"Maybe you can use these." Jabar set the clothes down and sat next to Jasim. They both ate, and at sunset, left on foot.

They walked for quite some time on canal roads and through deserted farms before they turned and headed for the border. By the time they reached an area near the border, the sun was gone, and Jasim was left trying to follow closely behind Jabar. He feared he would lose him in the darkness if he didn't. Jabar knew the trail by heart and didn't need a flashlight, which would have given them away anyway. As they crossed the border, they cut through some farmland and into a sea of sand. They walked in silence. Jabar had no problem pressing forward and was not tired, but Jasim was beat. After a few hours of walking, Jabar suddenly sat down. Jasim immediately dropped to the ground. He didn't know if Jabar saw or heard something that he didn't.

Jabar let out a hearty laugh. "We are taking a break. I don't want to give you a heart attack, old man."

Jasim let out a sigh and sat up. He placed his bag behind him and leaned against it.

"We're almost there."

Jasim leaned his head back; he couldn't remember the last time he had placed such a stress on his body. With all the walking, hiding, and cringing at the thought of going back to jail, his entire body ached. He leaned his head back and started to nod off to sleep. After ten minutes, Jabar nudged him. "Let's go."

They walked for another hour through the sand and dirt. Jasim couldn't tell if they were on a trail or if Jabar was just walking aimlessly through the desert. They stopped again, and Jabar pulled out a satellite phone. He dialed a number, said nothing, and then hung up. He started to walk again. Jasim tiredly lifted his bag up to his shoulder, and Jabar stopped again. They were at a road. Jasim couldn't believe his eyes. He didn't see it a few steps ago, but here it was—asphalt stretched out over the desert road. Just then, a car pulled around a corner and opened its trunk. Jabar grabbed Jasim's bag from him and placed it into the trunk. Jasim stretched across the back seat and fell asleep before the car started to move.

Jasim woke up when the car came to a stop in Kamishly. The driver, Jabar, and Jasim got out of the car and went to a nearby restaurant. After breakfast Jabar gave him his satellite phone number and walked him over to the Alapo garage.

"Just take one of these taxis to Alapo, and you're there."

15. Shift into a Low Gear

When Ali walked in to work after a three-day break, he felt refreshed and rejuvenated in his desire to fight. He had a lot to live for and a lot of fighting to do. Ali found out the day before that his wife was finally pregnant. This was the best news he had received since Yassin's death. Ali felt reborn; he was going to stop the killers who called themselves *mujahideen*, so his child—hopefully a boy—could grow up in a safe, free Iraq. Free from the terrors of Saddam Hussein and free from the nightmares imposed by the godless terrorists. He walked in to work pumped and jittery. The tired policemen in the station instantly noticed his excitement and high morale.

Ali said aloud, "Today I'm going to make a difference, and I swear to Allah, to my dying days, I will stop the criminals that plague this land. I swear to Allah." He spoke half to himself, half to anyone who would listen. Everyone seemed confused and exchanged looks as they filed into a small briefing room to wait for instructions on the day's mission. When Ali took a seat, there was about fifteen other police officers in the room. Ali loved knowing they were there. These men went to work despite the threats, despite the kidnappings, despite the assassinations and beheadings, because they knew they had a job that had to be done. The men knew they might die for this, but it was something worth dying for. It was better than sitting at home, waiting for something to change. They were going to *make* the change.

Ali couldn't sit still. Finally, the policeman sitting next to him said, "Ali, what's going on? Why do you keep bothering me with all of this moving around?"

"I, thanks to Allah, found out that my wife is pregnant." Ali paused and turned in his seat toward the inquirer. My son will not grow up in the oppressions of Saddam or the wrongdoings of the killers that now walk our streets." Everyone took heed of Ali's words, and congratulations spread throughout the room.

Just then, Salem walked in, and all the officers took their seats and became quiet. Salem took command of the room from the front. "Today we will be conducting presence patrols and random checkpoints ..." He went on to explain where they would go and the places they may set up checkpoints.

After the meeting concluded, all the officers grabbed their gear and lined the vehicles up outside the station. Everyone knew that this was a dangerous mission. All they had for protection was one man in the back of each pickup truck, totally exposed, with a PKC rifle. Men were piled into the back with the gunner, and two men, a driver and one passenger, sat in the front. They weren't going far, and they weren't going to very dangerous areas, but the mere presence of five police trucks attracted danger. They would drive through a couple of markets, and somewhere along the way, an officer would have them stop the trucks to set up a checkpoint.

Ali was assigned the gunner position in the fourth truck in the convoy. There was a slight haze in the sky, as the sun was rising to bathe the city. It was not as hot as usual. They started off by going through the downtown market. It was calm, and vendors had just started to fill the streets with their carts. The customers were just beginning to trickle in. Nothing was out of the ordinary. They left the market and headed toward the smaller neighborhood markets, which were close to downtown.

They turned down a main road, and as they rounded the corner, Ali felt things shift into a low gear. The hair on the back of his neck stood up. He frantically scanned the alleys and rooftops ahead. The road was four lanes across, and they drove in the lane closest to the small concrete median. Smoke started to come from the median up ahead of the lead vehicle, and the convoy shifted to the right. Ali felt slight relief.

The bright sunlight made it hard to see what and who was gathering on the side streets. He focused in on what he thought was a person in a ski mask—the earmark of terrorists who were about to attack, along with wearing a head scarf securely wrapped around their face, protecting their identity. The man stepped out of the shade of the building, but there was no mask.

Ali then felt a burst of energy and heat slam into his side. It was followed by a blast that seemed to break his eardrums. He ducked but felt a slight twinge in his stomach. He didn't notice the blood soaking into his shirt. Instead, he concentrated on what might become an ambush. As he stood up, he was hit again with a blast, this time from the other side. Then Ali saw them—the masks. Then he heard the gunfire. Everyone climbed out of the back of the truck and took cover from the bullets coming from behind. Ali pulled the heavy PKC with him as he hit the deck. The ambush was coming from the right side of the road, and it was intense. They had hit the second and last truck in their short convoy. People desperately needed medical aid in both trucks, but no one was moving.

Ali barked at three men from his truck, "I will lay down some cover fire. Get down to that truck, and pull the men out." He pointed at the last truck in the convoy, which was billowing with smoke. Ali then let loose with the PKC and hit one man who was getting ready to kneel down with an RPG. Another blast came from the front of the convoy, probably an RPG.

The three men made it to the last truck. Two of the occupants were obviously dead, and one needed medical help right away. The other three could still fight back, but they were clearly hurting. The driver of Ali's truck climbed back into the cab and backed the truck up, to make it easier to load all the men in.

Ali went around to the front of the truck, stood up, and started to fire. He needed the masked men to back off long enough for the injured men to be loaded in.

Boom ... another RPG hit farther up in the convoy. The ambush was heavy, a lot heavier than their usual hit-and-run tactics. When they fought the police, they weren't afraid. Ali estimated that there could have been fifty insurgents somewhere along the side streets. The insurgents had the police pinned down, and there was nowhere for them to go.

Jeremiah was sitting as the gunner in his Stryker while the team was out on patrol. They were going through a relatively friendly area, and there were always plenty of kids out playing in the streets. Jeremiah liked to see them out and about; it made the area feel safer. Lieutenant Colonel DeLuca and his personal security detachment were in with their patrol on this day. They had been out for about an hour and had stopped a few times to talk to the locals about how things were going.

Just then, a call sounded over the radio. Jeremiah could hear it through his helmet, which allowed him to hear the radio and others as they talked in the vehicle.

"Iraqi police are requesting backup in a heavy ambush in the vicinity of Route Vanilla and Route Sky."

"Roger. En route," came through the speakers. The Strykers kicked into high gear, tearing through the streets at full speed. Jeremiah sank down low in his position as gunner and kept his eyes wide open. They rounded a corner onto Route Vanilla, but they were still about another kilometer away from reaching Route Sky. Traffic was stopped, and they had to drive down the wrong side of the road.

"Jesus Christ!" Jeremiah said when he saw what was left of the Iraqi police convoy ahead. The ambush was over, but the Iraqi police trucks were all damaged. The Strykers scrambled up into the area and set up a perimeter around the police trucks, blocking traffic in both directions. When everyone was in place, the backs of the Strykers opened up, and out spilled a sea of soldiers.

Jeremiah stayed and held his position as gunner, just in case there was more trouble that had not been dealt with.

Soldiers pushed into the nearby buildings and side streets, checking for any signs of the terrorists, but it was apparent that the terrorists and all the civilians had left the immediate area. The only signs of their previous presence were blood and bullet casings and a few bodies.

DeLuca found a policeman who seemed to have taken charge of the situation in the absence of leadership, which was either inept or had been injured during the attack. He was a corporal, but he had everyone listening to him. DeLuca had the interpreter tell the corporal to get all his men ready for transport. Soldiers assisted in first aid of the wounded and got them into the Strykers. The soldiers and police loaded up the dead policemen and dead insurgents in body bags and placed them in the only two working police trucks. When everyone was ready to go, they took the police officers back to the American base hospital. DeLuca kept a close eye on the corporal and had him ride in his Stryker.

When they got to the hospital, everyone made sure all the critically injured made it in first. In all, six police officers were dead, two more were hurt so bad that they probably wouldn't make it, and seven others needed immediate medical help, but they had a chance. The rest of the police sustained some kind of injury. The Iraqi police officers with minor injuries sat in the waiting room, while the doctors worked on those who needed help right away.

DeLuca wanted to know what happened, so he grabbed his interpreter and pulled the corporal he found in charge earlier outside.

"How are you doing? Okay?"

"Thanks to Allah, but I got hit with something in my side; it is not bad, just minor cuts. One of your soldiers bandaged it up already."

"What's your name?"

"Corporal Ali."

"Corporal, what happened out there?"

Ali thought back to the incident. He hadn't had a second to think about what had happened. He was so focused on what to do next, he didn't have the time to digest all the events. He looked at DeLuca with almost a blank stare as he thought back to the smoke and the blast.

"There was smoke in the road, and then an improvised explosive device hit the truck in front of me, and then the one behind, and we stopped. They started shooting with all kinds of guns and RPGs. We tried to hold them back, because we needed to help the guys in the trucks behind us, but there was too much fire. There was so many of them." Ali stopped for a second. "Do you have any water?"

The interpreter ran into the building and came back with some water. "They are ready for you."

Ali walked inside with DeLuca. Someone came up to DeLuca and talked to him for a second as Ali was escorted back into the hospital to get treatment for his cut.

"Your colonel is on his way here," DeLuca said.

Ali nodded as he lay down on his side, per the medic's instructions. A medic walked up to him and took off the makeshift dressing covering the cuts. He cut away the part of the shirt that was soaked in blood and started to clean out the wounds. Ali cringed when he wiped across it with disinfectant. DeLuca watched and waited for a moment to interrupt. The cuts were across his side and onto his stomach and some on his back. They weren't very deep, but Ali would still need some stitches. The medic then placed a dressing on the wounds.

"You're going to need stitches. Hold this here, and don't go anywhere." The medic left to attend to another patient.

Ali looked up at DeLuca, guessing he was waiting for the rest of the story. "The fire started to come in heavy, and the last truck really needed some help. I don't think I was thinking when I stepped out in front of my truck and started to lay down fire with the PKC. I unloaded the entire belt, and I must've hit at least five or ten of them. When I ran out of ammo, I tossed it in the back of the truck and traded a pistol with one of the more seriously injured soldiers. I tried to get a look at the trucks farther up in the convoy through the flames and the heavy smoke, and noticed that they were not doing much better than us. They looked like they took the brunt of the attack." Ali turned his head, which jerked his body, and he winced in pain. He didn't really notice the cuts before, but now that he had looked at them and they had been cleaned, he was well aware of their presence. "I took three of my men and moved forward to signal for the guys up front to cover for us as we moved up to the flank. We moved back to the rear of the convoy and gave the signal, and the front end of the convoy lit up. We ran up to the wall and moved across them from the side. I don't think the insurgents saw us run up there. We started to hit them and must have shot a lot of them as we worked our way up. They hit one of us, but it didn't slow us down. Before we knew it, they had disappeared."

"How many of them would you say there were?"

"Thirty, fifty, I don't know; I was kind of busy and didn't have time to count." Ali said it as a joke to lighten the mood of the situation. DeLuca didn't seem to get the joke. There was a moment of silence between the two.

"We lost a lot of men, too many men. It was a horrible day; too many men lost their lives," Ali said, repeating it to himself in disbelief. He let it sink in. First he had to lose Yassin, and now more men. Ali couldn't help but feel responsible, and he started to cry. DeLuca made a veiled attempt to console him as the medic came back with an officer to stitch up his cuts.

DeLuca then turned to leave; he had many more things that he had to get done that day. As he passed through the waiting room, he noticed all the police and others were outside smoking. All had some sort of bandage on, and they were all quiet. When he got outside the door of the hospital, the Iraqi police chief appeared, escorted by some of his bodyguards and some American military police. DeLuca stopped the police chief and told him what he knew about the day, giving praise to the brave Corporal Ali. Colonel Ilyas thanked DeLuca for personally responding to the distress call they had made to the Americans, and they parted ways. Ilyas went into the hospital, and DeLuca left for his office, impressed with Corporal Ali and planning to visit him again, perhaps under better conditions.

16. Three Opels

Ever since the death of Mustafa and the disappearance of Juma, Mahmoud was forced to work as a general laborer. It was one of the most grueling jobs, one that took all a person's time and energy, with minimal pay, and surprisingly, it was still hard to find. Every morning, Mahmoud would walk the kilometer or so out to the main road and hitch a ride into Mosul. Once in Mosul, he would go wait at a laborer's square and was willing to take any job that came his way. For the last week, he had been working at a construction site, moving concrete blocks, one at a time. The pay wasn't bad at eight thousand dinar a day, but the work was exhausting, and he was sore all over by the end of the day. He would start his journey home around five p.m., after putting in a hard nine-to-ten-hour day. He tried to keep his spirits up by thinking about his children and sisters and how much they needed him, and the money this work was providing. He had to provide for them; otherwise they would starve.

Mahmoud got out of the car he had hitched a ride in at the top of the main road to his village. He thanked the driver and started to walk. The sun was to his back and cast a shadow that stretched far out onto the dusty road ahead. He crested the hill just before the village and started to make the short descent toward his house. Off to the right of the road, near some tomato gardens in the distance, he noticed three dark-colored cars, almost identical; the make of the cars appeared to Opel.

"No one in the village has those cars; they are too new and too expensive for any of us to afford," Mahmoud said to himself. He stopped and turned toward the cars, raising his hand to block the sun as he concentrated on the cars. Whoever was over there was taking something from the trunk, walking into the garden, and coming back empty-handed. Mahmoud then turned back and hurried into the village. He suspected they were *mujahideen*. He knew they were some of the people who could afford Opels, and he heard how they liked to hide things near the village, where the Americans probably won't check. If they saw him, they would threaten him or kill him.

He walked up to his house completely exhausted, and his children ran out the door and gave him a big hug. He squatted down to pull them all in close. He knew then that all of his hard work was worth it, and he didn't feel as tired. He still missed the days with Mustafa and missed Mustafa's shadow, Juma; those days were enjoyable, and the profits were slightly larger. He kissed his kids as they were called into the house to eat. Mahmoud stood back up. His back ached, and it was hard to stand all the way up. His muscles were fatigued from carrying the concrete blocks from the pile to where they were needed. He tried to crack his back by bending and twisting before following his kids into the house.

His wife had cooked a simple meal of rice and beans; it was all they could afford at the time and still have enough food to feed everyone. Mahmoud hadn't eaten all day, and the food tasted delicious, even though they had been eating it every day for the last two weeks. After dinner, his wife put on a pot of tea, and he walked out to the yard and sat down to watch his kids play, silhouetted by the sun sinking into the horizon. As it got closer, it cast pink and purple shards across the landscape. He saw this almost every day, but its beauty still impressed him. His wife brought the tea, and they sat quietly drinking. After he finished his cup, he decided he needed to pay a visit to Abu Mustafa. The poor man lost two of his sons in one fell swoop. Abu Mustafa was a like a father to Mahmoud, and he wanted to show that he appreciated him.

He pushed himself up out of his chair, which seemed like a monumental task, and walked out the gate. When he turned the corner onto Abu Mustafa's street, he saw the three cars he had seen earlier by the tomato garden. The cars were at Abu Mustafa's house. His jaw dropped, and he stopped for a second to take it in. Then he felt like something was coming up behind him. He spun around and saw his son following him. He was like a shadow and hated it when Mahmoud left. Mahmoud picked him up and kissed his forehead. He carried him back to the house and told the boy's sister to keep him there. Juma was up to no good, and he was going to find out about it.

As he turned to leave, he took a deep breath and walked back out the gate, rounding the corner just in time to see the cars leave the village. By the time he reached Abu Mustafa's house, his ears were pounding, and his heart had climbed up into his throat. He slowed as he turned the corner to walk in the gate. He searched the yard frantically. Nothing. He went and knocked on the door. Juma answered, and Mahmoud paused, not knowing what to say. He wondered why he didn't think about it until just then, but instead he stood dumbfounded in front of Juma. No words, just half-scared and half-angry. The two sat staring at each other like strangers who had never met.

Juma broke the awkward silence. "Are you okay?"

Mahmoud sat for a second. "No, actually, I'm not okay." The words were a surprise to both Mahmoud and Juma. "What happened to you, where have you disappeared ..."

Juma butted in. "Wait, Mahmoud. Please come in, and we'll discuss this like the brothers we once were."

Mahmoud calmed down slightly and followed Juma into the front room. When they reached the room, Mahmoud started to feel bad and gave a Juma a hug and kissed him on both cheeks. "I'm sorry. How are you? Is your father here?"

Juma sat and waited for Mahmoud to follow suit before answering the question.

"No, my father has gone to see his brothers," Juma said as he got up and walked into the kitchen. He came back with some tea that was already made. He poured a cup for Mahmoud and himself and sat back down. "Now, brother, what is it that you wanted to talk to me about?"

Mahmoud sat for a second, going through all the questions in his head that he desperately wanted answered. "I guess I should start with a topic that I know hurts your heart." Mahmoud paused for a second. "Mustafa ..."

Juma stopped moving; his cup was halfway to his mouth, and all the pain he felt at the death of his brother glazed over his body. He slowly placed the cup down on the ground and looked up at Mahmoud. The words from Mahmoud's mouth became silent murmurs, and as weakness started to seep into his body, he heard a clap.

"I guess that means you are not okay." Mahmoud looked at Juma with concern. "Is there anything I can do? Mustafa and I were very close."

"No, I'm taking care of everything."

"What does that mean? Taking care of what?" Mahmoud was starting to get agitated with Juma.

"Everything will be settled, and you don't need to worry."

Mahmoud glared at Juma. He could feel the anger rising up inside of him, and he tried to hold it back. He saw Mustafa's twin, but he did not hear Mustafa. Mustafa was a forward, honest, great man. He couldn't hold back any longer, and it took all his self-control not to yell at him. "What you're doing is not solving anything. These people got rid of Saddam, the man that killed my father, and what have they done that is so harmful?" Mahmoud couldn't stand the thought that his lifelong friend could be working with the terrorists.

The Land Between Two Rivers

"What have they done?" Juma was offended at the thought that Mahmoud was so oblivious to the situation. "You need to ask that question?" Juma stood up and stared down at Mahmoud. "Have you forgotten the murder of my brother?"

"Murder? What are you talking about?"

"His death; he was murdered by the infidels."

"Stop, stop, Juma. If the terrorists would stop their activity, *accidents ... accidents* like your brother, my brother, would never, *never* happen.*"* Mahmoud then rose and stepped up to Juma, staring at him face-to-face. His instinct was to punch him in the face. He then took a deep breath and shook his head. He turned to walk toward the door.

"I can't believe you would call that an accident!" Juma called after him.

"I can't believe you think what you're doing is right," Mahmoud said over his shoulder. As he got to the door, he stopped and turned around. "He wasn't shot by the Americans, nor was he shot by the terrorists. He was killed in an explosion by the people *you* now work for and support." Mahmoud then walked out the door.

He walked at a fast pace toward his home, very angry at Juma. As he got closer to his home, he started to slow and felt very disappointed in Juma. "This is not what Mustafa would want," he said aloud, wishing that Juma could hear his words. "What am I going to do?"

Mahmoud entered his yard and sat down in a chair outside. He contemplated the events that had occurred since Mustafa's death, the drastic speed and change of events. *Before, Mustafa, Juma, and I would always talk about how horrible terrorists are and how they were destroying the country, but now Mustafa's dead, and Juma is one of them.* He thought about Jasim talking to Juma at the funeral, Juma returning from Jasim's house, Juma being gone all the time, the three Opels, the stuff those strangers were unloading into the tomato garden. It was all too much. *I should keep out of this business,* he finally decided. He got out of the chair and went into his house. He sat down next to his children and pulled them in close and watched TV with them.

17. What Do I Do?

Jasim was temporarily settled in his old friend Khalid's extra room until he could get an apartment. Khalid was a branch member in the Ba'ath Party in Syria. After Jasim's arrival, Khalid explained his situation to the Syrian Intelligence Community, which was preparing to provide full support in the operations Jasim was going to conduct. As a sign of good faith, Jasim was invited to a large gathering of Ba'ath Party officials who were celebrating the promotions of many of the members to the division and branch levels in Khalid's district. The party would be a great chance for Jasim to make connections within the party in Syria. Members of the intelligence community were also expected to attend. Jasim was not sure what to expect; he was surprised with the level of support he was already receiving. After he received the invitation, he went out and bought a nice suit to wear to the party. He wanted to look trustworthy and professional.

After Jasim got ready, he went downstairs and waited in the reception room of Khalid's house. Jasim was impressed with the size of the house. Khalid lived in a neighborhood of Alapo nicknamed the millionaire neighborhood. The houses were vast. Almost everyone in the neighborhood was a high-ranking Ba'ath party member, government official, or officer in the military or police. Khalid came into the room with a big smile. "Are you ready?"

"I am," Jasim said, spinning around. He had been busy staring at a picture of Khalid's family on the wall.

Khalid was accompanied by his eldest son, who was an intern at a hospital where he was working on becoming a resident doctor. They left the house and were driven in a nice Mercedes. On the ride over, they discussed Iraq and what was going on, and why Jasim had left and was now in Syria. Khalid and Jasim had already touched on the topic, but his son was very interested in finding out on his own. Khalid's son was intrigued by the story.

Jasim was surprised when they arrived at the party; it was a much bigger event than he expected. The hall where the event was being held featured beautiful architecture. The decorations within the hall were very elegant and must have cost a lot of money. By the time they arrived, there were already well over two hundred guests inside. An overdressed usher, in a tuxedo three sizes too big, took them to their table.

The table was at the front of the room, where the guests of honor—the newly promoted—were seated. Among those men were Sultan Mohammad Sultan, who just was promoted to division member; Ismayil Ghalib Nur, new to the branch level; and Bakr Ghanim Bakr, also branch level. There were several other high-ranking members at the table. Jasim was seated between Sultan Mohammad—a man who seemed very comfortable at a table full of high-ranking members—and Khalid.

The main course was lamb. Jasim decided it was a good time to start making contacts. He didn't think these people could help him right away, but it would be good for him to know them in the future. Almost everyone at the table was interested in knowing about Jasim's plight, and he was peppered with questions about being in jail in Iraq and what was really going on the in the country. Jasim was very surprised by the interest he received from the group. Sultan Mohammad asked the most questions, but everyone at the table was just as interested in learning and getting an inside scoop. Jasim was careful to conceal his involvement, not knowing what would happen to the information, but he was more than willing to talk about the atrocities committed by the Americans against him and his family. He told them about having to sneak out of the country once he was sure the Americans were going to try to arrest him again.

After dinner, Sultan asked Jasim to meet his son. "My son talks about Iraq all the time. I am sure he would love to hear what is going on—more than what he sees on the news."

"I will be happy to talk with him."

"He gets so annoyed with the news. I mean, you can only take so much of what they say and work into what is really going on. After all, the Americans control most of the news coming out of the country."

Sultan escorted Jasim over to a small area with chairs, off to the side of the large room. Jasim took a seat and leaned back; he had not eaten so much and so well in a very long time. Just as he was getting comfortable, they were approached by a young man. Sultan rose to his feet, and Jasim followed suit.

"This is my son, Mohammad," Sultan said with a proud smile. "He is a college student and my eldest."

Jasim extended his hand to meet the young man. He looked uncomfortable meeting someone new but gave a Jasim a hearty handshake.

"Son, this is Jasim. He just got here from Iraq; he was escaping from the Americans there."

"It is a pleasure to meet you," Jasim said. "Your father speaks highly of you."

"It is nice to meet you also. Did your family come with you?"

"No, unfortunately, I did not have the time to prepare them to come with me, but Allah willing, they will be able to join me here, or even better, I will go home to Iraq when it is better."

"I hope they are all well then," Sultan said in the absence of his son's words.

"Yes, thank you."

"So, why did you pick Syria?" Mohammad asked.

"There are several reasons."

"Do you mind if I ask?" Mohammad said.

Just then, Sultan was called to go and meet some other individuals. Jasim could see that Mohammad did not want to be at the party. He leaned in close, as if to tell Mohammad a secret. "Let's go outside, get away for a second. I need to smoke anyway."

Mohammad followed, as if on command. They went outside and around the corner of the building, where not too many people would notice them. Mohammad seemed relieved to get away, as did Jasim. They leaned up against a railing that lined the outside porch. Jasim lit a cigarette.

"As to your questions of why I left," Jasim said, not really pausing for an answer, "well, first off, as your father said, the Americans are trying to arrest me. They can't do that if I'm in Syria."

"Why do they want to arrest you?"

"I was high in the Ba'ath Party in Iraq."

"That's it?" Mohammad asked, confused.

"Well, that's why they arrested me the first time," Jasim said matter-of-factly.

This immediately piqued Mohammad's curiosity. He started to become jittery with questions. He stood up straight and turned toward Jasim. "The first time?" The words stumbled out of Mohammad's mouth.

Jasim tried to ignore his excitement; he didn't want to scare the kid off. He puffed his cigarette and stared out onto the streets of Alapo. "After the invasion and the collapse of our government, Americans rounded up all the high-ranking officials in Iraq. I was one of them."

"How long were you in jail?"

"Let's see, I spent about a month, maybe more in a jail in Mosul, and then Abu-Ghraib for about …"

Mohammad cut him off, "Abu-Ghraib, you were at Abu-Ghraib?"

"For about five months," Jasim continued, temporarily ignoring the interruption, "then Um Qasr, near Bucca, until I was released just a short while ago."

"That means you were at Abu-Ghraib when the Americans committed those horrible atrocities against Muslims."

Jasim paused for a second and looked at Mohammad and then back out into the city. He couldn't decide if he should go down the road this kid was begging him to go down. It would be very easy to take a kid like this and push him into going to Iraq. *He is the son of a high-ranking member, and if I do …*

He left his self-doubt for a later time. Mohammad wanted answers.

"Worse than you could imagine," he said as he turned and focused his gaze directly into Mohammad's eyes. Jasim thought to himself that Mohammad's father should be proud of his son, and he will be a hero when he returns.

"They would march us around without clothing and make us do disgraceful things in front of women and each other. These are things I cannot talk about; discussing them only makes the acts that much more demeaning, and I will not give them that satisfaction. They have it on the news, but imagine worse than that, and it is worse than even what you could imagine." Jasim only knew stories from other prisoners who were in Bucca with him. He didn't even know if they were telling the truth or if they were reacting to the stories and pictures that were all over the news. He had not been through such things, but he knew it was a powerful component in swaying people's opinions. It sounded better in the first person than if he was to say a friend went through such things. It didn't matter either way; the fact is that those things did happen, and he wasn't going to let the occupiers of his country get away with it.

"I saw that on TV. I was so mad. That whole situation in Iraq, those stupid Americans thinking they can do whatever they want. Meanwhile, they have no regard for our faith. Someone needs to stop them."

Jasim was caught off guard by the passion this young Syrian had toward the Americans, but at the same time, it felt right. "You should see Iraq; Americans arrest all these people for no reason."

"I know; they also kill innocent people, and they are destroying not only the country, but Islam."

The two continued to talk about Iraq, about what Mohammad had seen on TV, attacking mosques, everything. After a while, they decided they needed to go back inside. After all, Jasim was at the party for a whole other reason than to talk to this kid. Jasim gave Mohammad his cell phone number and told him to call him the following day, and they could meet somewhere and continue to talk.

They walked in the front doors, and Khalid immediately rushed over and grabbed Jasim. "Where have you been? There are several men who are looking to talk to you."

"I ..."

"No time, we will talk about that later." Jasim was hurried over to a group of men whom Jasim could only guess were intelligence officers. Jasim followed them over to a corner of the room, where they sat and discussed Jasim's plans to recruit and send people to Iraq to help in the fight. The men seemed impressed with his crude plans and asked Jasim to meet them the following day in their office.

The following morning, Jasim woke up to a phone call from Mohammad, who was on his way to school. He asked to meet him in the afternoon, maybe around 1 p.m. Jasim agreed; he would be downtown to meet with intelligence anyway, and Mohammad's school was in that area. Mohammad then got up, got ready, and took a taxi to the intelligence office.

When he arrived at the building, which looked like a house, he was searched at the door. He was then allowed to proceed into the front hall area, a small room with little lighting. It had a no windows, just a hall coming from the front door and a hall heading into the back. Situated at the end of the hall from the door was a desk manned by a secretary, who was a young, low-ranking soldier in a Syrian military uniform. Jasim told him he had a meeting. The young soldier directed him to take a seat in one of the four chairs that lined the wall just behind his desk.

Jasim took a seat. He noticed that the soldier had no phone on his desk, nor did he bother to get up to notify anyone that Jasim had arrived. There was a fan sitting across the room, blowing cool air around. The front door remained open, and strong, glaring light made it difficult for Jasim to look in the secretary's direction.

After thirty minutes of waiting, Jasim went back up to the secretary. "I was wondering how long it would be."

"Have a seat, sir. They will get you when they are ready."

Jasim sat back down and continued to stare off into space. Another hour passed, and someone had come in through the front door. Jasim sat up straight and tried to see who it was, but the person was silhouetted by the glare of light at the door. Jasim stood up. He figured it would be best, just in case it was someone he had met the night before. As he rounded the secretary's desk, the new arrival's face came into view. The man looked Jasim up and down and walked past him down the hall, which seemed like a forbidden zone to Jasim. After the man passed, Jasim sat down. After another hour of waiting, Jasim started to get restless in his seat. He didn't understand why they were making him wait so long.

He walked back up to the secretary, who had been sitting and reading some kind of manual the whole time Jasim had been there. "Do they want me to come back another day?"

"They will call you when they are ready."

Jasim didn't know what to do with the answer. He had been sitting for over two hours, and nothing had happened. He stood there for a second and decided he could step outside and stretch his legs. The sun seemed to be brighter than usual, after he had been in the dimly lit waiting room. He stepped to the side of the guard at the door and lit a cigarette.

Just then, the secretary's head popped out the door. "They are ready for you."

Jasim threw down his cigarette and followed the secretary down the forbidden hallway. He was led into an office of one of the gentlemen he had met the previous night.

The man explained that it was hard to get the details worked out, but they had decided he would be given money on a monthly basis, as long as he could prove that the money was reaching the fighters in Iraq. Jasim explained about Abu-Zah'ara, his fighters, and their missions. He explained the smuggling of fighters into the country. The gentleman took copious notes and then stepped out of the office. He came back thirty minutes later. He explained that they would provide him with up to a hundred thousand US dollars a month if he could prove the money was reaching Abu-Zah'ara and his fighters. There would have to be explanations for where the money was spent, not detailed, just enough that they could justify giving him the money. They needed five more days to get all the paperwork and money in order. The man explained that Jasim's story would be checked for accuracy before he would be given the money, and he would be held accountable for the money. Jasim agreed and stated he would ship the money as soon as he got it. Jasim agreed to return in a few days to give the man more information that was needed to fill out his paperwork.

By the time Jasim left the office, it was past 1:00 p.m. He walked down the street to the nearest main road and hailed a cab. Once inside, he called Mohammad and asked to meet him for lunch somewhere near the school. Jasim got to the market next to the school and went into the restaurant with a green awning, as per Mohammad's instructions. He sat wondering if he could really convince this Syrian student to join their group. Jasim had recruited many young individuals in Iraq, but that was different. The fight was at their doorstep, and they had to deal with it one way or another. Jasim would just sit and wait for an opening to get them to join their side. For Jasim to get Mohammad, it would take real convincing. He didn't know what Mohammad's intentions were, and it may take time. He might use Mohammad to get to other students in the area.

Mohammad entered the small restaurant. It was empty, and he was able to pick out Jasim right away. He walked over and sat down next to him. They ordered some food from the waiter.

"I've been thinking about what you said," Mohammad started, after ordering. "I mean, what you said about Iraq." Mohammad was shifting from side to side in his chair. The waiter brought them some cans of Pepsi. Mohammad stopped and opened his drink, fiddling with the pop top.

"What about Iraq?" Jasim said as he watched the awkward young man.

"Well, I'm sick." Mohammad stopped. "I just can't believe what those occupiers are doing to our Muslim brothers."

"It is appalling," Jasim said, knowing he had heard these words from several other people before. He could tell Mohammad was headed down the right road, which was surprising to him. He only had to wait for Mohammad to say the words.

Mohammad didn't seem to hear Jasim. He seemed to be reaching back into his memory for words he had practiced all day long. "I was thinking in school today. The teacher was talking, and all I could think is there was no point in me going to school and learning things I don't care about. School did nothing; it didn't help anybody. I can't sit here, going to school, while innocent people are being killed, mosques are being destroyed, and my religion being disgraced to the world. Kids my age in Iraq can't even go to school anymore; they have to worry about the Americans. I want to help them, just as they would if I was in the same situation here in my country."

Jasim was pleased with the words coming out of Mohammad's mouth. All the rhetoric had already been instilled in Mohammad, and it was as if he was waiting for Jasim to come along and point him in the right direction. Jasim started to bring up some of the atrocities he had seen, and Mohammad listened intently. "There is this kid from my village, maybe a few years older than you, who worked in the market, selling vegetables to take care of his mother, father, and brother. Then, one day, out of nowhere, the Americans came to the market and shot him. No explanation."

"That is what I mean," said Mohammad. "How can I sit in school and do nothing when things like that are happening?"

"What if I told you there is a way you can help the Iraqi people?"

Mohammad stopped playing with the pop top to his Pepsi can and focused on Jasim. "Like what, what do you mean?"

Before Jasim answered, he waited for the waiter to place their plates of lamb kabob in front of them. "Well, I have friends that can help you, train you. You can be right with them, helping them rid our country of the occupiers." Jasim paused for a second to let the information sink in for Mohammad. "Think of the duty you would be giving to Allah, your fellow Muslims, and the Iraqi people."

Mohammad glanced up at the TV in the corner of the restaurant. The volume was turned down, but it showed pictures of American tanks. "It is my duty as a Muslim. What do I do?"

Jasim said, "I will give you five days to think about it."

"Why so short?"

"Like you said, they are fighting and dying now. They need help now. Look, it will take three hundred US dollars to get you across the border and down to Mosul. I will call you in four nights and tell you where to meet me on the fifth day. Then, if you show up, I know you are choosing to do the right thing, and you are not just talking a big game."

18. Coordination and Supplies

The vegetable market was thriving in the warm, sunny morning. Abu-Zah'ara leaned against his car, watching some men as they loaded a truck with large bags of rice. One of the loaders looked like he was barely fifteen years old, and he struggled to lift each sack and throw it in the back of the truck. Abu-Zah'ara turned his head to look down the other side of the sidewalk and found Abu Ahmed approaching.

He greeted him with a kiss on each cheek. "Have everyone meet in New Mosul for lunch, after prayer."

"I will see you there, Allah willing," Abu Ahmad said as he turned and left in the direction he came from. Keeping meetings short helped keep coalition forces off of them, and if there were any spies around, they wouldn't be able to get any information.

Abu-Zah'ara leaned up against his car again and watched as the fifteen-year-old tried to lift a bag above his head to be put in the truck and promptly dropped it on the ground, spilling its contents. Another man nearby yelled at the frantic kid as he tried to scoop the rice back into the bag.

Abu-Zah'ara's phone rang, and he fumbled through his pocket to answer it. "Ten minutes," the voice on the other end rang out and then hung up. Abu-Zah'ara placed the phone back in his pocket and turned around and leaned his elbows on the roof of the car as he looked around the market.

"This is it; these are the people I fight for, the laborers, the poor ... they need to thrive and do so free of oppression," Abu-Zah'ara said to himself as he watched crowds of people mull through the market. Down the busy market street, he saw Salahadeen approach. He lit up; it had been a long time since he had seen him, and today he could make Salahadeen proud. Salahadeen had given him all the tools to make up everything he was today.

Accompanying Salahadeen was one individual Abu-Zah'ara had never seen before, but he trusted if he was with Salahadeen that he was on their side.

"*Salaam alaikum*," Salahadeen said as he stretched out his arms for an embrace. Abu-Zah'ara pushed off his car and kissed him on both cheeks.

"Welcome, friend," Abu-Zah'ara said as he walked around to the driver's side, and all three men got in. As they fought the market traffic to get out, Salahadeen introduced the other man as Towfiq, but they kept conversation to a minimum. They had good reason to be fearful. Abu-Zah'ara took a long, roundabout way toward New Mosul. The house they were going to was nearby in comparison to the market, but they had to be sure no one was following them and that they didn't run into a checkpoint. Salahadeen's protection was very important.

They arrived at a two-story home and entered through the gate. When they got into the house, Juma was there, setting up for lunch.

Juma had a stack of supplies that Abu-Zah'ara had asked for, sitting on one of the nearby cushions that were sprawled around the room for seating. Juma was busy spreading food out on a serving tray and didn't hear them come into the room. He heard a noise and turned to find three men staring down at him, one of whom was Abu-Zah'ara. They weren't talking, and Juma knew they wanted him out of the house. He stood up and kept his eyes on the ground, scooting along the wall to go around the three men as he went out the front door. He went down the steps to the yard and sat on the last step. He pulled out his cigarettes and lit one.

As soon as he was out of the house, the other three sat down and made themselves comfortable.

"How do you afford such a large house?" Salahadeen asked Abu-Zah'ara.

Abu-Zah'ara grinned. "The people of Mosul love and support us, and they provided us with a home."

Salahadeen nodded with approval as he peered around the room and out the doorways that led to other rooms, knowing full well that was not quite how Abu-Zah'ara had come by the house. "You have become everything I hoped you would," Salahadeen said as he continued to look around. He then sat up and pointed to Towfiq as he looked at Abu-Zah'ara. "Towfiq is an expert who will be very vital to you in the future."

Abu-Zah'ara was leaning against the wall with his head back; he turned his head toward Towfiq, still resting it on the faint yellow painted wall. "And what is your specialty, may I ask, Towfiq?"

"Salahadeen, thanks to Allah, found me in Kirkuk. I was working as a laborer. Before that, I had graduated from Baghdad University with a bachelor's degree in electrical engineering. Then Salahadeen saw me, and I went for training. I am skilled in assembling all sorts of bombs—small, big, cars, people; different types of explosives. You name it, I can make it."

Abu-Zah'ara perked up, and his eyes widened. He sat up, and the wheels in his head began to turn. *There are so many possibilities available with an expert in explosives.* "Yes ... indeed, your skills are very welcome, and so is any brother that is willing to fight, skilled or not. Thanks to Allah."

"Thanks to Allah," Salahadeen repeated.

Abu-Zah'ara continued, "One of my men, Abu-Zakiriyah, who you'll meet later, has come up with simple mines, but perhaps he will work with you and learn your skills. He is smart and a fast learner." The idea of having an explosives expert opened so many possibilities to Abu-Zah'ara. Abu-Zakiriyah had done a very good job up to this point, and the two of them could create exactly what he needed to complete many missions.

"*Insha-allah,* Allah willing," Towfiq added in.

The three sat and discussed their past as they waited for prayer. After prayer, they waited for the other to arrive.

Juma knocked on the door with some more food in his hands. Abu-Zah'ara helped him bring it in from the car. Juma, sensing the group wanted him to leave, moved toward to the door just as Abu-Ahmad and Abu-Zakiriyah walked through the door. This made Juma feel more uncomfortable as he leaned against the wall to allow them to pass, and he went for the door.

"Stop," Salahadeen called after him. "At least come enjoy the food that you brought for us."

"Thank you, sir," Juma stuttered out, "but I should be going. I'm not hungry."

"No, come, sit."

Juma reluctantly agreed after looking at Abu-Zah'ara, who shot a look conveying that Juma should do whatever Salahadeen asked him. Juma was frightened to sit down right away and stuck to answering the door as everyone arrived, making sure the gate was locked once Abu-Sayf and Abu-Aiya arrived.

After sitting down with the rest, Juma silently ate his food, as quiet introductions were made between the two newcomers and the rest of the group. He tried not to make it obvious that he was rushing, but knew if he took too long, he might make everyone mad. He kept to himself and concentrated on the food he was eating, careful not to make eye contact with anyone. He thought if he left too fast, he would offend Salahadeen, and likewise for everyone else there. Juma had not felt accepted by anyone other than Abu-Zah'ara, who at times had taken him under his wing and other times would snap at him without warning.

As lunch began to wind down, Juma thanked them all for lunch and rushed out the door. When he had made it down the steps into the yard and was getting the keys out to open the gate, he heard the door open. Juma spun around to see who it was, just in time to catch a set of keys, dropping his in the process.

"Grab that notebook out of my car," Abu-Zah'ara called as he disappeared back into the house.

Juma fumbled with the keys as he tried to open the car door. He knew he had long overstayed his welcome; this only prolonged the feeling, and he wanted to leave. He pulled the notebook out of the car and locked the doors. He then turned to walk around the car and tripped over the small row of rocks that separated the garden from the driveway. In the process, he threw the notebook in the air and its contents spilled all over the dirt of the garden. He pulled himself up and bent over to pick up the notebook. It was open to a page that had a list of police stations, and nearby there was a map of Mosul, a good map that looked like a picture taken from the sky. He picked it up and started to dust everything off. He then carefully made his way back to the house, not wanting to fall again.

When he opened the door to go into the house, he heard Salahadeen saying, "They'll hear about this attack around the world." The conversation abruptly stopped, and everyone turned to Juma. They all had cups of tea in their hands, and all seemed to freeze with Juma's presence. Juma handed the notebook to Abu-Aiya, who was sitting nearest to the door, and left.

Abu-Aiya leaned forward and handed the notebook to Abu-Zah'ara. "Are you sure about that one?" he said, half out of disgust at the presence of a newcomer, but careful enough not to overstep Abu-Zah'ara's authority.

"Don't worry. Americans killed his brother for no reason, and he has done a great job since he started working with us. He is very dedicated and reminds me of myself when I was young. He could be a great leader someday. Plus, Jasim trusts him, and he has known him since he was born, so I trust him too," Abu-Zah'ara said as he opened his notebook.

Abu-Aiya nodded but didn't really accept the answer.

Abu-Zah'ara pulled out the map and unfolded it, hanging it up on the wall with some tape. There were markings all over the map. "I've been drawing this up with the help of Abu-Ahmad. It has been a work in progress for the last two months." Abu Ahmad shook his head in agreement.

"No one is taking notes, because we want as little as possible to be found of our planning. Today, all we are going to cover is coordination and supplies. The rest will come as we get closer," Abu-Zah'ara said, as he made sure to make eye contact with everyone in the room, so they knew how serious he was about the subject. He trusted his men, but he did not trust a note taken on a piece of paper. If the Americans got a hold of anything, they might exploit it and ruin all the work the group had put into this.

"Abu-Zakiriyah," he said, pointing to him, "I want you and Towfiq to coordinate and make at least eight car bombs and as many roadside bombs as you can. Go and see Abu-Ahmad for any money you need, and he might be able to acquire supplies for you also."

"Do we have a place to work?" Towfiq asked. He was new to the group and obviously had no idea as to the size and capabilities of this new team.

Abu-Ahmad chimed in, "I should get one in the next few days, Allah willing."

"Abu-Sayf," Abu-Zah'ara said, shifting his gaze over to him, "I need you to get with Abu-Sa'ad and get some martyrs. I think it will really help us out if we are going to use these car bombs."

Abu-Sayf nodded, acknowledging the tough task ahead to find, recruit, and mold someone into a desire to blow himself up. Whether for religious duty or not, it was not a task taken lightly or hastily, nor thought of as being easily done.

Abu-Zah'ara continued with his instructions for Abu-Sayf. "And I need you to do some reconnaissance of the police headquarters, in addition to Yarmook and Sheikh Fathi police stations."

"We'll get on it."

"Abu-Aiya, I need three mortar teams on the same locations. Help each other out. Find a good spot to launch from and some backup locations. I don't want word getting out, so give as little information as possible to your soldiers. Abu-Ahmad will handle the money and weapons for all of this. In addition, he will find a place for Abu-Zakiriyah and Towfiq."

Salahadeen listened to Abu-Zah'ara's instructions with awe; he knew Abu-Zah'ara was smart, but he didn't think about how well this was thought out.

"I think that is enough for now," said Abu-Zah'ara, looking around the room at each of his men. With that, they all got up and started to exchange good-byes. "Abu-Zakiriyah, take Towfiq to Abu-Sa'ad, and get him set up with a place. Keep close contact with him," Abu-Zah'ara said as everyone exited through the front door.

He then picked up his phone and called Juma. "I'm leaving soon," he said without explanation and hung up the phone.

Salahadeen and Abu-Zah'ara were left alone to discuss the details of the attack. "I was wondering if you need coordination with some out-of-town groups for this?" Salahadeen asked.

"I could use the men. I have talked to three other groups in Mosul, and more men are always welcome."

"When do you need them by?"

"The attack is in nine days."

"Don't you need more time than that?" Salahadeen asked.

"The weapons are collected, the explosives are ready to be made into bombs, and as I said at the beginning, Abu-Ahmad and I have been planning this out for two months. Coordination with other groups already began."

"I will get you the men, but it might not be until right before you need them, Allah willing."

"Allah willing, and thank you."

Just then, they heard a creak as the front door slowly opened a bit, with Juma cautiously standing behind it, waiting for an indication that he could enter.

Abu-Zah'ara waved him in, and Juma began to clean up all the teacups and food that had been left around the room. Abu-Zah'ara got up, took down the map, and placed it in his notebook. Salahadeen accompanied him as he left the house.

19. Coin of Excellence

It was going to be a normal day. Jeremiah woke up at six a.m., went to breakfast, and went to call his family. It was nighttime back home, and he was sure that someone should be home to answer the phone. The phone center was pretty empty at this time of day, but there were still a few soldiers murmuring away to their loved ones. The dust was heavy, and the light allowed in by the rising sun made it glisten. Jeremiah sat down at a phone in the center, allowing for some semblance of privacy with space left between him and the few other callers. He dialed the number shown on the phone card, and then his PIN, then his parents' phone number. The process was tedious, and anytime he messed up a number, he had to hang up and start all over again.

He heard, "Hello," from the other end of the line.

"Dad, it's me," Jeremiah said, hoping they had a good connection.

A few seconds later, he heard an answer. "Hey, son, how are things?"

"Great, I really ..." He heard a garbled noise on the other end. Jeremiah thought to himself, *Great, a delay in the call makes the conversation difficult.*

"Dad, there is a delay, just so you know. Like I was saying, I'm great; I'm enjoying it over here. How's the homefront?"

"Same ol', same ol'," his dad answered. "Your mom is constantly worried with all the stuff she sees on the news ..." He paused for a second and started in with his normal disgruntled voice, "To tell you the truth, I can't watch the news."

Jeremiah rolled his eyes and propped his head up with his hand, which he had leaned against the small wall between him and the booth next to him. He'd had this conversation with his dad a million times. "Why, Dad?"

"To watch all those young soldiers lose their life over oil ..."

The Land Between Two Rivers

Jeremiah interrupted. "Dad, you don't even know what's going on. You can't say that. They are men anyway, and they are fighting for you, not for oil." Jeremiah was getting annoyed with his father, who never listened to him. He tried to avoid the obvious topic of his being in the military and in Iraq to keep some sort of peace between them, but it arose constantly. "Can I talk to Mom?" Jeremiah said, in an effort to change the subject.

Hers was the next voice he heard. "Hi, how are you?" She had already picked up when he was talking to his dad.

"Good, Mom. How are you?" There was a click, indicating his dad had hung up his extension.

"I'm good. McKayla and I went looking for dresses the other day."

"She told me." McKayla had sent Jeremiah an e-mail every day since he left, and he was up to date on every move she made. It was nice to know what was going on at home, but sometimes he thought he could deal without the stress of knowing everything. He would never tell her that.

"I miss you so much," she said in the silence.

"I miss you too, Mom. Dad tells me you are still a worrywart."

"I can't help it; you're my only son."

"Don't watch the news. It's too negative."

"It's my only connection to you."

Jeremiah couldn't believe how annoyed he got with these words. He knew his mom meant well, so he tried to leave it alone. "Okay, but don't worry so much. What's Dad's deal?"

"You know he hates the war."

"Try to explain it to him. You should see these people, the Iraqis; they've gone through so much crap, and I want to give them every opportunity that we have as Americans but take for granted." Jeremiah tried to keep his cool with his mom; he knew his frustration with the situation was toward his dad and not her. "This is not some stupid thing for oil."

"I know, son," Jeremiah could hear the annoyance in her voice.

"Just once, that's all I want, just one time for him to look at me and be proud of what I'm doing. I believe in this one, Mom, more than anything else I have ever done or will do."

Silence fell over the conversation for a few seconds, and Jeremiah felt bad that he wanted to get off the phone. He could feel the heat start to creep into the murky call center, and he wasn't looking forward to sweating so early in the morning. A soft wind was blowing dust in from outside, making the air uncomfortable to breathe. "Mom, I have to get going. I got work to do. I just wanted to call and say hi.."

"Okay, I love you."

"You too, Mom." Jeremiah hung up and picked up his weapon. He had just cleaned it last night, and there was already a fine coat of dust on it. He wiped it off as he stood up and slung it over his back. He stepped out of the call center and stopped for a second to adjust to the sunlight as he put on his cap. There were soldiers everywhere, walking, chatting with their friends. It seemed odd to him how quickly everyone had adjusted to living in this foreign country, on this small base, with the few amenities it had.

He crossed the gravel road, which had deep ruts from tanks that rolled down the street on a daily basis, turned, and headed toward his room. He had been at the base long enough that he learned the fastest way to his small hut was to cut through the small lot in front of the post exchange, cut around the side, and walk in front of the kabob stand, which was commanded in midday by local Iraqis serving food. From there, he could cross another gravel road and cut into the tall cement walls surrounding a group of trailers where another unit lived. Once he passed through their living quarters, he would go past the cement walls on the far side and cross yet another street, which led right into the area where he lived. Before he learned this trick, he would walk around everything on the side of the roads, dodging Humvees, Strykers, and tanks, which took up most of the road, and taking a considerable more amount of time. It was starting to get hot, and he was choking on the dust kicked up by the warm wind whipping across the base. It pelted his eyes, making it difficult to see.

As he entered his unit's living area, he stopped by his soldiers' rooms, making sure they were up and moving and hopefully had already made their way to the chow hall.

"Ali, you are wanted in Colonel Ilyas's office with Lt. Salem," a policeman said as he poked his head in the door of the sleeping area, where Ali was sitting talking to everyone. Ali instantly became nervous. Chuckles circulated around the room, and everyone shot glances at Ali. He started to rack his brain for anything he could possibly have done wrong in the last week. He quickly adjusted his uniform and buttoned up his shirt covering his dirty tank top. He made his way out the door and went straight for Lt. Salem's office. If Salem was still in his office, he could warn Ali of what was to come, and it wouldn't be such a surprise when he walked in Colonel Ilyas's door.

He knocked on the open door to Salem's office, which also housed three other officers. They all had rickety desks along the walls that were covered in paperwork, which seemed to be strewn about. No one answered, so Ali stepped in. One of the officers was on the phone.

Salem and the other two were buried in paperwork and must not have heard him knock. "Sir, Lieutenant Salem, Colonel Ilyas is requesting our presence in his office," Ali mumbled.

"Now? What is it about?" Salem said, not glancing up from his work. He was busily writing something down.

"Yes sir, now."

Salem slammed his pen down, stood up, and pushed his chair back, bumping into the officer who was on his phone. That officer adjusted his chair to allow Salem to get out of his small corner of the world. Salem looked up at Ali and seemed very frustrated. As they made it into the hallway, Ali blurted out, "Do you know what this is about?"

"You were the one that came and got me, as I recall."

"But, I was just ..."

Salem cut Ali off. "You must have done something. Corporals are not usually needed in the colonel's office. It's about time they did something about this," Salem said as he hastened his pace down the dimly lit hallway and winked over his shoulder. Ali trailed behind him.

The walls were painted green on the bottom half and cream on the upper half. The floor tiles desperately needed replacing. There were men everywhere; as they were unwilling to go home in between shifts, offices overflowed with men who spilled out into hallways. They smoked, drank tea, and tried to listen in to whatever TV was on inside the buzzing officers' offices. When they reached the end of the corridor, they turned left before the staircase, which was unnecessarily guarded by a weak, young officer. This was where the higher-ranking officers and administration of the police department were taken care of. At the end of the hallway was the colonel's door.

Ali could not figure out what was going on, and he started to sweat in the nicely air-conditioned hallway. Salem knocked on the door. "Come in," came the shout from within, as someone inside pulled the door open before Salem could grab the handle. Inside were three other officers—the colonel's usual entourage of two and a young kid who was brought in to serve the colonel. His office was large, and he commanded a large desk at the far end of the room. Two windows reached from floor to ceiling off to the right, but as a precautionary measure, sandbags were stacked in front of them. Trickles of light came in from in between the bags. The room was ringed with several chairs and a table in the corner with fresh tea. Salem walked in and moved straight for the front of the room. Ali paused at the door for a second, as the young kid inside pushed his way past, out the door. Ali took a deep breath and proceeded inward for his undecided doom.

He went to the center of the room and stood next to Salem, who was talking to Colonel Ilyas. The colonel had come around to talk to Salem.

The other men were talking, and they stopped as Ali came to attention in front of his commanding officer. Ali could feel their eyes burning into the back of his neck, and Colonel Ilyas had a devious grin across his face. Ali then started to feel weak and realized he hadn't taken a breath since he moved from the doorway. It felt like he had been standing there for twenty minutes before Colonel Ilyas turned his attention to Ali.

"I heard about your heroic actions that saved the lives of many of our men." Ilyas stood and walked directly in front of Ali. "Your motivation, hard work, and dedication to our mission of protecting this city have paid off. At the request of many men and officers right here in this room, I have decided to promote you to the rank of lieutenant. You are taking charge of your squad, and Lt. Salem will be moving to other duties. You proved that you know what you are doing," Ilyas said as he extended his hand in congratulation.

Ali exhaled; he wasn't in trouble. He hadn't even thought about something good happening. Ali reached out for his hand as the men in the room chuckled. Salem turned and handed the new rank to Colonel Ilyas, who placed on the shoulder boards of Ali's uniform. "As your first duty, I want you in charge of the checkpoint on the road headed south out of Mosul."

"Yes, sir. Thank you, sir." Congratulations went around the room, and Ali shook the hands of his new peers and received their hugs and kisses on each cheek. He was nervous with his new appointment but knew he could always ask questions of Salem. Just as he finished shaking the last person's hand, he turned to walk out of the office and was surprised to see some Americans coming swiftly down the hall toward him. He took a few steps back into the office and got out of their way. Lt. Colonel DeLuca was the first in the door. "Corporal Ali," he said, quickly followed by interpretation by a tall, elderly gentleman who usually accompanied DeLuca, "how are you?"

Ali was shocked that a US commander remembered him and his name.

"Sir, we have just promoted him to lieutenant," Salem said from behind Ali.

"Congratulations, Lieutenant. You are well deserving of the rank."

Ali stepped to the side as DeLuca made his way up to Colonel Ilyas and greeted him with a strong handshake. "Good to see you, Colonel."

"I thought you would be arriving much later. Let me get you some tea."

"I would appreciate it. You are always so welcoming to us, and you are a gracious host."

Colonel Ilyas gestured to one of the men in the back of the room, who promptly left.

"May I?" Lt. Colonel DeLuca asked Colonel Ilyas. Ilyas nodded. "Ali—excuse me, *Lieutenant* Ali," DeLuca said as he turned in his direction. Ali promptly stepped forward, again confused by his newfound recognition with these individuals.

"I wanted to present you with this," DeLuca said as he extended his hand; in it was a large coin. Ali took it from his left hand and shook DeLuca's right hand, looking bewildered. "It's a coin of excellence from the 2/38 Infantry Battalion, recognizing you for your bravery during that patrol. I hope that more policemen will follow your lead. This is what Iraq needs to help the people take control of your country."

Ali smiled, said, "Thank you," and stared back at DeLuca, still shaking his right hand. An awkward silence fell across the room, and Ali instantly looked around, dropped his hand, and left.

As Ali walked down the hallway toward the guarded staircase, he asked himself, "What just happened?" as he glanced down at the coin in his hands and looked at the new rank on his shoulders. He couldn't help but wonder if this was a dream, or had any of this actually happened? Did he really get married, and was his new wife really with child? Did Yassin really die? Did he really fight the terrorists? Did he really save lives? Was he promoted, and did a lieutenant colonel in the US Army remember him and recognize him for his actions? He had heard of Lt. Colonel DeLuca and always looked up to him and all his men, and now they were looking up to him.

He rounded the corner to walk back to the room where the rest of the men were hanging out and sleeping. What would they think of what had just happened? Would they accept him? Ali slowed his pace to contemplate, as fear ran over him. He wondered what his fellow policemen would think of him. Ali started to fill with a strange mixture of pride and confusion. As he got near the sleep room, some men were standing in the hallway and patted him on the back and congratulated him. Ali was not quite in the moment; he was still wondering if he was dreaming. As he started to hug his comrades, he knew that he had to do everything he could to fight the terrorists.

20. A Jacket

Mohammad decided it was best not to tell his father what he was doing, in order to avoid any sort of opposition. He gathered up all the money he had saved over the past few months and took it to a money exchanger the previous day, yielding him just over two hundred US dollars. He then went to his mom and dad separately and asked for fifty US dollars to buy new clothes and things for school. He packed the money in the bottom of his backpack, which he only filled halfway, believing that anything he'd need would be provided for him once he arrived in Iraq. As he strutted down the empty sidewalk toward the mosque where he agreed to meet Jasim, he felt like he was on clouds. He was proud and anxious to arrive in Iraq and fight the Americans, but he knew everything was right.

For several months now, he'd been downtrodden, angry, and edgy; now he lost all those feelings. He knew it was his turn to fight. He got to the mosque a little earlier than he was supposed to, climbed the three small steps to the front doors, and turned around, hoping the steps would give him a vantage point to peer in each direction down the road. When it became clear that he could not see Jasim, he went and sat on the small, concrete garden wall adjacent to the mosque. He couldn't sit still, and instantly he was up again, leaning against the railing that ran down the center of the stairs.

Jasim pulled up in a red Mercedes, which was given to him by Syrian Intelligence. "I'll drive you to Kamishly, and I'll explain what to do on the way," Jasim said after Mohammad ran around to the passenger side and climbed in. As they started their drive, Mohammad was jittery in his seat and could not sit still. He started to rattle off what he had done to get the money for the trip. Jasim realized that it would be a long trip if he didn't calm Mohammad down, so he put in cassette tape, singing songs about jihad. Mohammad seemed to enjoy them and calmed down enough to listen to the words. Jasim noticed this instantly; he reached into the center console and pulled out some CDs with similar music and gave them to Mohammad.

Mohammad took them and stared at the booklet covers. Jasim then reached behind his seat and pulled out several DVD cases. "You might like these too."

Mohammad looked at the cases and placed them into his bag. "So where am I going to get training, and how much training? Is there a specific specialty I'm going to have, or am I going to be a foot soldier?" Mohammad began to rattle off questions before Jasim had a chance to answer. "What kind of missions will I do?"

Jasim turned down the music. "Mohammad, you are going to be with a very elite fighting force, led by a good friend of mine, Abu-Zah'ara. They have been fighting this fight since the beginning." Jasim continued to tell embellished stories of Abu-Zah'ara and his men. He had no idea what was in store for Mohammad, but what he did know was Abu-Zah'ara. These stories seemed to satiate temporarily Mohammad's unquenchable thirst for knowledge.

In the heat of the day, the drive to Kamishly seemed to take forever. As they finally pulled into the city, Jasim picked up his phone. "Where are you at?"

"Same place me and you ate," the voice on the other end replied. Jasim had already guessed that was where they would meet, and it took him another fifteen minutes to remember exactly where the restaurant was located. The daytime traffic did not help in this effort. When he finally found the restaurant, it took him another ten minutes to find parking. After parking, both climbed out the car and stretched. The long drive had taken a toll on their bodies. Mohammad shut his door.

"This is your time," Jasim said to Mohammad. "You brought your bag this far; wouldn't you like to take it the rest of the way?" Mohammad immediately opened the door and grabbed his bag. Jasim then reached into the back seat of the car and pulled out a jacket.

"Isn't it a little warm for a jacket?" Mohammad said staring at Jasim who had sweat dripping down his face. Jasim didn't reply, just smiled and winked at Mohammad. They walked over to the restaurant and were greeted with a blast of cool air upon opening the door. The sudden change in temperature made the restaurant feel like a freezer, even though an ice cube could still melt in a few minutes in the room. Jabar met them by the door. Jasim introduced Mohammad, and they escorted him back to where Jabar had been sipping tea. Jasim took a seat next to Jabar, and Mohammad placed himself across the small, round table.

Mohammad was eager to get answers to all the questions that swirled in his head about his future and couldn't help but immediately interrupt

Mohammad and Jasim. "How long does it take to get there? Where will I stay when I'm there? Who will I get to live with?"

Jabar chuckled at the myriad of questions posed by Mohammad. "Don't worry, young man; things will be taken care of," Jasim chimed in and then turned his attention back to Jabar.

"Looks like you are being treated well, and business is good. You're moving fast in this country, as if it is your own," Jabar commented. "By the way, nice car."

"My people are in harm's way, and they don't have time to wait for the Day of Judgment. They have lives and families; they need to live in their own country without the presence of occupiers." Jasim paused and turned around to pull the jacket off the back of his chair. "Which reminds me," he said as he turned back around, "these are the gifts of people who wish for our situation to stabilize." Jasim handed the jacket to a puzzled Jabar. "Of these gifts, the right-hand pocket is for you. The rest is for Abu-Zah'ara."

Jabar smiled and shook his head while he placed the jacket on the chair next to him. "You're faster than I thought."

Mohammad peered at them over his teacup, which was placed up to his mouth. He was confused but knew that since he couldn't get answers to the questions he had asked before, he wouldn't get them now.

Jasim glanced down at his phone, took one last sip of tea, and stood up to leave. Mohammad stood up next, followed by Jabar. Jasim embraced Mohammad. "Go with Allah," he said as he pulled back.

"And you also, and Allah willing, I will see you again," Mohammad said as Jasim left for the door. Jabar nestled back into his chair. "Young man, sit down. We have a long time before we can begin our journey."

Mohammad reluctantly took a seat. He had learned by now that no one was willing to answer his questions. He leaned his head against the glass and stared toward the corner of the dusky coffee shop. He wondered what it would be like down there—his trip, his future work, training, where he would live, and where he would work. He imagined it was like the videos he had seen on the Internet, ones put up by the Taliban in Afghanistan. Training in the mountains was intense. The fighters looked strong and very well-equipped to do their jobs. They had the newest weapons but still seemed effective with the old ones. He couldn't wait until he was just like them. He never really understood politics; his father's arena was never his style. He liked to get into the fight. When he and Arab were little, they would find every excuse to start a fight with the kids in the neighborhood. Mohammad always thought the other kids believed he was weak because so much was given to him by his father, and he didn't want that to be part of his image. Arab would talk him out of it at first, but in the end, he was just as excited to fight.

The feeling of raw power and adrenaline rushing through his veins was the only thing that made him really feel alive. Now he was going to be a fighter for something he believed in. The excitement of it all started to come over him.

21. Good News, Ladies

Mahmoud was sitting in the car of a man who was nice enough to give him a ride toward his village, but they were stuck in traffic. The road was blocked off, and the way it usually went, they would be stuck for several hours. The Americans probably found a bomb in the road, were fighting, searching homes, or something of the sort. Any way it went, it would be several hours before the road cleared up, and it was the only way to get home.

Mahmoud peered out the front windshield and thought about the terrorists and how they were causing so many problems. People couldn't accomplish the simple, everyday tasks others took for granted. Rush hour was bad enough without the road being blocked off; now it would be hours before he could see his family. Their misdeeds had caused the death of Mustafa and countless other Iraqis who had nothing to do with anything but were just trying to live a normal life. Mahmoud flashed back to being in the store at the market, when he realized Mustafa wasn't in the store but in the street. He wondered how many other Iraqis had experienced similar things everyday as women, children, babies, and men—anyone innocent of any wrongdoing—were being killed by these people who called themselves *mujahideen*. Anger rose up in him. "Juma ..." he quietly said under his breath.

"What was that?" the driver said.

Mahmoud looked over at him. "Nothing, I was just thinking," he said and went back to looking at the long line of cars in front of them and listening to people needlessly honk their horns. He thought of Juma, the last time he saw him, and how brainwashed he sounded. Then he thought of the Opels and the tomato garden. As Mahmoud's eyes reached the front of the long line of cars, he could see the Americans pointing their weapons down the street. They seemed so cautious of what they were doing. *I should tell them,* he thought to himself as he shifted forward in his seat. He cocked his head to one side and concentrated on the soldier with the big weapon sitting atop his Stryker, and he knew he had to tell the Americans. That soldier looked too cautious, and Mahmoud knew if he got too close, he might be shot.

He grabbed a hold of the door handle and leaned his body into the door. "I suppose I could get some shopping done. I mean, we have to wait anyway," he said as he pushed the door open with his left hand. "Thank you so much. May Allah bless you."

Mahmoud decided to go to the American base, which was stationed on the old Iraqi base called Ghlizlany. It was the closest one to his present location. He walked a few blocks away from the traffic jam and hired a taxi to take him to the intersection nearest the base. The taxi dropped him off, and as he exited the car, he saw the American checkpoint nearby. He took a deep breath and walked toward them. He was cautious as he approached; he didn't want them to be alarmed and shoot him. He held his ID card in his hand and showed it to them as he got up to the checkpoint.

They searched him. He started to talk, but before he could get a sentence out, he realized that they didn't understand his Arabic. He then tried to speak in English: "I know ..." He couldn't remember the words it had a been a long time since he thought about English. "Not good, bad man ... uhhh ... *Arhabi*." He settled on *Arhabi*, the word for "terrorist" in Arabic.

"*Arhabi?*" one of the soldiers repeated back to him. "You know *arhabi?*"

"*Na'am*, yes, yes." Mahmoud felt like he had accomplished a lot with the short exchange. The soldier smiled, finished searching Mahmoud, and called an officer over. Mahmoud stared at them and tried to decipher what they were discussing. The officer, accompanied by an interpreter, pulled Mahmoud to the side of the checkpoint, around the side of a vehicle.

"Hello, sir," the officer said, with his words echoing in Arabic through the interpreter. "What were you trying to tell my soldiers?"

Mahmoud was confused; he wasn't used to the interpreter and two people talking to him, one in a different language and the other with a thick Sudanese accent. He took a few seconds. "Ah yes, my cousin is a terrorist and he has ..." He was abruptly cut off by the interpreter. Mahmoud became anxious, but the interpreter soon told him to continue. "My cousin, he has weapons, and his brother was killed by terrorists." He was cut off again.

Before he could continue, the officer started to talk. "Okay, look, I have someone you can go talk to. It sounds like you have something very interesting to tell us, and I want to make sure someone has your full attention. I know someone that will be interested in hearing what you have to say," the officer said before Mahmoud had time to object. The officer wandered back toward a small shack, leaving Mahmoud with the Sudanese interpreter and a soldier. The interpreter escorted him over to a bench and sat down next to him.

"Wait here," the interpreter said as he wandered back to the checkpoint to talk to the other American soldiers.

Sitting on the dusty bench, his back to a large barrier, with his legs crossed, he started to tap his foot. He tried to control it by uncrossing his legs, leaning forward, and resting his hands on either side of him. He rocked forward, placing all his weight on his arms, which were weak from all the work he did that day. He had lifted and moved what felt like a hundred cinder blocks, moving them over to the masons and back again. His back ached. He started looking around, first straight ahead at the small shack that the officer and interpreter disappeared into. Then his focus shifted to the scratches and engravings on the bench. He could tell that there was something in English scratched into the bench, but he couldn't make out the words. Perhaps someone wrote the name of a loved one who was all the way over in Iraq, far away from family, fighting a war. It made Mahmoud think about his family. He thought they must be wondering where he was; these days, someone not coming home could mean he or she was killed. He didn't want to wait anymore, so he stood up and turned to walk back out of the checkpoint.

As he turned the corner, a man came up to him. "Sir," an interpreter, this time with a Jordanian accent, said, "How are you today?" The interpreter was with another soldier. The soldiers blended together in Mahmoud's mind. They all looked the same, with their uniforms and same haircuts. He couldn't tell one from the other. The man began to speak to him in English and was closely followed by translation: "You wanted to talk to us?"

"Um ... yes, but it is getting late ... and my family ..." Mahmoud stopped. He came all the way here; no reason to stop now. "Yes, I would like to talk to you."

"Would you like some water?" the soldier said as he handed him an ice-cold bottle of water, dripping water that was sweating from the melting ice inside. Mahmoud took it as the man waved him toward the entrance to the base. "Come on, we will just go over here to talk, away from everyone else," the soldier said with a smile.

Mahmoud took a sip of the water, which was too cold to handle in the heat. This soldier seemed to be a very warm, gentle man, and the interpreter echoed the soldier, as if they were long-lost brothers. On the other side of the entrance, which was guarded by towers and large guns and soldiers everywhere, there was a small path that wound up to a large concrete barrier wall. They each stepped through the small opening in the wall, first the interpreter, then Mahmoud, and finally the soldier. There were several small metal buildings in there. They stepped into the entrance of the first one. The interpreter turned on the light, which took a second to flicker on. The room was simple, just a table with some chairs. The dust was thick in the room, and it looked as if no one had taken care of it, minus a few footprints on the floor.

"Is that water enough," the soldier asked, "or would you like something more, perhaps tea or Pepsi?"

Mahmoud was amazed at the kindness of this young soldier, who couldn't have been more than twenty years old. He had glasses that skewed his large, brown eyes, but that was enough to bring attention away from the large, dark circles under his eyes and the zits that lined his forehead. "I'm fine," he said, answering his question. The interpreter sat down beside Mahmoud, across the table from the soldier.

"My name is John," the soldier said.

Mahmoud smiled; he remembered saying his name in English class when he was growing up. It was one of the first things he had learned. "My name is Mahmoud," he replied, proud that the interpreter did not have to translate this part of the conversation.

"Why have you come here today?"

"Well, my cousin died a few months back, and this Ba'athi came and asked my cousin's brother to be a fighter. And now he has become one of these terrorists, and now I saw with these Opels, and I think he has many weapons in my village." He wracked his brain, making sure there wasn't anything he left out, while the interpreter went on explaining what he said, and John scribbled on his notepad.

John looked down at his notes and pointed with his pen to one section. "Let's start with this. What is your cousin's name, the one that passed away?"

"Mustafa." Just saying the name brought back much of the pain of his death. He tried not to think of it. So much had changed since that day in the market. His life had turned upside down. Everything he knew, loved, and depended on had changed. He didn't have time to grieve; he had to find a way to take care of what he had left of his family.

He painstakingly went though the story of what happened in the market and choked back tears as he detailed Mustafa's death. Then he told the soldier about Jasim coming to the funeral and Juma falling for his stories. He told him about how they used to work together and how things had changed. John seemed genuinely concerned for what Mahmoud had been through. He stopped taking notes while he listened to the stories.

"... and that is it," Mahmoud said, as his stomach turned upside down inside of him.

"You mentioned weapons earlier."

"Well, I don't actually know if they are weapons, but I did see something. A week ago in our village, there were three cars, and they were strangers' cars. They were parked by this garden, and the men were unloading large objects and carrying them into the garden. I didn't check to see what they were, but there is no other reason for that."

John and Mahmoud started going into the details of what Mahmoud saw that day. As they talked, the conversation shifted toward Mahmoud's family and his children. Mahmoud then became anxious; he needed to get back to his family.

John stood up with Mahmoud and shook his hand. "Thank you for coming in here today."

As they started to walk back toward the gate, Mahmoud told John he would come back if he learned anything else. As Mahmoud exited the checkpoint, he questioned if he did the right thing. He felt like he had betrayed his cousin in some way, but at the same time, he need safety for his family, for their future.

They had the lights off in Wynn's room; five of the soldiers and Jeremiah were squished in there, watching *Team America,* when they heard a knock at the door. Duncan reached from where he was sitting on his bed for the door handle.

"Good news, ladies," said their platoon leader as he took account of the people in the room. "We are heading out first thing in the morning. Be up, dressed, and ready to go by 0500." The door shut, and the moaning and groaning began. The movie was only halfway through, but they had all seen it several times. They didn't have too many DVDs to choose from.

"I'll be at your rooms by 0400 to wake you all up. Get some sleep," Jeremiah said as he picked up his uniform top, hat, and weapon and left the room. Jeremiah went straight to bed.

It seemed he didn't even sleep. He swore he had just laid his head down when his alarm jolted him awake. He grabbed his toiletry kit and climbed out of his little room. As he headed to the bathroom, he pounded on his soldiers' doors. He missed being home, where the bathroom was only a few feet away and still inside the house.

He felt tired. The heat was more than he cared to handle during the day, but each day he was closer to going home. He missed McKayla and couldn't wait to get home to her. He was surprised at how well his mom was getting along with her; she usually hated the girls he brought home. Maybe she felt a connection to McKayla because they were both separated from Jeremiah. Maybe it was because McKayla wasn't like other girls he had brought home. She was in college and wasn't there for the parties. She was getting her degree in business administration and would probably do very well with her life. The other girls had no real futures that they thought about.

He finished in the bathroom and walked back past everyone's room. The light was on in one room, but Duncan and Wynn were still in the dark. He knocked on their door again. "Just got up," Duncan said, looking clearly sleepy and disheveled.

"Get ready and be out here by 0440."

"Roger," he said as he flipped on the light that blinded him and then shut the door.

They were riding out to a small village they had been to quite a few times. Jeremiah remembered being out there, and everyone seemed so happy—not like the people in the city. This visit to the village wouldn't be very friendly; they were first going to hit the house of a suspected terrorist and then going to look for a weapons cache. As they pulled into the village, they all prepared to leave the back of the Stryker. The vehicle came to a stop, and the ramp dropped. Jeremiah flashed back to the first time he had been to the village; they were in front of the same house. Last time they were there to break up an insurgent meeting. He could have sworn that it was all a mistake last time, but now that they were poised to open the gates to this home, belonging to a guy named Juma, he wondered if that really *was* an insurgent meeting last time he was there. And was the dead man not an innocent but a terrorist who had died in a battle, killing Americans?

The ramp hit the ground, and his mind cleared. Time to think of the task at hand: knocking down the door and spreading into the house like a forest fire. He realized the mystery and danger that lay behind a closed door, and it gave him that extra bit of adrenaline rush. When they reached the gate, an old man was in the process of opening it up. This didn't stop the machine that they had created while clearing a house; he was set aside with a guard, and they swarmed into the home. Jeremiah was with the second team in the house, and the rooms he searched had no one in them. He came back to find women and children all huddled together in the main room.

Jeremiah went outside to see if any other men and been captured. The old man was being questioned by Jeremiah's platoon leader. Apparently, he was the father of the man they were looking for, but the answer did not come quickly out of him. He claimed he had not seen his son in over a week. The man was also the *mukhtar* of the village and claimed to know everything that happened in the village and that he was responsible for all of it. At the same time, he admitted to no wrongdoing. Jeremiah went back inside to help search the house for anything illegal—weapons or anything else that could indicate the man's son's involvement in terrorist activity. Jeremiah searched through one of the bedrooms and couldn't find anything. He went back to the family room and was looking at the bookshelf, which was covered in pictures. Most of the pictures were of two men, who looked almost like twins. Jeremiah picked it up and pointed to one of the men and said, "Juma," as he turned to one of the women in the room.

"No, no," she said as she took the picture from him. "Juma," she said as she pointed to the other man. She pointed back at the first man. "Mustafa," and then said something in Arabic and started to cry. He didn't get quite what she was saying. Jeremiah decided to take the picture so it could be used on a wanted list.

He stepped outside to get orders for what he should do next and handed over the picture. "That guy is the one we are looking for; I got it from the woman inside." The picture was placed in a plastic bag, to go along with the old man's things. They decided to take him in for questioning. Jeremiah yelled to his team to come out of the house; it was time to move down to the garden on the edge of town and fan out to look for weapons. Jeremiah could see that a perimeter had already been put in place so they could search the area.

"Line up on me at double-arm intervals. Look for signs of overturned dirt or anything that would indicate something has been hidden here," Jeremiah yelled out to his soldiers as he stood on the edge of the garden. The sun cresting the horizon made it hard to see who was walking his way. He knew they were soldiers by their outline, but he couldn't see their faces. He heard them echo the orders and recognized their voices. He pulled out his sunglasses and traded out his clear lenses for something better suited for the current lighting. He wiped the dirt off the glasses, while he waited for everyone to line up on the edge of the tomato plants. Then everyone turned and started to walk into the poorly tended garden. It was hard to tell if the dirt had been messed with, but as he passed the fourth row of plants, he noticed the soil was no longer the hard, brittle soil that surrounded the other plants, but a fresh, brown soil. In most gardens, that is what you would expect, but in this one, it was definitely different.

"We got something over here!" he called out as he started to push the dirt aside with his foot. Just below the surface was a wood plank. "I think I found it," he said as Duncan came to his side and helped him carefully brush off the rest of the dirt. There was a handle at either end, made of rope that was encrusted with dirt. The two of them hoisted up the large box, and the surrounding gravel began to fall, revealing several more boxes, each about the same size. Each was a perfect size to hide all kinds of weapons. They set the first box down, and the makeshift wooden lid slid off, revealing RPG rounds. "Oh, shit!" they called out in unison and backed away. They looked around and saw many boxes being pulled out of the ground.

"All right, everybody stop!" The order echoed across the field. "Mark the areas with weapons or where you think the weapons are; we are calling EOD to find the rest of what is hidden in here." Jeremiah turned Duncan around and reached into his bag, revealing the roll of tape he made sure one of his soldiers always had. He marked their cache and did another sweep of the area, looking for anything else that might show more weapons.

22. At Their Fingertips

"We'll figure it out. I mean, we can wait a few extra days," Abu-Ahmed said, leaning forward with his hands gripped onto Abu-Zah'ara's shoulders.

Abu-Zah'ara sighed out, "That was a good amount of the supplies for the mission," as he slunk down into the pillows of the living room of his current home. Abu-Ahmed sat down beside him. "Sometimes we just work so hard, and it starts to slip away," Abu-Zah'ara said, gazing up at the ceiling and shaking his head. He would never act this way in front of anyone else, but he had known Abu-Ahmed for a long time, and the stress of their work could be overwhelming at times. Abu-Ahmed had brought him bad news from a phone call he just finished with Juma. Juma had called and told him what had happened in their village earlier that day. Most of their weapons had been destroyed, and Juma's father, an innocent man, had been detained.

"He was more concerned with a place to stay than with our weapons," Abu-Ahmed snorted at the nerve of someone who obviously had his whole life handed to him.

"He probably cares about the weapons. What would you do in that situation?" Abu-Zah'ara said as he propped himself up onto one elbow.

"We all have been through that situation. I mean, look where you live now, and this will last, what? A month at the very most. That is if you're stupid enough to stay that long."

"He can stay here."

"Are you sure? As it stands, I am the only one that ever knows where you live. Why ruin this place? It is nice, and the Americans will never expect it. The neighbors will never say anything. If you let that kid in here, this house is ruined."

"It's just for a night, and plus, we both know we have to go underground after the attack or at least change everything. The spies will come out of the woodwork when the Americans are spewing money to figure out why all their hard work means crap when people like us have a heart in the fight."

"Weren't you just saying all your hard work for the attack had gone down the drain?"

"Nah, we just need to re-adjust and get the word out. There isn't that many people to tell," Abu-Zah'ara said as he stared across the room and out the window. The tall walls of his current home let him leave the curtains open; it was a nice change. Abu-Ahmed jumped up, which shook him from his daze. "Aren't we late? Everyone is probably waiting for us in New Mosul." Abu-Zah'ara looked up at him as he extended his hands and pulled him to his feet.

"We'll take my car," Abu-Ahmed said. They rushed out the door and climbed into Abu-Ahmed's newly acquired car, a '93 Opel Omega. He usually stuck with Opels because they were as common as could be, cheap, and fast. Abu-Zah'ara climbed into the passenger's seat and leaned his chair back partially, leaning his head on the head rest. Abu-Ahmed backed out and ran back to close the gate to the house.

Abu-Zah'ara was tired. All week, he was running around, doing little errands and meetings; he didn't even get a chance to watch an attack, let alone participate. Every few hours brought a meeting with someone, somewhere. He missed the days of picking a nice place for an ambush, the rush of detonating a bomb on a passing convoy, the adrenaline that came over him when gunfire erupted all around him and he got a chance to fire an RPG. He felt Allah was shielding him from bullets, because he stood so unguarded from the people who were trying to shoot him. He would usually leave right after he shot his rocket, and he never got to see the end result. It didn't matter, though. The fact that he was fighting in the name of Allah, for the sake of his people, was all that mattered. These days, remembering *those* days was difficult. He was stuck in the organization and the politics of it all. Getting money from this business, or this organization, people from that group, weapons from those people—he never realized it would be so complex. In the past, he would still find time to go out and at least watch an attack, and sometimes participate in things like a checkpoint that would stop people looking for *qafirs,* traitors, who were working with Americans, police, or National Guard.

Today seemed to be going all wrong. He woke up with a headache, and with the loss of all of those weapons, it was going to be hard to recover. "I think I'll make Juma my driver," he said, out of the blue, breaking the silence. He turned his head, still leaning against the head rest, to make eye contact with Abu-Ahmed. "It would leave you free to get stuff done. Besides, the kid has got nothing left but us."

Abu-Ahmed glanced at Abu-Zah'ara and turned back to concentrate on the traffic.

"No opinion, Mister I-have-an-opinion-on-everything?" Abu-Zah'ara said to Abu-Ahmed's silence.

"I like driving you around, but you're right. I do have a lot to do, and I don't have time to take care of your laziness."

"Shut up!" he shot back as they both chuckled. Abu-Ahmad suddenly stopped laughing. "Umm ... I, ahh ... figured out what the traffic problem is," he said, looking ahead at the row of slowly moving cars.

Abu-Zah'ara sat up in his seat. "Don't tell me."

"It's too late now. We can't turn around or run. We have to go through it."

"You don't have weapons in here, do you?" Abu-Zah'ara grimaced and looked over at Abu-Ahmed.

"No, we do have that on our side," he said, trying to cover up the fact he was supposed to keep his boss out of these situations.

Abu-Zah'ara was suddenly fully awake. His heart was pumping loud enough for the taxi driver next to them, listening to loud Lebanese pop music, to hear it. He thought of the events of the day and how the day seemed to crumble in front of his eyes, and there was nothing he could do about it. He pulled out his fake ID card and looked at the name. He knew it, but he studied it anyway, not wanting to mess it up. The line of cars slowly crept forward. Abu-Zah'ara leaned back in his seat, trying to act natural. The two of them sat in silence for a long time.

"Let's watch these stupid monkeys not even notice us, even though they have been looking for you all over the place," Abu-Ahmed said, breaking the silence. The two of them chuckled, and it settled the tension for a brief moment. They pulled into the checkpoint and presented their ID cards. Abu-Zah'ara took a moment to think about what his life would be like if he was captured and interrogated. He thought about the jails that housed his friends and fellow fighters. He had heard it all—from the worst of stories to tales of the kindness of Americans. Who knew where the truth lay? He stared back at the Americans, who had no clue who he was. They all probably knew his name and maybe even saw an old picture of him, and now they stood next to him, searched him and his car, and yet had no idea that he was right there, at their fingertips. They continued about their business like he was just another citizen. Abu-Zah'ara felt good as they finished searching the interior of the car. Then one of the soldiers searching the trunk stopped and backed up and called over another soldier. Abu-Zah'ara threw a glance at Abu-Ahmed, who seemed just as confused as he. Both of the soldiers laughed and shut the trunk. One of them motioned for them to get back in the car as he handed back their ID cards.

They started to drive off, and Abu-Zah'ara exhaled. "What do you have in your trunk?"

"I honestly don't know, but it scared you," he said with a big smile on his face.

"I ought to smack you," he said back as he let out a slight chuckle. They knew they were lucky to get that close to the Americans and just slip by.

"I can't wait to eat," Abu-Zah'ara said, trying not to think of what just happened. "It has been a long day."

By the time they arrived at the house, everyone was sitting inside, waiting for them so they could eat.

"We decided to go through a checkpoint, to see if they knew who we were," Abu-Ahmed said as he shied away from Abu-Zah'ara and plopped down between Abu-Aiya and Towfiq. He knew he messed up, not knowing where the checkpoints were.

Abu-Zah'ara sat down next to Abu-Sayf. "You look very tired. What's the matter?" Abu-Sayf asked with genuine concern. "How is your health?"

"Most of our weapons are gone," Abu-Ahmed butted in before Abu-Zah'ara could get off an answer.

"The attack will just have to be pushed back a few days," Abu-Zah'ara said, reassuring his compatriots.

"About that," Abu Zakiriyah said, trying to lift the situation, "I already talked to the Kurds. I put in a large order, because I knew it was very time-sensitive, but it's expensive, at least 100K US." He looked around at the group for a sign of approval.

"And what money were you planning on using?" Abu-Ahmed shouted. "We don't have much left."

"I was just trying to fix the situation," Abu Zakirayah said, looking at Abu-Zah'ara for support.

"Well, nice try; now the Kurds won't do business with us, and we are screwed for all future missions. Nice thinking, Abdullah." Abu-Ahmed stopped himself. He wasn't supposed to use their real names, but he had known Abu Zakiriyah his whole life, and it kind of just slipped out.

The two of them continued to bicker, and the others sat looking down at the floor and at each other. Abu-Zah'ara realized then that he had to stop them. "You sound like a bunch of old women," he said as both men fell silent. He turned to Abu-Ahmed. "How much money do you have left?"

"Not enough to cover this genius's order."

"All right, everyone," he started in as he looked around the room, "it is time to call in some favors. Hit up all the businesses that support us, and pull in as much cash as possible."

"That has already been done," Abu-Ahmed objected. "How do you think we got enough for this attack?" The room fell silent.

"Let's eat," Towfiq said as he salivated over the food in front of him. Towfiq fit in nicely with the boys. He seemed to be just like them and didn't seem to mind the way they lived. He worked just as hard as everyone else to get the mission done.

Everyone turned and looked at Towfiq, who acted as if he had been starved since arriving in Mosul. Abu-Zah'ara grabbed some food, giving the go-ahead for everyone else. For a second, they all forgot about their problem. Abu-Ahmed told them about the checkpoint and exaggerated every point, claiming he wasn't scared the whole time. Abu-Zah'ara was sure everyone saw right through him but humored his heroic event.

After a few bites, Abu-Zah'ara sat silently as he tried to conjure up a plan of what to do. The plan formed in his head: they would cross-level some weapons with other groups, and if he could not get that organized by the following night, he would push back the attack.

He listened to everyone tell stories of all the missions they used to do together in the beginning; he knew they were all showing off for Towfiq. One of their favorites was when Abu-Aiya decided that the PKC was the best weapon, and he didn't want to use anything different. On one day, they were running from the Americans when their car wouldn't start. Everyone ditched their weapons and took off. Abu-Aiya tried to lug that huge weapon as he ran down the alleys and nearly cried when he was forced to drop it in order to get away. He was so upset, he went and stayed with his family for a few weeks before checking back in with the group. He even tried to help his dad out at his store.

Abu-Zah'ara stood up and walked outside. Abu-Sayf stopped him. "Speaking of weapons, what are we going to do?"

"I will work it out and let you know what, if anything, will change. In the meantime, let's try to get some dough for the Kurds," Abu-Zah'ara said as he stretched and walked outside.

Everyone else stayed and talked till about an hour before curfew. They all started to filter out. In the end, it was just Abu-Zah'ara and Abu-Ahmed. Abu-Zah'ara called Juma and asked him to come over to the house to pick him up.

"You got a plan?" Abu-Ahmed said to Abu-Zah'ara as they stood on the front steps.

"Allah willing."

"I guess that means you figured it out."

"Allah willing," he said as he smiled and turned to pat Abu-Ahmed on the back. "Juma is coming to take me home. Go, be with your family."

"I have to say, you're risking a lot having him be with you."

"You're right. I mean, we should just let this kid live on the streets after everything he gave up to be with us. That seems like a much better plan," he stated sarcastically. "He has nothing left."

Abu-Ahmed shook his head, walked down the stairs, and got in his car.

23. The List of Names

Ali felt a little twinge of nervousness as he stood with the slowly gathering group of men who now would have to rely on him as their leader. He knew they trusted him, especially after that convoy they were on, and it seemed everyone would listen to every order he gave. Being a leader felt natural to Ali; he fell into the position without thinking, just reacting and ordering people what to do. When he thought back to the convoy, it all seemed like a dream. In front of him now was the proof that none of it was a dream. Friends of his were missing from the group that he now led.

Ali told his wife about the convoy. He was excited to tell her how he acted so heroically and how everyone was happy for him. All it did was upset her.

"How am I going to raise this child by myself?" she screamed at him. "And with what father, what money?" It was the first time she had yelled at him, and after that, she didn't talk to him for a few days. Then he brought up the promotion.

She seemed excited for him at first, but Ali could tell that under her sly congratulations, there was something stirring in her mind. He found her in the bedroom, crying later that night. He quietly walked in and sat down beside her, trying to console her. He didn't know why she was upset.

"Ali, you have to quit. You can find other work. Work with your family or in the market," she pleaded. "You can't keep working here; this job is too dangerous, too much."

Ali didn't know what to say. She had never said anything about him quitting before, and he had never seen her this upset in all the time he had known her.

"What about Yassin? Do you think of him ever? When is the last time you saw his family? Have you seen how they are doing?" she squeaked out as the tears ran down her face, making a river of black mascara. Ali stared at the vulnerable face; she looked like an innocent child who had lost something very dear. The shock of seeing this side of her cut him deeply, and he didn't know what to do.

"Yassin's family, they are still grieving. His mother, his father, they look dead to the world. You can see it in their faces. To lose a son that way, can you imagine, Ali?" she said, breaking up the shallow breaths and wiping the tears with her sleeve. "What if ... what if ... you know, they want to kill you; you saw the threat, they know who you are? You have to quit. What would I do if I am to raise this baby by myself?"

"I can't ..." Ali began, but she wouldn't let him finish.

"Today there was another explosion down the street. Every gunshot, every creak of the door, every strange car, I wonder about where you are and if the last time I kissed and touched was the last time. Do you know what that is like?" She stopped and then lay back on the bed, and as she sighed, the tears welled up again and streamed down her cheeks, making her frazzled hair stick to her cheeks. Ali just stared at her and touched her belly. He hadn't realized the pain he was putting her through.

She sat back up and got in his face. "Then you, you are gone for days at work, and I don't know if you're okay. You can't call me, and I'm just supposed to sit here and wonder. Sit here and cry," she said sternly as she brought her finger up to his face. "Now, now you are in charge. What are the terrorists going to think now? Before you were a nobody, just another cop, but now if they kill you, they have killed an officer. Allawi ..." She said his nickname as she cupped his face, staring deep into his eyes. "You have to quit, for the sake of your unborn child, for the sake of me, for our love, for us; you have family now."

"With the promotion I will be protected, people ..."

"People will nothing. Will they protect you here? I see no guards. It is just me and you. Am I, your pregnant wife, going to stop those animals from kidnapping you?" This time she rose and left the room.

Ali was dumbfounded. She had never really mentioned any of this. This was the first time they had fought. He had never thought of things on those terms. He sat for a long time, thinking of everything she had said. He needed her to know that he was doing something more than just getting a paycheck; he wanted her to understand. Ali considered what it would be like to go back to working in the family store or being a day laborer in the market, but he knew that wasn't for him. He was a police officer now, and that is what he should be; that is all he could ever be.

A few hours passed, and the room was getting dark. He slunk down the hallway to the front room. His wife was watching TV with the sound off. He could tell she was deep in thought. Ali softly sat down next to her, looking at the red in her face and her hair, which was now frazzled and all over the place. She didn't look back but stared into the glowing lights of the TV.

"I love you, and I love our child," he started as he leaned his head in front of her, trying to get her to pay attention. "It is these things that keep me going every day. What is a life for our child if it is not safe? I don't want to raise a child in a place where shooting and killing is commonplace. The destruction of these men, these criminals, is no place for our child to grow up. It must be a safe place, a better place than it is now. These things, they don't just stop; someone has to stop them. Men have to be brave to step up and say enough is enough. We cannot cower in the corner and wait for things to change. It is up to us to be brave and not quit when things are rough. I want my child not to worry about these terrorists. I want him to worry about school and soccer, not explosions and kidnappings."

She turned her head slightly toward his.

"I know it is difficult, but you should be proud that I will risk my life to raise our child in a safe place; a place where not only can he be free of terror, but free of tyranny. That is something that we have never experienced. That is something worth fighting for. That is something I must fight for."

She turned back to the TV. Ali didn't know if she heard a word he said, but the subject did not come up between them again.

Ali looked down at his watch; he had given the men plenty of time to show up, and it was time to take roll. As he called out their names, he assigned each of them their duties.

As he was finishing providing the last assignments, he was joined by Salem and Major Saleh.

"As you may already know, you are going to the checkpoint near the vegetable market," Major Saleh said as he handed out a stack of papers. "Those are the names we need to be out on the lookout for. They are wanted men. Some may try to lie about who they are, and there are pictures of some of them in there also."

"Go and get the trucks ready," Ali yelled out to his men as he dismissed them. Ali went inside and sat down. He checked his gear to make sure he wasn't forgetting anything.

Major Saleh sat down beside him and dropped a bag of gear. "I will be joining you for your first mission," he said.

"Yes, sir." Ali stood up and came to attention. Major Saleh gave him a dirty look, picked up his gear, and headed for the door. Ali picked up his vest and swung it on. He checked each of his pouches and pulled out each magazine to make sure he put bullets in every one. As he picked up his bag and headed for the door, he saw Salem in front of him, all geared up.

"You too?" Ali called after him.

"Me too, what?" Salem barked back.

"Well, Major Saleh is coming."

"Yes, me too, I guess," he said as they both walked out to the trucks.

The drive to the checkpoint was uneventful. The air conditioning in the trucks did little to combat the heat they felt wearing all their gear. The team that was there let them know the night had been quiet and nothing significant had happened, and left them there to take over.

Ali fell happily into step putting his men to work but found it agreeable that he had oversight from Salem and Major Saleh. He moved from place to place, helping where needed and making sure no one was slacking off. Everything seemed to be running smoothly; he had a list for each direction of traffic, and each name was checked carefully against it. Cars were randomly inspected, but so far they found mostly just people coming and going from the market. After an hour, Ali decided to go and help with the incoming lane, double-checking the names across the wanted list. It felt like the names had become ingrained into his brain, the more he looked at it. After a while, he got a report from one of his men that there was a man in a white Opel Astera who appeared very nervous. Ali told them to make sure they checked his car.

When the car got near, they instructed the driver to go into a different lane and had the man get out of his car. Ali went over and took the identification from the man. He seemed very upset but was not talking. He was just staring at the men doing their work and back at Ali, who ran his name down the list of wanted men. The men opened the trunk and immediately found an AK-47 and some magazines hidden under some loose clothing. The driver was then detained and brought to the side for questioning. Ali was being peppered with questions and found the rather daunting task of reading all the names again impossible, because he kept forgetting the name on the ID card. Major Saleh took over questioning the new prisoner, who claimed the weapon was for personal protection only. Major Saleh ordered him arrested and loaded him into the back of one of the trucks.

Just then, they noticed a car coming toward them at high speed. The men out front were trying fruitlessly to flag the car down and stop it. Ali noticed that none of his men had pointed their weapons at the car but were struggling to position them correctly. Ali turned his weapon toward the car and started yelling as he fired warning shots. The car wasn't slowing down, and his men scrambled to get behind the barriers of the checkpoint. Shots rang out, this time from the gunners positioned in hardened bunkers on either side of the road. The rounds hit the hood of the car, in an effort to disable the vehicle. The car wasn't slowing. The rounds rose up and were shot into the windshield. The car slowed and came to a stop right outside the checkpoint.

Ali had the man next to him approach the vehicle. As the two of them leveled their AK-47s they slowly approached the side of the car. Inside was a man with his hands in the air. In the back seat was a woman who was screaming. "I'm having a baby!"

Ali ordered the man next to him to go get an ambulance.

"Why didn't you slow down?" Ali asked the man.

"I'm shot," he said, as if shocked by the blood that he had just noticed running down his left shoulder.

"Sir?" Ali said, annoyed with the man.

"She was yelling at me. I didn't ... I'm shot." By this time, Ali was joined by other men. "Take care of this man, and make sure she is doing okay. Search the car too," Ali said as he turned and headed back toward the checkpoint and over to Salem, who was enjoying a cigarette not far from the trucks. Salem appeared unfazed by what had happened, as if he had seen it on TV. Major Saleh seemed to be the same way. He was still interrogating the prisoner.

Ali stood shoulder to shoulder with Salem, watching the unfolding scene in front of them.

"Before he got there, how were you to know? It could have been a car bomb. You didn't do anything wrong. Don't worry about it, Ali," Salem commented on Ali's nervous behavior.

Ali felt jolted, the adrenaline still pumping furiously through his veins. He tried to control his now-overflowing nerves. He recounted each step, trying to decide if he had handled the situation right. Salem's words were barely enough to calm him. His heart was beating out of his chest, and his hands were shaking, but he tried to act like Salem and Major Saleh, who appeared fine. Ali decided that is what the men needed to see, but it was very difficult to portray.

The ambulance came, and Major Saleh left with the prisoner and an escort. Operations resumed a regular pace, free of the incidents from earlier that day. The day was starting to wind down when a red pickup truck pulled into the checkpoint. One of his men brought over the identification of the driver. Ali checked the name; it looked familiar. He had read the list thousands of times by this point, and all the names felt familiar. He went down the list. "Juma, Juma ..." he said, repeating the name as he read through the names. Juma Ahmed Agoub ... he paused, read the identification and the list; the name was the same, a dead match. He had never heard of a dead match at a checkpoint. "Detain him. He is a match," he ordered the man who had brought him the identification. "Search his truck too."

Ali walked over to Salem. "We got ourselves a terrorist," he said to Salem, showing him the list and the identification.

24. Mosul

Mosul seemed vast as it stretched along the banks of the Tigris River, sprawling out into the land and shadowed by the small mountains far to the west. The beating sun glared off the sand that loomed in the sky, in the place of any other major city's smog. As the road crept into the city, Mohammad noticed that the edge of the city was pockmarked by the poor. The houses were barely above the level of mud huts, with their crumbling walls. They appeared tattered and worn, and much to his surprise, they were far from abandoned. As they pressed further into the city, they came into the industrial area. The large warehouses screamed for help, for not only were they old and in desperate need of restoration, they bore the scars inflicted by battle. Bullet holes riddled the walls, with some buildings reduced to mere rubble. Each building wore distinct markings of graffiti and were clearly unkempt, many of them looking abandoned.

Mohammad was taken aback by the empty storefronts along the main road as they passed. They were boarded up, windows were broken, and many of the stores were burned. He saw very few people in this area. Mohammad could not understand why such a good location for a store would be abandoned. He was then reminded that the whole reason he was here in Iraq was because of what was going on—was war. He knew that the Americans caused the pain here, and they didn't want Arab businessmen to succeed.

The driver of the car Mohammad was in made a sharp turn into a parking garage and parked. Mohammad couldn't believe that he had finally arrived, after all this traveling, walking, driving, and staying with strangers, his moment was finally upon him. The driver pulled into a space just beyond the taxi stand and got out of the car.

"Don't go anywhere," he said as he got out of the car.

Mohammad got out of the car to stretch his legs. He felt cramped and needed to breathe in his arrival at Mosul. He walked around to the back of the car and leaned up against the trunk. At the taxi stand was a woman who was distraught and frantic, going to and fro, talking to cab drivers and anyone who had a car. With her was a quiet young man, probably about Mohammad's age. He went to his mother to help her calm down, and he took over the task of talking to the drivers. They were just out of audible range; many drivers seemed very concerned but also unwilling to do whatever the young man was asking.

Mohammad then let his eyes leave the interesting scene to find his driver, but he could not see where he had gone. He didn't know the driver's name and hoped that the man was not just going to leave him here. In light of this, he decided it was not wise of him to get away from the car; if he talked to anyone, his accent would clearly mark him as a Syrian, and with what was going on, there was no reason for a Syrian to be in Iraq. Mohammad tried to peer out of the garage, to take a look at Mosul, but he could not see much. He settled in, leaning against the side of the car, and waited, keeping entertained by the people in the garage. After what felt like an eternity, the driver emerged from the crowd by the taxi stand and came and leaned up against the car, next to Mohammad.

"It will only be a few minutes," the driver said.

Mohammad nodded but did not really acknowledge what the driver had said. He was fixated again on the distraught woman and what appeared to be her son. "What is happening with those people," Mohammad said, pointing his head in the woman's direction, "do you know?"

The driver turned and leaned against the car, facing Mohammad. He had a very serious look on his face that commanded Mohammad to mirror his actions. "Now that you ask, I realize that until this moment, I didn't see that as abnormal. I suppose that is what makes it the most depressing—for such tragedies to take place and for no one to take notice because it is so commonplace. I've seen similar things happen so often that I fear I have gone numb."

Mohammad was intrigued and confused by the driver's comments. He glanced back at the unfolding scene, back at the driver, and back to the woman, who was now near hysterics. Her son continued trying to calm her down. "And that would be ..." he said, trying to understand.

"I guess after years of oppression under Saddam, we should have never thought it would be better. What America brought here were false hopes. It was better to wake up and know your position, and no hopes could be crushed, because with Saddam, you were born without hope. Then the Americans came here." He then turned and mimicked, as if he was giving a speech. "They came and told us, fear not, Iraqi people;

your days of oppression are over," then rested his elbows on the top of the car, "and we believed him, George Bush. You know his father, he was the same. After the Gulf War, we waited for George Bush Senior to rid us of tyranny. Now his son comes to deliver us what his father couldn't, and he feeds us the very tyranny we were trying to get rid of." By now the driver was serious and waving his arms in Mohammad's face. "Under Saddam, we had security. Now we have freedom, and people die for no reason. Look at that boy." The driver pointed to the young man with the woman. "Do you know what he is doing?"

Mohammad didn't know what to say; he was not expecting a speech, just a simple answer to his question. "I believe I asked you that very question only moments ago," he said with a baffled look on his face.

The driver didn't hesitate. "He is looking for a driver headed in the direction of his village."

"I don't see what the problem is; this is normal, is it not?"

"It is when you need room for the coffin of you father, sister, and baby brother."

The words crushed Mohammad's chest. He turned to the driver as he felt the blood drain from his face. He shook his head in disbelief. Mohammad began to pray for this family and found it difficult to control his emotions. "Wh—why ... Who?" Mohammad said as he opened the passenger door to sit down.

The driver followed him. "Brother," he said, resting his hand on Mohammad's shoulder, "this is more common than you can imagine. These are the animals that we fight. The father and baby brother of that man were escorting his sister to the university. She was studying law. This is what the drivers are telling me. They were stopped at a light, and somewhere nearby, there was a shooting. An American vehicle then came around the corner and crushed the car like a Pepsi can. The child lived until he reached the hospital."

"Back in Syria, I had imagined the atrocities that were occurring in this country, but never did I imagine the full way it is here. Before I left for here, I asked myself if I should go, but I know now that Allah needs us to fight the infidels. My fellow Muslims need us, and I cannot leave their side until they are living life the way it should be."

The driver stared down at Mohammad and looked out onto the bustling street just a few feet away. "Ahh, there they are," the driver said with a smile.

Mohammad looked up, in mid-prayer, and he started pulling all his stuff together as the driver walked off holding the jacket. He met up with the gentleman from the other car. The driver then motioned to Mohammad. As he approached, he heard the driver say to the other man, "Gifts from Jasim to Abu-Zah'ara." He handed over the jacket. Mohammad went around to the front seat.

"My name is Abu-Sa'ad. What is yours?"

"Mohammad."

"You have nothing else to go by?"

Mohammad thought back to all the people he saw on TV and realized they all went by nicknames, presumably to protect their real identity. "Abu-Sultan," he said thinking of his father and how he had always known that he wanted his first child to be named after his father, as it was tradition in his family.

With that, they were on their way. As Abu-Sa'ad navigated the morning rush-hour traffic, he would explain bits and pieces about the city. From the garage, they headed east into the city. First they came across Yarmook Circle.

"This is the busiest circle in all of Mosul, and therefore vital for everything we do. The Americans can be expected here several times a day, and we will have to use it to get where we are going when we do operations here on the west side."

From the circle, they headed south along the Baghdad Highway, aptly named because that road would take you all the way to Baghdad. As they started down the road, Mohammad noticed the destruction to the road. Abu-Sa'ad had to pay as much attention the various potholes and debris in the street as he did to the traffic that surrounded them.

"Why is this street so desolate?" he asked. "I see that there is a large amount of traffic, yet there is no stores and almost no people walking on the side of the road."

"As I have told you, the Americans can be expected in this area all the time, so it is the easiest place to hit them."

They hit the first traffic light, which seemed to be more of a suggestion to everyone, so nonetheless, there was gridlock, making the left turn more of a game of Frogger than driving. Immediately after they made the turn, the area improved. Mohammad could see the large, new homes of New Mosul, which made the Baghdad road seem like a dream. They continued down the road into Old Mosul, which was butted up against the Tigris River. The houses were packed together tightly, and the streets became increasingly narrow. Abu-Sa'ad then pulled into a neighborhood he called Zinjili. The roads became confusing, and he was surprised that a car had room to move down winding alleyways. The roads became almost too narrow to navigate, and Abu-Sa'ad found a parking place. Mohammad picked up his things, and they were off on foot to continue into Zinjili. Eventually he opened the gate to what would be Mohammad's new home. Mohammad didn't know if he could find his way back here if he wanted. He wasn't sure how Abu-Sa'ad was able to discern this house from the rest.

"This is where you'll be staying, for now," Abu-Sa'ad said as he made his way through the very small courtyard to the door of the house.

"How long is *for now?*"

"Well, until it becomes too dangerous for you to live here, of course," Abu-Sa'ad said matter-of-factly, like Mohammad should know such things. Immediately inside the door was a room covered in bedding that had a small laptop computer in the corner. There were seven other men there, gathered around the computer, trying to watch a video about a recent martyr. They didn't pay attention to the door opening and shutting. The video was about an amir who died during the fight in Fallujah.

Abu-Sa'ad cleared his throat, and the video was paused. They turned around and greeted the man they called Abu-Sultan.

"You guys need anything?" Abu-Sa'ad asked over the commotion of the new arrival. One of the men showed Mohammad another room where he would be sleeping with two of the other men, while the others plagued Abu-Sa'ad with requests. Mohammad put his stuff down in the room, and when he returned, Abu-Sa'ad was gone, and the martyr video was back on.

Mohammad learned about his new roommates and fellow fighters. He was struck with the eighteen-year-old who had traveled from Chad and the nineteen-year-old who was married with three kids and came all the way from Yemen. Mohammad became engrossed in the stories of their hometowns and their travels. Finally, when a quiet man, maybe only twenty years old, began to talk, he said that he traveled from Egypt with every intention of being a martyr.

"My family is proud of my decision," he said with his thick Egyptian accent. Mohammad was blown away with what he had said.

"Do you know the difference between a *mujahid* and a martyr?" the young Egyptian asked Mohammad. Mohammad shrugged his shoulders, not realizing there was a difference. "A *mujahid* goes into war realizing that he will die, but a martyr goes to war knowing he must die because he believes it is the only way for him to truly give himself to the cause and Allah."

Mohammad leaned back with the heavy words looming over the now-silent room. He thought back to the reason that made him come down to this country, so torn and twisted. He had never thought of the *mujahideen* in such a manner.

25. The Station Wagon

Ali jolted awake to the whistling of incoming, and then he felt a wave of power taking his breath away, immediately followed by a large blast. He was instantly on his feet, putting on his boots and yelling at his men, who sat up in their bunks with blank faces. They began to move, but not as fast as Ali needed them to move. Salem rounded the corner into the room just as Ali was ready to go, fully suited up with his weapon and protective gear. Ali caught a glimpse of Salem and was instantly at a trot to go and talk to him.

Salem leaned over to his ear and whispered, "This is huge! The New Mosul and East Side police stations are gone. Most of the men ran, and the rest got hit with a car bomb. It's a full frontal attack. Get your men reinforcing the towers and along the fence line."

Ali turned around and checked out his men; most were ready, but the few who weren't enraged him. He ran over to them and shouted the anger that he really wanted to direct at the enemy, but in the back of his mind, he wanted them to just be ready to go. Ali picked out his best shooters to relieve some of the men who had been in the critical positions with the heaviest weapons the whole night. When they hit the front doors, Ali was first and directed his men exactly where he wanted them.

"Shoot any moving car or person. It is night and a full-force attack. Civilians will be smart enough not to be around. And for Allah's sakes, don't start shooting at the Americans." With that, his men were off. Ali first went to check on his newly assigned gunners, to see if they had enough ammunition and that there weren't any problems. On the way, he noticed Maj Saleh down by a tower on a cell phone, huddled up against the tower legs.

"Incoming!" was being shouted from the rooftop. The round hit outside the building. No one was hurt; everyone joggled. Ali pressed himself up in the small, secure building his gunners were in, and he could see everyone hunkering down.

A third, fourth, and fifth round came in. There was a break; no movement outside the walls. Then six, seven ... each round was getting closer to the main building.

Vaboom, the noise was too much; the building was being hit, eight, nine, ten. Suddenly movement broke loose outside. Ali made room for his gunner to do his work. He stepped out to move down the line to check for gaps. He could hear the screaming of men up on the roof, but he knew someone else would take care of it. Gunfire then started to erupt from all sides. Ali made sure that he checked each of his men, to ensure none them was injured during the incomings. After he found them all in good standing, he went inside to provide an update and get one.

Ali pressed through the front doors and back into the control room with Colonel Ilyas and Lt. Colonel Subhe. "Just lost three more police stations," Salem said as he watched Ilyas and Subhe shout orders to the scurrying room full of men on phones and radios.

"My men are in place and have plenty of ammunition. I'll keep an eye on that line and provide them whatever they need. Gunfire has already erupted, but I think it is just my men being anxious. Nothing has really come at us yet since the mortars." Ali turned and left the building. He went up to one of his men, who seemed particularly nervous, and held down a position a few feet from him. In the distance, a large vehicle rounded the corner. *Car bomb,* Ali thought to himself. He squinted at the object and noticed a second one swing around the corner.

"Americans. Don't shoot!" he shouted. Everyone began repeating it. There was some joy in the ranks. Reinforcements were what they needed. The gate was lifted, allowing the Strykers to enter at full speed. Everyone's eyes seemed to be on the Americans' entry when an RPG whizzed over the far fence line and struck a police truck sitting in the parking lot. Ali looked at his men, who were all focused in. He started to run down his line. "Eyes out; don't worry about what is going on in here. Hold your position, and keep them from getting in."

The Strykers spread out across the compound, positioning themselves around the police station, using their vehicles as mobile towers. Ali could feel the pulse in the air; his men, who had been scared, now had a surge of energy. He knew that they could do anything without the Americans, but not all of them had gained the same confidence that he had. As the last Stryker pulled through the gate, fire erupted. Ali climbed up on the wall to see what was going on. An old station wagon was barreling toward the wide-open front gate. It didn't seem deterred by the heavy amount of lead that was being thrown at it. Ali screamed for everyone to take cover. The maroon station wagon became ingrained his mind as he jumped down into one of the bunkers. The gates were halfway closed when it slammed into them and slid down the drive into the Stryker that was taking up position and dropping the back ramp, seemingly oblivious to what was happening. The blast knocked everyone over, and fire hid the flying shrapnel as it pelted everything around. The glass on the surrounding buildings all broke. Many men began to cry out. Ali could not see much of that station wagon left; he could only smell what he could only imagine was hell.

He checked the man with him and headed back toward the gate, making sure each of his men was okay. Ali encouraged, "Hold your positions, men." Some of the men complained of minor cuts and bruises. He was forced to ignore them as the small-arms fire erupted again. As Ali approached the front gate, he found two men who were dead and being carted off by men in the other unit. Ali called down the line for two of his men to help defend the area until more reinforcements could arrive.

As Ali went about his work, he noticed an American on the ground. He did not have much body left, maybe there was another body. There was really too much blood to tell. Ali was more worried about the fence line and knew that the Americans were taken care of.

"God damn it, *God damn it!*" Jeremiah mumbled under his breath. The back of the Stryker was full of blood. "You'll be okay, man. Looking good. Hold on, all right?" Jeremiah said as he peered into Duncan's eyes. He wanted to exude confidence in him, but it was hard to. The tourniquet on what was left of Duncan's arm didn't seem to be working. For a moment he got lost in what was left of his face and wondered if it was Duncan; it was hard to tell. He got pretty messed up when the blast went off, and he was smashed by the Stryker door flying up and closing itself. Duncan ... or was it? This boy's face was badly mangled. Jeremiah leaned his full body weight into him, trying to stop the bleeding. He glanced around, and everything was reddish-brown, and he felt like he was pressing on a bowl of soup. Other soldiers were hard at work on the other major problems Duncan had. The medic then ran up and immediately relieved Jeremiah. The bleeding seemed to have slowed in Duncan's arm. Duncan peered up at Jeremiah; he was very afraid and probably crying.

"You're fine, buddy; you're going to be okay." He knew Duncan needed to believe him. "Stay with me; hold on, okay? Don't you ever fuckin' give up. You fight, okay, you fight." A stretcher then arrived, and Jeremiah helped the medic and the few others move him over. Duncan was shaking and just stared back at Jeremiah.

Jeremiah stopped and checked himself for damage. He realized he was having a hard time hearing. He touched his ears but couldn't tell if they were bleeding or if it was just blood that was covering him. He peered out of the back of the Stryker and could see tracer rounds, but he did not really hear gunfire. The medics were back, picking up what seemed to be a rucksack smothered in blood. Jeremiah leaned forward; it was Wynn. Jeremiah couldn't believe his decision to exit the Stryker last would be his saving grace but his team's downfall. He puked and saw his other men were helping run the stretchers.

Jeremiah felt slight movement in the Stryker and could hear the ever-so-slight pinging of bullets hitting the armor. He looked over at the gunner's hatch and found it empty. He popped out the top and swung the .50-cal into position. He saw a small gathering of men and fired several rounds and just kept firing. He laid down heavy fire, and soon thereafter, many of the opposition had disappeared. Some lay in the street, mortally wounded. Jeremiah watched intently for any movement in the distance. He waited for it; he craved it. There were still several hours until morning, and he knew he would have his chance.

26. The News

"Breaking news about the war in Iraq. US military officials just released information that insurgents have launched a heavy attack on the Iraqi security forces in Mosul. We go now to Baghdad with Rob Jansen to get more information on this late-breaking story. Rob."

"Yes, US military officials here in Iraq have just released information about a large-scale insurgent attack in Mosul. The attack was aimed at Iraqi security forces made up of Iraqi police and Iraqi army, not at coalition forces, even though some American soldiers were killed and several others wounded. The exact numbers and names have not yet been released. Officials are saying it was a very well-planned attack, which caused a near collapse of the Iraqi security forces. Apparently there is still fighting as we speak in Mosul. The attack started last night, and most of the heavy fighting has ended. Now US soldiers stationed in Mosul are fighting to regain control of the city. Susan."

"Do we have any pictures of this, Rob?"

"No, officials have not released any pictures. In fact, fighting in Mosul has been so heavy recently that there is virtually no press in that area of Iraq."

"As we have seen the situation develop in Mosul, experts were saying this city was becoming a new insurgent stronghold."

"Yes, in fact it has become apparent just how strong the insurgents have grown in that area of Iraq, in order for them to plan and carry out such a large-scale attack."

"Thanks, Rob. We turn now to a former military official who has looked at the situation. Retired Colonel James Arbogast."

"Thanks for having me here."

"Thank you for coming. Now what we see here in Mosul, is this considered to be a large threat to our troops who sit there now on the ground?"

"Well, Susan, what we see here is a large-scale attack aimed at the Iraqi security forces, not at the troops on the ground, and although it has worsened the situation, it's not clear if it is a threat directed at US soldiers."

"And what do you see happening next? What is the next step for the military in Mosul?"

"First of all, it seems that with the near collapse of the Iraqi security forces, the insurgents have become free to conduct operations. The next step would be to regain control of the city, re-establish the security forces, and then begin again to rebuild the government."

"How does this situation affect the upcoming elections in Iraq?"

"I think it is too early to determine what effect, if any, this will have on the first elections held in Iraq since the collapse of Saddam Hussein's regime."

"For the last half year, we have seen insurgent forces conduct similar attacks in the Sunni Triangle. Most predominant is the situation in Fallujah. Do you think there is any relationship between these attacks in Mosul, as compared to past attacks in Fallujah?"

"In fact, I see that these situations are very closely correlated. Two months ago, coalition forces in Fallujah went on a major offensive against the insurgents' operation there. Marines and soldiers swept through, clearing out most of the city. Although attacks continue in Fallujah, it is clear the significant reduction in the sheer number of insurgents operating in Fallujah. Perhaps the offense in Fallujah pushed many of the fighters to seek refuge in the developing stronghold for insurgents located in Mosul, and made the attacks that started yesterday, and that are still occurring today, possible."

"And just how many insurgents are operating in Mosul today?"

"For that, I just don't have an answer."

Mckayla turned off the TV and picked up a pillow and held it close. "Please, God, say it's not Jeremiah, please, God," she repeated over and over. The phone rang and Mckayla jumped to her feet and her heart leaped. She was confused at the first ring, but upon the second she recognized it. "I hope it's Jeremiah," she said, scurrying across the small apartment she and Jeremiah wanted to make a home, to the kitchen, where she picked up the phone.

"Hello?" she said, out of breath.

"Hi Mckayla, this is Pamela." Jeremiah's mom's voice was comforting, but all too upsetting, because she wanted to hear her fiancé's voice. "You need to turn the news on."

"I just turned it off," Mckayla interrupted. "Jeremiah told us not to watch the news too much because it would be upsetting."

"I can't lie. I am pretty worried about him."

"Ohh, you are always worried about him. We are just overreacting. I'm sure he is fine," Mckayla said not too convincingly. "What does Dad think?"

"He is off ranting and raving about how his boy was injured or killed because of Bush's stupid war on oil."

"That upsets Jeremiah so much. He keeps saying it is not a war for oil, and he just wishes he could explain it."

"Well, his dad won't take that."

"Do you know the good news?"

"What's that?"

"We haven't received news from anyone but the TV. That's good news."

"I guess."

"Keep me posted if he calls, or you know."

"Don't you worry, Mckayla. We are just overreacting."

"I'll keep you posted, and you keep me."

"I'm sure he'll call you first; he always does. He loves you so much. He is just crazy about you."

Mckayla smiled. "Okay then, I'll talk to you later, bye."

"Bye."

27. Mullah Abdullah

"It went well," Abu-Ahmed said to Abu-Zah'ara as they rounded the corner near the mosque. They strolled along without a worry in the world. Their men had taken control, there were checkpoints to get the remaining police and Iraqi army, and all other major operations were finished. Almost all the weapons systems were recovered, except the few that were in use and the two lost in battle. The day was warm, and the sun gracefully touched the treetops and painted a beautiful blue sky, unfettered by the events that had occurred a few nights before. The sky wouldn't be able to hold the memories of that night; if it reflected the sorties of so many nights in the history of Iraq where men tried to seize the fruits of the Tigris and Euphrates River, it would no longer hold its beauty.

Abu-Zah'ara and Abu-Ahmed were extremely early, as they were every Friday to meet with Mullah Abdullah, who greeted them at the gate, extremely excited. "I remember when you came to see me after your exodus from Mosul. I wondered what you had learned, but here you are today. People are going crazy. I get mixed reactions from people who come to me for advice. Some ask if there is a fatwa, others ask if it is right; some are upset, some seem eager to join us, and all too many are just confused. I believe there will be a large number of people here today." The three of them sat down inside the mosque walls and soaked in the cool morning breeze.

Abu-Zah'ara was content with the events and hadn't spoken much about it. He listened to the war stories of Abu-Ahmed but felt disconnected. He couldn't believe what had happened. He couldn't believe it happened so well. So much had changed over the last year, and he thanked Allah for his introduction to Salahadeen, the guidance of Mullah Abdullah, and the companionship of Abu-Ahmed.

"Hey, Abu-Zah'ara." Abu-Zah'ara snapped his attention back to

Abu-Ahmed; he had drifted off for a few moments. He looked at Abu-Ahmed with a half-smile on his face, making fun of the situation.

"Did you find out what happened to Juma?"

"Juma ..." Abu-Zah'ara had all but forgotten about Juma. "Umm ..." Abu-Zah'ara thought back to the few nights before and realized that he was so busy getting the last few suicide bombers ready, he didn't notice his driver never showed up. "No."

"I heard they picked him up at a checkpoint."

"Americans?"

"No, I think it was the police."

"Allah will take care of him."

"After the attack, most of the Iraqi police prisoners were given to the Americans."

Abu-Zah'ara didn't think Juma knew that much, and he didn't think he would betray the cause.

"Which reminds me," said Abu-Ahmed, "here is your new SIM card; everyone else already got one." With that, Abu-Zah'ara's worries over Juma floated into the treetops. Abu-Ahmed had the angles covered. A couple of people began to trickle in through the gate. The three of them stood up and went to prepare themselves for prayer.

Ali finished his breakfast around noon. He had slept in because the events of the last few days did not give him much chance to rest. His wife was cleaning up. "I'm going for prayer. I will be back soon." Ali washed up and put on a white *dishdasha*. With the morning, it felt good to put on lighter clothes and not carry around all of his gear. He walked out of his gate and turned to walk to the mosque. He saw Yassin's father in front of him, and he called to him and asked him to wait. They greeted each other. Yassin's father seemed to have aged quite a bit since the last time he saw him. He looked very tired and worn.

"It is a graver day in Mosul than I could've imagined," Yassin's father said as he stretched out his arms. He seemed to have trouble walking. The death of his son seemed to wound him deeply. Ali didn't feel like talking, and it seemed to suit Yassin's father. They were at the mosque a few minutes before the call to prayer. They washed and entered the mosque.

"I look forward to the guidance of what we should do on this day," Yassin's father said as he made his way to the front of the mosque.

Ali was weary of being in the middle of a group of people and decided to stay near the door. He didn't feel like he had slept well the previous night. He dreamed of the attack, remembering it like it was a dream. He remembered watching himself run from place to place, resupplying ammo, helping with first aid. He saw his men's trust in his actions and his words. They seemed to feel confident with his words. Ali remembered the men who were gone; thanks to Allah, none of them were his own men. Some of his men did get injured, but not seriously so. Ali began to think of his dreams; he drifted into his own world, and was immediately snapped back as the call to prayer echoed through his bones.

He began to look around. *Something is not right,* he thought to himself. He scanned the crowd. The mosque was packed, and more people were coming in. He held his position near the door, but to the side to prevent assailants from getting him from behind. It was dusty in the mosque with all the people moving around, and it bothered Ali's eyes. The call to prayer finished, and Ali settled down and watched as people began to line up. As the prayer started, Ali slowly relaxed. By the end of the prayer, Ali was at peace and was no so edgy. Mullah Abdullah started his speech by having everyone greet the people around them. Ali greeted a man next to him who seemed very excited. He was in his mid-twenties, good-looking, and carried himself as if he were a prominent politician. The man reminded Ali of one of his old schoolmates from elementary school. Ali looked at him for a second and decided he must be some sort of distant relative. On the other side of Ali was a young boy, probably fifteen, accompanied by his young father.

Mullah Abdullah spoke of the events of the last few days. It was comforting; he usually avoided the topic of the insurgency altogether. "My Muslim brothers, as you know, the police of Mosul have failed, as we thought they would when they are supported by and working for infidels. They were nothing but puppets of the non-believers, and therefore traitors, and here in Mosul, it has begun, the cleansing of the city of the traitors and occupiers."

Ali froze; he stopped hearing, focused on Mullah Abdullah. The words were not sinking in, and Ali wondered what the Mullah was trying to say. He realized that his mouth was wide open, and he closed his mouth and leaned back. He listened back in to see if he was dreaming.

"And in the name of Allah, the most merciful and gracious, I call upon my brothers of Islam to do what must be done and conduct jihad."

Ali got sick to his stomach and dizzy. His eyes darted around the room. There was a lot of movement and whispers. As he moved his head, his eyes could not keep up, and his vision bounced from side to side. He closed his eyes for a second and took a few deep breaths. His heart seemed to slow to a stop. The child next to him put his hand on Ali's knee. "Sir, are you okay?"

Ali turned and smiled at the boy and put his hand halfway up to indicate he was fine. The boy removed his hand and gazed at Ali with a puzzled face. Ali looked back at Mullah Abdullah and to the men to his left. They were smiling and glancing at each other.

Ali gained control, and his heart rate skyrocketed as sweat poured down his face. He gripped his knees and stared into the crowd in front of him, the rows of heads, listening so intently. "What do I do?" Ali asked himself, half under his breath. "If there are terrorists here, which there probably are, I can't leave." *Stay calm, you'll have to wait it out,* he thought to himself. *How many of these people are terrorists? How many will become terrorists?* Ali glanced back to the boy on his right, who seemed to be in awe of the words the Mullah was spewing. Ali looked back ahead and watched where the boy gazed and looked back at the boy. Ali's eyes began to mist. Had all of his work become fruitless? Was he on an unwinnable mission? A tear dropped from his eye. Ali wiped it away and looked straight ahead. He sat and tried to regain his composure. He tried to imitate the posture of the men around him, sitting up straight and nodding when others did. He did not hear Mullah Abdullah, and he considered it a blessing. All he could think of was his wife and his child who was on the way.

The speech came to an end, and everyone began to file out. Ali was in shock as he pushed himself to his feet. The mosque erupted with loud conversations, people questioning, some opposed, some for. Yassin's father came to Ali and looked him in the eyes. Yassin's father was scared, and his face was almost white. Ali knew he was very proud of his son and that he was a policeman. He truly believed that Yassin had fought and died for something he believed in. Ali escorted him out of the mosque. Both were silent but bursting to talk. Yassin's father was holding on to Ali's arm. As they passed the gate outside and started down the street, Yassin's father stopped Ali and glanced around to see who was close by. "Do not worry. People cannot believe this man. This is not right, and he should not be doing or saying these things."

Ali tried to talk but he was cut off. "I know what you are thinking, but you must keep your job. Don't give up now, don't quit, or they will win."

Ali nodded and pulled at him to keep walking. "Keep a lower profile; don't go to this mosque anymore, and don't go anywhere really. Just to work and home."

"I know, I will."

Just then, someone came up behind them and passed them. The rest of the walk home was in silence and very slow.

28. Wood Splinters

"Did I tell you about the e-mail from my dad?" Jeremiah said to his platoon sergeant, Jeff Straus, who looked back him with a blank stare. He had big dip of Copenhagen shoved in his lower lip, and his teeth disappeared in the tobacco. He spit into the frothing pile of spit in the gravel in front of him. They were sitting outside the quick reaction force building, waiting for action.

Jeremiah continued, "It's a whole bunch of bullshit about this war. I just can't seem to explain it to him, ya know, this war."

Jeff was only a few years older than him, but Jeremiah looked up to him. He was from the middle of nowhere, Arkansas. He grew up as a hard-working farmer on a ranch, and you could see the added years on his face. He stared straight ahead. "What did the e-mail say?"

"I guess you have to understand my dad. He was drafted into Vietnam, and the thought of the military haunts him. He doesn't talk about it. When he found out that I joined the army, we almost got in an all-out brawl. He tried to talk me out of it—with his fists. It's like he had such a bad experience, he figured everyone else would too, and he didn't want his kid to go through the same stuff. If he did talk about the military, it was about how bad it was. I didn't believe him. I tried to tell him that after all this time, the military was different, but he didn't listen. Anyway, he always refers to this war as a false war. You know, a war for oil," Jeremiah said, reaching into his pocket to pull out a cigarette. He lit it and leaned back against the concrete wall that was protecting their building. "He thinks we are brainwashed because we believe in what we do, and he thinks we think it's okay to lose soldiers."

Jeremiah took a drag on his cigarette and started to talk, but he was cut off by Jeff, who finally turned his face out of the sun and stared directly at Jeremiah. "Who said it was okay for those soldiers to die? Don't listen to your father. If he served in Vietnam and thinks that of his comrades ... Your, *our* guys made the ultimate sacrifice for a freedom that people back in the States will never take the time to understand."

"Well ..." Jeremiah started but was cut off by his platoon leader coming around the corner. "Line 'em up; we're rollin," he said to Jeff. Jeremiah acted immediately and started rounding everyone up.

They were all geared up and ready to go within a minute. "Okay, we are headed after the top guy. We're going off a tip that he is supposed to be at this meeting, so there will be a ton of guys there and probably a ton of resistance," the platoon leader said, giving off marching orders.

Jeremiah started to get pumped up. This guy was responsible for the death of Duncan and Wynn. He was ready, and there would be no mercy. They mounted up on their Strykers. Jeremiah decided to be air guard, and the glare of the sun spewed rays of light from the west, which disappeared in the dust kicked up in the sad semblance of a dirt road as they sped from the base. They were headed for the "death street," which was infamous for a number of attacks. It was reminiscent of a ghost town, making it hard to believe it was a main road in this godforsaken city. The only sign of life was the traffic, which was not so comforting to Jeremiah. Cars were what killed his men, and it was damn near impossible to tell the difference between a regular old person going about their business and someone who was intent on harming them.

Just then, Jeremiah slammed to one side. The Stryker was jumping the median to go around the traffic stopped at the light. As they approached the intersection, they made a sharp right turn and then a left into a neighborhood. They were zipping down side streets that the Stryker enveloped with its massive size. The familiar sound of the choppers zipped above and started circling. *The house was near,* Jeremiah thought.

The call came through the headsets, "There it is: red gate, yellow awning." There were no people in the street, which was a good sign. The gate was slightly open; nice to know they wouldn't have to blast through it. Jeremiah and the others slithered out of the back out of the Stryker and went in for the kill.

The gate was slammed open, the yard clear. They climbed the stairs and set the stack. *Slam,* front door open. Two men slid in, followed by Jeremiah. Jeremiah saw a man slide around the far corner as he entered. They followed him down the hall, clearing the rooms as they went. *Last room on the left, he is in there.*

They set up again, another stack. The first man kicked the door, and as it opened, the door made a dramatic push in the opposite direction. Wood splinter cracked from the middle of the door, and the door shot outward, knocking the kicker down, followed by a ball of flames that spread into the hallway. Jeremiah fell back against the wall. The kicker started screaming, and the shrieks were eerily and painfully familiar to

Jeremiah. "Not again," he said, pushing the thought out of his mind as he pushed past the front two men and entered the dank room. He found part of the body of one man and a badly ripped-apart man in the corner. The window was shattered, and Jeremiah could see two men fleeing over the wall into the neighbor's yard. Jeremiah started shooting and could see they were blindly shooting behind themselves. They cleared the wall; Jeremiah climbed out the window and jumped for the wall. By the time he made it up, they were clearing the next wall. Jeremiah sat up on the wall, aimed in that direction; he would get them when they climbed up the next wall. He started yelling at others, pointing out where they went. Jeremiah was joined by another man on the wall.

The helicopter swooped in and unleashed the chain gun. One man hit the ground hard; the other slowly fell to the ground.

"Get 'em," Jeremiah heard the order echo forward. He and the soldier next him jumped off the first wall and headed for the next as the helicopter moved off. Jeremiah slowly climbed the next wall, cautious of the men who lay in that yard. One of them pulled a pistol, and before he could get it aimed, Jeremiah and the soldier next to him shot three rounds into the man until he dropped his pistol. They dropped off the wall and slowly approached, checking both men. The one with the pistol was surprisingly still alive. Jeremiah kicked his gun away and searched the man. The other soldier opened the gate to let the other soldiers in. A medic came in and started to provide first aid to the man who somehow lived through the helicopter's attack and the shots from Jeremiah.

Lt. Colonel DeLuca came out of a Stryker with an interpreter. "What's your name?" he said to the badly injured man, who just looked at him, disgusted. "What's your fucking name?" he said again.

This time the man responded. "Ra'id," he struggled to say, "Ra'id Abdul Kareem."

"Your *other* name," he ordered.

"Abu-Ahmed."

"Where's Abu-Zah'ara?" The man didn't answer, paying more attention to the man who was bandaging him. "Is he here?"

"You only wish," the man said smugly.

DeLuca leaned in very close and whispered something in Abu-Ahmed's ear. Abu-Ahmed grunted as a bandage was tightened around his leg. "He's safe and protected."

The man was rolled onto a stretcher and didn't talk any more. Jeremiah went back to the yards they had passed over. There were already soldiers inside the houses, looking at the unsuspecting residents. Jeremiah searched the yards to see what they had left or thrown. The dead man had an ID card and nothing else. The sound of the helicopter was comforting and put Jeremiah's mind at ease. They entered the next yard and found an AK-47.

"Must've dropped it on his last little run," Jeremiah remarked.

After the search Jeremiah made his way back to his Stryker. "What happened in the first house? Was anyone killed?" he asked Jeff.

"Suicide vest; one man in the house had it on. Jason is hurt, but not bad."

"Any sign of our guy?"

"Not yet, but we are hoping he is one of the guys in that room with the suicide vest."

29. Remember Your Training

"I don't know what happened," Abu-Zakiriyah yelled as he walked through the crowds up to Abu-Zah'ara in the vegetable market. The market was buzzing with hundreds of people, and Abu-Zah'ara felt cramped and claustrophobic as he stood up from leaning back on his newly acquired black BMW. He looked down at the ground and turned to face the quickly approaching Abu-Zakiriyah. Abu-Zakiriyah had what people always referred to as beautiful eyes; they were bluish but had shards of gray and green interlaced. They pierced through crowds and popped out against his dark skin and short, buzz-cut black hair.

Abu-Zah'ara sat wondering who had ratted them out. He was supposed to be there, but he was late. He thought that since Abu-Zakiriyah was still here, maybe it was him. He gazed in through the beautiful gates he presented to the world and could see the panic and pain set in them and quickly discounted his involvement. When he got up close, he was jumpy and fidgety. Abu-Zah'ara thought back to all that led up to this point. Abu-Zakiriyah had always shown a keen involvement in the cause, and there was no way he would put his best friends in peril.

"Well, what did you see?" Abu-Zah'ara said to Abu-Zakiriyah, who was now constantly looking around them.

He leaned in close and spoke very low. His voice was almost indiscernible against the hagglers at the nearby stands and the noise of the passing trucks. "I was headed toward the house, but the roads were blocked, and I could hear the helicopters near. I turned down a different road and decided to get out of the area. That's when I heard an explosion, and then the helicopter started shooting. I knew it had to be our house, and I had to get out of the area. I feared the worst. I didn't know who was already there. That's when I started calling people, so they didn't get near the house, but you were the only one that answered the phone immediately. I went across town and switched cars with my brother and came back. I was going to go in for a closer inspection, but I didn't want to get into some sort of sniper trap." With that, Abu-Zakiriyah stepped back, looking for affirmation that his actions were indeed correct.

Abu-Zah'ara turned his attention down an alley nearby. He was trying to imagine what had gone wrong.

"Have you heard from anyone else, Abu-Aiya, Abu-Sayf?" Abu-Zakiriyah said, breaking the silence.

Abu-Zah'ara kept looking down the alley. He started to feel the fear of losing everything he had worked for, and it made him nauseous. "Not them, not Abu-Ahmed," he said calmly.

"Towfiq, well he finally called back; he is safe. How long have you been here?"

"Came about an hour and half ago, hoping one of you guys would show up." Abu-Zah'ara reached in the window of his car and grabbed two cell phones. "Give one to Towfiq," he said, handing them over. "Move the factory, now. Tell the others to check in if you see them. Find out where the hell they are. I want to know what happened," he ordered.

Abu-Zakiriyah nodded and turned to walk away and then turned back and hugged Abu-Zah'ara. "Thank Allah you are okay; we would be lost without you."

"No, you wouldn't. Follow Allah, and he will tell you what to do."

"If Allah wills it," Abu-Zakiriyah said as he turned and disappeared into the masses that swarmed one of the oldest markets in Mosul.

Abu-Zah'ara leaned back onto his car. He felt some comfort in seeing one of his men, mixed in with the people he fought for. He liked to see the civilians out and about, going about their lives. He was taking care of them. After watching the ebb and flow of the market for another thirty minutes, he decided he probably should leave; remaining stagnant in one place for too long was never a good idea. He pulled his car keys out of his pocket and started to twirl them as he stood and turned around, searching the crowd for another familiar face. He wanted to know if Abu-Zakiriyah was the only one who made it out of that meeting house. He climbed in his new BMW with its leather seats and started the engine. The market traffic was horrible, and it was hard to find a space for him to pull out of his parking spot. He was concentrating on the cars when he heard a pounding on the passenger window. Abu-Zah'ara jumped and glanced over to find Abu-Aiya. "Get in," he yelled, motioning to him.

Abu-Aiya opened the door. "I gave up on you," Abu-Zah'ara said.

"I noticed," Abu-Aiya said as he sat down. "Nice new car."

Abu-Zah'ara concentrated in pulling into the mess of cars.

"I went to find out what happened," Abu-Aiya started. "One of my guys asked the neighbors. Apparently, Americans hit the house, and some people fled out the back window into the neighbor's yard. Someone inside the house blew himself up; I think there was someone else in the house with him. Some of the neighbors say four people were in there with him. The two that went into the neighbor's backyard were shot by the helicopter. One survived; the other one died. The one that lived was arrested."

"Who was in the house? I just saw Abu-Zakiriyah; I know he is fine. Same with Towfiq."

"Thank Allah. With that knowledge and seeing you, I'm guessing it was Abu-Ahmed and Abu-Sayf and their drivers. Or maybe that guy Abu-Ahmed hired to be your driver."

"Abu-Sayf's driver usually has on a suicide vest, or at least he claimed he did. Now we know the truth." Abu-Zah'ara reached into the seat behind him and pulled out a phone, "Here," he said, handing it over.

"Thank Allah, you weren't at the house. I feared that most."

"You men are trained, and I believe Allah will direct you. Wait here in the market a little longer to see if someone resurfaces. We might have got it wrong, and maybe Abu-Sayf and Abu-Ahmed are okay. I'm going to check with Abu-Sa'ad and go get a new place to live." Abu-Aiya pushed the car door open and walked back the one hundred meters or so from where he was first picked up. Abu-Zah'ara waded his way through traffic and thought about the possible loss of his brothers. He couldn't believe that he lost his best friend and hardest worker, Abu-Ahmed. He held out hope for him. Abu-Ahmed was always his inspiration, and he really should have been in charge of the group, the way he ran everything. Abu-Sayf was a dedicated hard worker. Now he had to figure out reorganization and get new amirs. It would be hard to get in contact with his previous amir's cell leaders. He would send someone to their houses to find their closest friends; they would know. He decided then to give Abu-Aiya that duty, since he was able to get information on the meeting house so quickly.

Abu-Zah'ara could see he was getting toward the end of the traffic jam and decided he'd better call Abu-Sa'ad to figure out what was happening. "Is it ready yet?" he said when the other line picked up.

"Yes, I'll meet you at ..."

Abu-Zah'ara cut him off. "Not there."

"I'll go to your place," Abu-Sa'ad said. Abu-Zah'ara promptly hung up his phone.

He then cut down an alley into one of the worst neighborhoods in Mosul, one that flanked the industrial section. He decided this would be the safest route to travel. Most people didn't bother with the industrial neighborhood; the roads were made of dirt and riddled with large potholes. Not to mention the high crime rates. This place was bad when Saddam was in power; now with terrorists capitalizing on the government's focus on terrorist activities, they were pretty much free to do what they wanted. He passed the large factories and darted across the road to Tal Afar before arriving at the place he had called home for the last month. It had been home for too long, and he needed to move on. He pulled past the house and around the back, the entrance to the alley, and parked his car.

He headed back to his house, to enter via the back way, and as he grabbed the gate, his phone rang. "I need a little more time to get there," Abu-Sa'ad said.

"I need to clean up and get my stuff anyway," he said and then hung up the phone and walked in his back door.

He headed straight for the shower. Afterward, he put on a clean track suit, packed his few belongings, and decided to pray before leaving. As he turned to face Mecca, he could hear the distinct hum of helicopters and hoped they would just pass by. The noise became so loud, he could not hear his own thoughts. He stopped praying. "They must be circling," he said aloud. He decided it was time to get out—now. He had already planned out several escape routes. Before he could get to his feet, *BOOM*. Abu-Zah'ara hit the ground, and pieces of the front door sprayed over the top of his head, "Too late," he said to himself. He was disoriented and dizzy and tried to crawl toward the kitchen. He could hear the yelling in English and then felt the distinct feel of the barrel of a rifle press against his head. He lay back down flat on his stomach and stretched his hands out in front of him.

Abu-Zah'ara started to mutter prayers under his breath while the soldiers were searching him. Abu-Ahmed was the only one who knew where he was, and the thought of him being alive gave Abu-Zah'ara a fleeting thought of happiness. Just then, his arms were pulled behind his back, and he was flexi-cuffed. He snapped back into reality. *Remember your training*, he thought to himself, while his chin dug into the ground. It was terribly uncomfortable to have his hands behind his back while he lay on his stomach. He remembered what his people had said: "Americans treat all prisoners well." He knew this part was the only part that wouldn't be that comfortable. A soldier pulled back his shoulders, forcing Abu-Zah'ara onto his knees, and then helped him to his feet. He was then pressed back against a wall.

"What's your name?" he heard, but he did not answer. Abu-Zah'ara had a hard time believing what was going on. He thought about his fake identification and tried to remember the name. This time someone yelled in his ear, "What's your fucking name?"

"Ahmed ... Ahmed," he finally answered.

"Your full name."

"Ahmed Mohammad Hussein."

"Nickname?"

"I don't have one," he said with defiance. Did they really believe he would simply just mutter his infamous name?

"Who lives here with you?"

"No one. I'm finishing the house for my family," Abu-Zah'ara said. It was the story he always had planned, because he always stayed by himself and wanted a good excuse.

"What are you doing here?"

"Painting."

"Bullshit." The exchanges became quicker and louder. "Do you have weapons here?"

Abu-Zah'ara closed his eyes and tried to drown out all the noise that unfolded around him. Soldiers were searching the place and going up and down the hallway. Abu-Zah'ara knew they wouldn't find anything; he never kept evidence where he was staying. He could hear the soldier start to scream in his ear, but he couldn't hear the words. A blindfold was then slipped over his eyes, and someone grabbed his shoulder and made him start walking. Abu-Zah'ara couldn't see where he was going and decided to drag his bare feet across the ground. He stubbed his toe as he got toward the remnants of his door. He could hear people yelling orders, but he didn't understand anything. He felt his way down the stairs and out the front gate and then felt a push as he was hoisted. "Up," one of the soldiers said, as he pushed him into the back of the vehicle. Abu-Zah'ara thought to himself, *It's probably one of those Strykers*. They were his favorite target to blow up. Now he was finally getting an inside look, or rather *feel*.

He was sure that the Americans would take Baghdad Road back to their base and knew that his group would probably attack the convoy. In some ways he hoped, but then again, this time he was in the Stryker. Everything seemed to be a dream. *How did they find me?* he thought to himself. He closed his eyes behind his blindfold, and when he opened them, he hoped he would wake up somewhere else. He tried it several times, but nothing was changing. He was still sitting uncomfortably with his hands behind his back, his blindfold on. He felt the twists of the road and the changing speed of the traffic. He was being jostled around with the rapid acceleration, stopping, and turning. He started to feel motion sickness. It was all too real, and he knew then that it couldn't be a dream. He then heard the gunfire erupt. The Americans were shooting, but they didn't slow down. Instead they sped up.

Just then, he thought about everything he had worked for, and a terrible feeling swept over him. He leaned forward and wanted to puke. One of the soldiers propped him back up. Everything he had said and done every day for almost two years was over. He tried to boost his self-confidence. *I can trick them. I was trained. Maybe they think I'm someone else. I can get out of this.*

The Stryker slowed down. They must have reached the base. He never saw them moving this slowly on the road. He knew everything about their movement. He studied it, looking for patterns and weaknesses. He heard the back of the Stryker open up, and he was pulled out. He felt the sun on his face; it felt different. After today, everything would feel different. He would be in jail, and the sun does not feel the same when you are in a cage. The beating sun made his heart ache. He was told to sit down and found himself sitting on gravel. He tried to listen to the people around him, to figure out what was going to happen next. The anxiety started to rise in him, and he could feel his heart race. He tried to calm down. "My name is Mohammad, No, Ahmed Mohammad Hussein. Everything else about me is pretty much the same. I live in Sukr neighborhood. I was just at this house, fixing it up for my family to move in. I do labor in the vegetable market, usually just loading and unloading trucks."

He felt the tug at his armpit again, being coaxed to stand up. He started walking in the direction the hand that had him beckoned. He wondered which base he was on and where he was on the base. He was searched again and then pushed through a door. He could feel the air conditioning blowing on his face. He kept walking, turning, and finally they stopped. His blindfold was removed, his handcuffs cut off. He was told to strip and put on the orange jumpsuit that sat in front of him. There were four soldiers watching him. Before he could get completely dressed, a doctor came over to him and started asking him questions and looking him over.

"Were you beaten?" the doctor said.

"No," Abu-Zah'ara said, almost laughing out loud. *They were right; they won't hurt me at all.*

He was escorted to a room, where they took his picture and his fingerprints and asked a lot of questions about who he was. He was then given a blanket, a Koran, toothbrush, and toothpaste, and taken out of the building and out around the side. They put him in a small cell by himself and closed the door behind him. He put his stuff down and sat down. He saw scratches on the wall, and mostly what he could make out was verses from the Koran. He thought then that prayer would be good to calm him down.

He laid out his new rug in the direction of the arrow that was painted on the ground of his cell. Just then, the door opened, and he was told to get out. He walked out and went to another small room with a table and chairs. The two people in there asked about his name, tribe, and other stuff about him, and then the guards came and got him and sent him back to his new little home. As soon as he got to his cell, he thought about how easy it was talking to those people. They didn't press him on his name. They just took the information as he gave it to them.

He washed his hands and feet and decided to pray—or rather finish. It was something he started a couple hours earlier in his house; now everything was different. As soon as he finished, the door opened again. He thought someone was watching him, but they didn't interrupt him. He was walked over to the bathroom and then led back to that same room with table and chairs. This time, two different people were there. There was a girl, who couldn't have been much over the age of twenty. She had dark-brown hair and reminded Abu-Zah'ara terribly of his sister Zah'ara. Her face was small and flanked by her large ears. Abu-Zah'ara was confident his sister, had she not died, would look like her. Next to her was an older gentleman, who sat smugly, puffing on a cigar. As they started to ask him the same questions as before, he could distinctly tell the accent of the man was that of a Syrian, one who was very educated. Abu-Zah'ara stared back at the girl and answered questions about his assumed name.

"Do you have any sisters?" the girl asked as she looked up from her notes.

"Yes, three," Abu-Zah'ara said, thinking of his family that he had not seen in quite some time. He felt like this girl was his sister sitting in front of him, and it made it difficult for him to concentrate on the task at hand.

"What are their names?" she asked with a sly smile on her face.

"Fatima, Esma, and Zah'ara," he chose his real sister's name because he didn't want to be caught up in too many lies.

"Fatima's full name ..."

Abu-Zah'ara rolled his eyes, but he knew that the Americans had been thorough since he arrived, and he expected that they would continue to ask questions like this. He chose not to fight it. "Fatima Hassan Sulayman." As soon as his grandfather's name slipped out, he realized he had messed up. He had given her real name, his real father and grandfather's name. *Maybe she won't notice,* he thought to himself.

"Really?" Abu-Zah'ara's young interrogator exclaimed. "Then what the hell is your name?"

Abu-Zah'ara's heart sank; all hopes in his mind that they didn't know who he was had sunk. He didn't answer for a long time. She stared at him and didn't let up. He had to cover for what he just did. Then a fleeting thought entered his mind: the Americans only knew his nickname, and perhaps they never learned what his real name was. He had gone by

Abu-Zah'ara for the last two years, and even his closest friends had not divulged to newer members his real name, nor he theirs.

"Abdul-Jahliel Hassan Sulayman," he said, looking down at the ground.

"Well, that is different than before," she said to his new name. "What is your nickname?"

"I don't have one." *Did she really think it would be that easy?* He tried to reinforce and regroup. *Remember your training,* he said to himself. *Sit up straight, put hands on lap, look directly at interrogator.* He could remember his instructors hovering over him: "Any movement tells them something, so stay still. Your eyes say more, so make sure you look straight ahead. Think about something else, anything else, but be sure to answer the questions. Be vague, change the subject, but always do as they say and be polite." It was almost too much to concentrate on at one time, but he knew it must be done.

Looking back at his interrogator, he thought of his mother and father and the last time they were all together. It was Eid, and just for him, they celebrated in a smaller group late at night, so he wouldn't be exposed to all the cousins who might turn him in.

"Answer the question," he heard the interpreter growl at him. He wasn't paying attention.

"I don't know," he said, figuring it was as good an answer as any.

"You're telling me you don't know what you do for a living?"

"Oh, that. I'm a laborer in the vegetable market."

The interrogator talked about every aspect of everything he said. She even started to ask about his best friends and potentially fallen comrades. He wanted to ask her if Abu-Ahmed was alive, but he knew that was impossible to do. He wondered if he was in this jail or if it was someone else from his group. He missed his best friend and wished he was there with him now, as he had been every time he needed him.

"Do you know Juma Ahmed Agoub?"

"No," he said instinctually. Then his eyes grew large. *Juma.* How did he forget Juma? He had that kid under his wing; he had taken him everywhere. He could feel the anger rising in him and tried hard to conceal it. He could feel his face going flush. He put it out of his mind and went back to denying everything and everyone he knew.

30. Imagining Things

Ali was weary, headed back to work yesterday. When he arrived, he felt at home. He knew that it was where he belonged, and he could feel it in his heart more than ever: he was meant to have this job. He was confident that he was to turn in Mullah Abdullah; he had been mulling it over the whole time he was home. He knew he had to do something about this supposed spiritual guide influencing the young people of this country to ruin their lives.

Ali lay awake in his makeshift bed at 5 a.m.; he thought about the mission they were going on today to capture him, and it made him restless. He didn't sleep much anyway; what happened at the mosque haunted him. Getting to work was dangerous, and he heard about the bodies of Iraqi police and National Guard strewn about the streets, but he knew what he was doing today was going to help change that. He rolled out of bed and looked around the room at his sleeping men and decided to let them have two more hours of sleep. Ali conducted his morning prayers, pulled on his uniform, and headed to the operations room.

He stopped outside the door, as he could hear Major Saleh talking inside. Ali took a deep breath and pushed the door open. As soon as he did, the two other men talking to Major Saleh left the room, leaving Ali uncomfortably alone with Major Saleh. Ali sat down at his desk.

"Good morning, sir. How are you?"

Major Saleh seemed angry as he looked up from his paperwork and spun around, meeting Ali's eyes. "Do you realize what you're doing?"

Ali immediately snapped to attention and hurriedly glazed over all his activities that morning to learn if he did something wrong. He stared dumbfounded back at Major Saleh.

"Well, do you?" he said with agitation and a raise in his voice.

"Sir, I am getting ready for the day."

"Not that," Major Saleh said, rolling his eyes. "This mullah may say what he wants. He has freedom of speech, and who are you to take that away?"

Ali was confused and couldn't help but stare at the angry officer. He couldn't discern if Saleh was mad that they were arresting the man or that they were stripping him of his freedom of speech. "I'm not sure what you mean, sir," Ali finally spit out.

Major Saleh began to breathe heavily. Just then, the two men who were in the office earlier scurried back through the door and stopped dead in their tracks, as Major Saleh rose and took a step toward Ali. Saleh then stopped and looked over at the men in the doorway and back at Ali. He turned and pushed his way through the two men who were standing stunned at the doorway. The pair looked at each other and then at Ali, just as confused as Ali was. They then looked back at each other and went straight to their desks and started working without saying a word.

Ali decided he should probably leave the operations room until there were enough people in the room that there wouldn't be another confrontation. Ali went to the roof and peered at the city, which was beginning to come to life. With the curfew at night, the city looked abandoned, in stark contrast to the day, when there were so many people running about their business, it was impossible not to get lost in the chaos. Ali sipped his coffee and watched as people started to creep into the streets in ones and twos. He looked down at his watch after a while and noticed it was fast approaching the time he should get his men up. He headed down from the roof to the operations room.

"Good morning, Ali," Salem's calming voice said as Ali walked through the door. He was going through a stack of papers.

"Good morning, sir," Ali said, sitting down next to him in the cramped, overcrowded office. Even with few people in it, all the desks and chairs made it feel full.

"What is it?" Salem said without looking up from his task at hand.

"Sir, when someone preaches jihad, is he exercising his freedom, or is he wrong?" Ali said in a low voice.

Salem put down his paper and turned with a grimace to look Ali in the eyes. "If you are asking about the imam, son of a bitch, that threatened all of us, including you and your family, you have a problem."

Ali nodded. "I don't know what I was thinking."

"Have your men ready by 1100. You get back here by 1000," Salem said as he returned to the task that had him searching through a large stack of papers.

Ali got his men up and had them clean half the building. By the time they were done, it was almost time for them to leave. He had them get ready and get the trucks ready to go. Ali headed back to the operations room; inside were Americans and Iraqi National Guard. Salem came over to him, "You can pick two men to go with you. The rest of your men are staying here. Have them help with guard duty. We will go with the National Guard."

Ali was annoyed but had his fill of confrontations with leadership for the day and decided not to protest; besides, his men would be happy to stay here. Ali went out to tell them the good news. As he reached the front door, Major Saleh stopped him. "You aren't going. I will go for you."

Ali stared back at him; he didn't like what he was up to but decided there was no fighting a man with such conviction in his voice.

"I need two of your men to accompany me," Saleh barked as he walked away.

Ali watched Major Saleh push his way down the hallway. He couldn't help but wonder what had transpired with Saleh that day. Why had he been so angry without provocation? Why would he go on a raid? His type never did. Ali knew everything about Mullah Abdullah, including where he lived, worked, hung out, and all the members of his family. He then turned his attention to changing the orders for his men.

After his men were sent out with fresh orders, Ali sat down in a small break room and sipped on tea. Salem entered the room, sat down next to him, poured himself a small cup of tea, and began emptying ten sugar packets, slowly stirring it into his cup. Ali didn't say a word and just watched his actions. He considered voicing his concerns about Major Saleh, but instead thought it was his duty to keep his mouth shut.

Just as Salem was stirring in his last packet of sugar, the front door to the building slammed open. Ali and Salem got up and rushed to peer down the hallway and found Major Saleh storming their way, his helmet under his arm and his vest undone and dangling from his shoulders. Ali stepped back into the break room and allowed the angry man to continue on his mission that would lead him to the end of the hallway.

Ali then went to find his men he sent with Major Saleh. He found them outside, sitting on the wall, smoking cigarettes. Their gear lay at their feet. Ali overheard one question the other: "Why is he is so pissed off? We got the guy, and nothing went wrong."

The other spouted back, "I heard him earlier, trying to convince the National Guard and the Americans that he knew him and he was not at the mosque."

Ali didn't say a word to them and turned and went back into the building. He was determined to tell someone that something wasn't right, but he had to find someone he could trust. Ali heard on the news in Baghdad all the time that corruption ran rampant in their police force, but he never imagined it occurring in his own police station, in his own chain of command. In Baghdad, they rout out the corruption and find it often goes all the way to the top. Many of the police were surprised to find out about their leaders. Ali paced to the end of the hallway and back, unsure of where to go or who to talk to.

Thoughts raced through his head. *There is no way that the chief of police is dirty, but then again Major Saleh is always with him. Is Major Saleh supposed to be with him? Is that his job? I can tell Salem. Can I? Would anyone believe me? Am I thinking too much into this? I can go way out of bounds and tell Americans. No, no! I need more proof, evidence; hardcore, irrefutable evidence.* Ali thought back to every time he talked to Major Saleh. *I didn't talk to him much before he got promoted. After I got promoted, he said very little other than giving me orders; he congratulated me when he found out my wife was pregnant.* He couldn't think of anything else that was strange.

Gunshots rang outside the police station. The noise flashed Ali back to the day of the big attacks. Major Saleh was standing by a truck, and his ear was covered. He remembered seeing Major Saleh turn; he was on a cell phone. Cell phones are not allowed for low-ranking guys. Was that okay? Ali's breath became rapid as the details of that split second of time filled his mind. The pain and anguish of that evening paused as he relived that moment at a slow, tormenting pace. He had Major Saleh in his sights when incoming was shouted, and he hit the dirt, Major Saleh still on his phone, still talking. No words could be heard, just the fact that he was still on the phone. Ali was crawling toward the wall as fast as he could and still would catch Major Saleh on his phone. Then the screaming, the screaming of his men drew his attention away from Major Saleh. Ali could feel the moment as if it was real and wanted very much to help the screaming man.

Ali leaned up against the wall in the hallway, overcome with the moment. He turned his back fully to the wall and slid down to the floor. Ali wanted to cry and found it hard to breathe, reliving this moment. In his mind, the event played again; the mortars came in, gradually getting closer to the building. It all happened so fast. When they stopped, Ali ran toward the screams. He called for medics, looking back at the station. Major Saleh was off his phone and running back into the building. Ali shook his head. Was he thinking too much into this?

Ali stood up and started to pace the hallway again; he found himself leaned against the door to Salem's office. He stopped and was poring over memories, circumstances. He felt a tap on his shoulder. Ali ignored it at first, not realizing he was in a hallway, but somewhere in his thoughts. Then he felt his shoulder being grabbed, dragging him back into reality, into the hallway of the police station.

"Are you okay?" he finally heard from Salem's lips. He didn't know how to answer or what to answer. "Ali," Salem repeated.

Ali turned his full attention to Salem and stood up straight, looking at Salem, finding his thoughts still racing. "Sir, fine, I am fine sir."

"Ali, you are clearly not fine. Come in; we need to talk." Salem walked into his office, beckoning Ali to follow. Ali reluctantly followed him, and Salem closed the door behind him.

Salem sat at his desk, and the two sat closed-mouthed, staring at each other. Ali couldn't decide if Salem was the one he should tell, but he could feel it bubbling up from inside of him. Several minutes passed. Ali finally squeaked out, "Major Saleh, I ... well, there has been strange things happening, and well, I don't know what to think."

Salem bounced back, "I thought I was just imagining those things. This is something we have to tread lightly on. If you have something to tell me, know that you can, and I will handle it."

With that, Ali started to talk about all he had seen.

31. It Was so Easy

Abu-Zah'ara woke up to the sound of footsteps in the rocks outside his door. It was hot. He gazed at the ceiling, pondering what he had to do today. At the sound of a loud clang, he sat up, and his heart broke. "I'm in jail," he whispered to himself as he pulled himself to his feet. The guard was telling him to do something. Abu-Zah'ara did not understand. He pulled on his orange jumpsuit that he had taken off to survive the heat that seemed to make his cell smaller.

"Badge," he finally heard. He pulled out the piece of paper that was given to him by the Americans and slid it through the small window that gave light from the sun. The guard threw it back at him and opened the door.

He slid on his sandals and stepped out into the sun, which seemed harsher than it ever had in his whole life. It was only harsh because it didn't bring him comfort. All his life, the sun reminded him that he was working hard. While he was a laborer in Kurdistan, it gave him strength to work and survive. In the past couple of years, the sun provided beauty over the land he fought for and believed in. He never felt more free his whole life than he did when he was accompanied by his men as they all worked together and then sat together to reflect on everything they had done. After the big attacks, he felt like he was on clouds. He was fighting for Allah, and he had followers. Today, the sun was beating on him and did not comfort him.

After using the bathroom, Abu-Zah'ara was escorted back to his dungeon. He was shattered. He reminisced about the day of the big attack, the chaos. It was so well orchestrated, it was hard to believe it happened. He was sure they were going to win, but within days, everything fell apart. This jail still stood, unaffected by all his efforts. Abu-Zah'ara wondered how many and which of his fighters and other fighters from other resistances accompanied him in this jail.

The little slit in his door was opened, and Abu-Zah'ara was handed his first breakfast in the jail. It was a plastic bag with the type of meal that was dropped from the sky after the Americans first came to his country. He remembered trying them before and recalled that they were not very good.

He sat with it in his hand and contemplated about his hard work, wanting to know just how much he had accomplished. He had never really thought about it before. The thoughts raced through his mind, and he didn't even bother to open his breakfast.

The guard came back, opened the door, and escorted him back to the room that was occupied by his interrogator and her Syrian interpreter. Abu-Zah'ara paused at the door and took a deep breath. The day would be long. He didn't feel like he'd had any sleep; he felt like he had closed his eyes, and when they opened, the night had passed by. He still was hoping it was all a bad dream. Now it had become very real. He stepped in the doorway and stopped.

The interrogator attempted speaking Arabic and asked him to take a seat. As he made himself comfortable in the plastic chair, he wondered what was in store for him today. He hadn't given it thought. Until now, he was trying to decide if he was actually in jail. Now he was staring at the face of his little sister, but the face sat on an American. It pained him to be reminded of his sister, but in a strange way it also comforted him.

He had been in jail less than a day, and he felt beaten down. Others who had been captured said the first few days were the worst; then it becomes normal. It was hard now to sit and downplay everything he was so proud of, all his accomplishments. He rarely boasted of the things that he had done, but he often relished them in private. Never in his wildest dreams did he imagine this day. He never took the time to think back on what he had done, from the day he walked away from the training camp, back into his life. Not even the day he got back home or the day he met with Mullah Abdullah. He often worked so hard for the future, he did not realize what had actually happened. Now as he brought his eyes to meet with the interrogator's, he could not handle the pain that soaked into his joints, muscles, heart, and brain. As they started to talk, his mind drifted off to someplace distant. Every answer was rehearsed. He tried to focus, and his interrogator's words finally settled in to his mind.

"Well, how is Mosul now?" she asked him.

"It's hard to describe."

"What do you mean?"

"Mosul changes all the time; it has its ups and downs," Abu-Zah'ara said, sure the ups for him were the downs for the Americans.

"Ups and downs?" she returned.

The Land Between Two Rivers

"Well, under Saddam, we were oppressed, and the Americans came and filled us with hope for a better life."

"Is it?"

"Yes." Again he knew that *better* for him was not the same as what she must have been interpreting it to be.

"How is it?"

"People are free."

"But are people safe?"

"That is the problem—people can make a living, but there is no stability," Abu-Zah'ara said.

"What is not stable?"

"People can get caught in crossfire between the Americans and the resistance."

"Why else is it not stable?"

Thoughts started to flash through Abu-Zah'ara's mind. There was so much he had wanted to say about the occupation of his country, but he knew the words would give him away. He held his tongue and said, "I don't know." That was easier than trying to think of anything else to say.

His small interrogator pulled out a pack of cigarettes, pulled one out with her teeth, and lit it. She had smoked during the last interrogation, but this time it hit him—he had never seen a female smoke. He himself didn't smoke because it was a prohibited act.

"Well, do you know anyone that has been harmed in the crossfire between the Americans and the resistance?"

Abu-Zah'ara didn't quite understand where she was going with her questions; this was not at all what he had in mind for questioning. He thought of his father and his sister. "I have heard about it; I don't know of anyone, though."

"Give me an example," she said leaning forward in her chair.

"Once I heard that my neighbor's cousin was in the market when there was a fight between the terrorists and the police. The police started to fire randomly into the crowd and killed him."

The interrogator probed for more information about the incident. Abu-Zah'ara had made it up at that moment and found it hard to produce details.

"Who do you blame for his death?" she asked as she sat back.

"The police," he said matter-of-factly.

"Why the police?"

She was incessant with her questioning of everything, "The police are always fast to shoot and arrest people, even though they are innocent. The police are no different than they were under Saddam's regime."

"What do you mean?"

"They are not helping people," Abu-Zah'ara said, rolling his eyes and leaning forward. "They are just making the situation worse."

"We are noticing that trend, and we are always curious to hear how they are affecting people," the interrogator said as she puffed on her cigarette.

Abu-Zah'ara couldn't help himself; the Americans were agreeing with him, and he relished just how much he hated the police—probably more than he should have.

The interrogator uncrossed her legs and leaned forward, resting her forearms on her knees. "It doesn't surprise me that they were attacked."

"Me either," Abu-Zah'ara blurted out, unable to deny his own masterpiece. "It was quite the sight to watch them collapse. When they ran away without a fight, anyone could tell they were truly cowards." Abu-Zah'ara suddenly sat straight up and shook his head, knowing he shouldn't have said that.

"And just how did you see that?" the interrogator said without blinking an eye.

"I didn't see anything; I only heard about it," he pushed out in a thinly veiled contradiction to his previous statement.

"That's too bad. I wish I could've seen them run away. The cowards they were. Ever since I heard about the attacks, I always wanted to know how they went down," she said, leaning back in her chair and extinguishing her cigarette in the ashtray that sat on the table to her side.

Abu-Zah'ara was taken aback by her comment and the thoughts of an American toward the police. He couldn't help but bask in what she was saying. He asked questions about the attacks as if he didn't know anything about it.

"I heard the police at Yarmook were in a standoff with the resistance for hours before finally giving up," she said when he asked about one of the smallest police stations. "I heard they put up the biggest resistance before giving up."

"It was so easy," Abu-Zah'ara said. That was one place he was physically at during all the attacks. "We walked up and told them to leave, and they did. There wasn't any fighting. After they left, we took the weapons, and I had them set the place ablaze and set off a small bomb."

"We?" she said, acting disinterested as she turned to her interpreter to light her next cigarette.

"The resistance," Abu-Zah'ara said matter-of-factly and continued on. "The Yarmook police station gave up so fast. Headquarters, though, that wasn't an easy task. But we gave it our best shot."

"What were you doing during all this?" she said as she jotted down a note on her notepad.

"They gave me an AK, and I was just there. I didn't even shoot," Abu-Zah'ara said, downplaying who he was. It felt good to talk about it all. He talked about pulling up to the Yarmook police station, and how two men went inside. A few minutes later, the police all left. Most of them had dropped all their police gear in the station and were leaving just in their white T-shirts that they wore under their uniform.

"I guess headquarters didn't quite go as easily as that."

"*That* was a battle!" Abu-Zah'ara said, grabbing her pen and flipping to a new page in her notebook. He drew a square and around it another one. "This is headquarters," he said, writing *headquarters* across the building. He then drew lines toward his squares. "First we hit them with mortars," he said, looking up to meet his interrogator's eyes, making sure she understood. "The mortars softened them up. The cowards there would run with the mortars. That's why we started with them." This time he drew dotted lines toward the square. "Then we started to shoot them. At first, we just hit them from this side," he said, pointing to one side of his makeshift drawing. "See, it's opposite the main road," he said, drawing the road.

The interrogator nodded as the interpreter leaned over from the far side of the table to get a better look.

"This was good; we wanted to distract them from the main road." Then the Americans showed up, which was great, because we weren't expecting it. "So we waited a minute but kept distracting them from the one side. Then the best thing happened: the brave martyr, Abu-Sultan, followed them in the gate and blew up inside the gate," he said, stabbing at the paper, indicating the place where the car blew. He leaned back, still holding the pen, nodding and waiting for approval.

"Abu-Sultan—you haven't mentioned him before. What's his real name?" the interrogator said, looking at the drawing on her yellow notepad.

"I don't know," he said, shaking his head. He leaned forward and started to darken the lines he already drew. "He came from Syria just to fight jihad, and he did very well."

"Were there others like him?" the interrogator said, trying to meet Abu-Zah'ara's gaze.

Abu-Zah'ara threw the pen back on the notepad and leaned back. He had said way more than he should have and knew he couldn't say anything else.

The interrogator kept probing for more information. Abu-Zah'ara went back to his old tactic. "I just heard about this stuff. I wasn't actually there." It was one of his best creations, and he was proud of it, but if he spoke any more of it, he could put his men in danger.

This didn't stop the interrogation; it went on for hours. She even stopped for thirty minutes to give him lunch, but he was so drained and upset, he didn't really eat anything. When they finally finished in the early afternoon, he was starving. He hadn't eaten all day, and come to think of it, because of the events yesterday, he didn't eat much then either. Went he got back to his little room, breakfast was still sitting on the floor. He started to eat it to quell his hunger. It wasn't long before the guard came back and took it away from him. He lay down on his thin mattress and thought about the last day. He talked some, yes, but he didn't give out names or places. This gave him some comfort; he hadn't put anyone in harm's way.

The interrogator incessantly asked him about attacks on Americans, ambushes, roadside bombs, and mortars. He kept saying he didn't know anything, but it got him thinking about all the attacks he had carried out. At the time, that was all that mattered: the attack being carried out. He thought back to each attack and couldn't think of much tangible evidence of success. Most of the time, they attacked and ran; there was no time to assess damage. He didn't know how many died, how many got injured, or what happened to their equipment. *The Americans took their broken equipment home or destroyed it even more so we couldn't even look at it.* He thought about all the roadside bombs. *Come to think of it, most of the time the Strykers were hit with a bomb, they drove off; maybe not at full speed, but drove off nonetheless.*

The Americans went nonstop, and it was hard to stay in front of them. In fact, as his group grew and attacks became more frequent, the Americans kept coming back, faster and stronger. He hadn't really thought of this before. He was so concerned with keeping missions going, expanding his group, and keeping the weapons coming in. He saw every mission as a success. Even if nothing happened, no one was hurt, no damage was done, it didn't matter; it was not a failure. Abu-Zah'ara thought of this as he tossed and turned on his little mattress for hours. Even after his dinner, he couldn't stop thinking of this. He couldn't sleep. Then he saw the Koran sitting in the corner, the one the Americans gave to him when he got there. He started to read and found his mind was finally starting to rest.

32. Someone Has to Fight

Ali and his men entered headquarters from a checkpoint that they were manning for the last twelve hours, covered head to toe in sweat. His men were exhausted but in good spirits because some of them would be headed home tonight. Because of the attacks, they were forced to stay at work for more than a week at a time; there was no real set shift. Some of his men would not be able to go home for a few more days.

The collapse of the police stations in Mosul put the city in chaos. People did not realize the importance of the police until they were gone. Coupled with the collapse, more than half of the remaining police force quit. The leftover police, and some who had quit, along with the National Guard members were being kidnapped and killed in the masses. The bodies were left all over the city, with their ID cards attached to their clothing. When they did go home, they would hide in their tribal relatives' homes and would not leave, not until they had to come back. Everyone was afraid. Going to their tribal village seemed to be the best option. No one in the tribe would let anything happen to them. Some of the younger men didn't leave work at all.

Ali's men started requesting to wear ski masks to hide their identity. He allowed them as soon as he saw the other squads all doing the same thing. They needed security forces, and if that is what it took to keep them at work, they weren't going to stop them. Most of the police stations' workforces had shrunk drastically, or they had been blown up, forcing the men at those stations to go to headquarters to ask for a job. Rumors spread quickly that it was an inside job. It had to be; there was no other explanation for them to give up without a fight. Of the men asking to keep a job, few of them actually got one. No one knew who they could trust.

Of Ali's men, only two quit at the request of the terrorists. They all stood along that wall and fought the terrorists during the battle and weren't about to give up. Ali thought they were very brave. It gave him strength. They spoke of a safer Iraq. They hated the terrorists and wanted justice for the men who had died. Every one of his men agreed that they were using the name of the *mujahideen* to kill innocent civilians, their own people, women, children, and men. Mercy no longer existed for the *mujahideen*. These men were giving everything up for the freedom of the Iraqi people. Even if it meant they stripped themselves of freedom to do so. They didn't go home, because they were watched like prey for a hawk. They couldn't go out, shop, drink tea, drive down the road; nowhere was safe. Despite all of it, they still came to work. They found strength in each other.

"Quit and the terrorists win," Ali repeated to his men before they would leave. He could see they needed a break. They were all working overtime, and break time was a thing of the past. He sent his men home. He was supposed to have a day or two off also, but he wasn't sure it was going to happen.

Ali went to check in with Salem. "Hello, sir. How was your day?" Ali asked him.

"Probably better than yours," he said to Ali as he was wiping the sweat dripping from his brow. "Actually pretty good, what about yours?"

"Could be worse."

"How is your family?"

"Allah knows, it has been some time since I have seen them. And yours?"

"Thanks to Allah, they are well. I have some good news," Salem said, pushing past the pleasantries. He motioned for Ali to take a seat, and Ali came in and sat down.

Salem leaned over. "They arrested Saleh today."

Ali smiled but was still in shock. "I was worried I was making all that up."

"I was worried we were paranoid too. A few days ago, I got the nerve to walk up to Lt. Colonel Ilyas, and he said several people have noticed Saleh doing odd things. Today they set some sort of trap for him, to see if he would release information. He did, and they arrested him."

"Wow," Ali said, pausing to feel the cool breeze from the oscillating fan in Salem's office. "So, who is going to take his place?" He looked over and noticed that he was now addressing *Major* Salem. "Congratulations," Ali said, standing up and reaching his hand out to shake Salem's. "When did this happen?"

"This morning," Salem said, standing up, shaking Ali's hand, and cupping his other hand around his. "They are looking at you to take my place. You didn't hear that from me."

Ali smiled; he didn't expect this.

"On a happier note, it's your turn to go home."

Ali sighed with relief. "How long?"

"Two days, but as always, keep your phone on. We may need you back sooner."

Ali immediately turned to leave; he wasn't about to let him change his mind. "Roger, sir," he said with one foot out the office door. He headed straight for the bunk room and changed into his civilian clothes. He called his brother and asked him to come and get him in the alleyways behind the market near the station. His brother was happy to oblige. Ali also asked to stay at his house; he knew going home wasn't really an option. Ali's wife had been staying there ever since the attacks anyway.

He left the office nervous for the trip home but in good spirits. The possible promotion was great news. He also missed his wife, who was increasingly concerned with his chosen profession. She was trying to provide support he need to continue, but he could tell that she was scared.

Ali's family was the same way. "You are married, and you have a child on the way. You have responsibilities now. Time to quit your job." His mother's words echoed in his ears. He was sick of explaining himself and tried to avoid the topic altogether.

His brother was waiting for him in the alley when he walked up. They hugged and jumped in the car. They needed to hurry to beat the curfew home. After the collapse, the Americans changed the curfew to 6 p.m. to hold down problems incited by the terrorists. It was already after five. They went straight to his brother's house, which was on the other side of the river. They drove around in the neighborhood for a little bit, to make sure no one was following them. They then quickly darted into his brother's gate and locked it behind them.

After dinner, Ali was left in the visitor's room with his wife. Ali was hesitant about telling her about the possible promotion, but he was excited and wanted to share it with someone. "I might be promoted to Captain," Ali finally said to break the silence between them.

She smiled in congratulations, but the fear exuded from her every movement.

"It's possible I will take Salem's job. He was just promoted to Major."

With those words, she put her head in her hands and started to cry. She paused for a moment and looked up at him, with the tears streaking her makeup that she had put on especially for his homecoming tonight. "This means you are a bigger target, and we will never be a family in our own home," she squeaked out between her sobs. "What about our child?" she said, crying louder. "What if something is to happen?"

At first, Ali leaned in to comfort her, but anger overcame him. He was sick of it. "What do you mean, *what about our child?* What about the terrorists? If no one stands to fight them, then our child could be killed. If no one stands up against them, they will walk all over us. We will be forced under their archaic laws and treated like nobodies, like Afghanistan." Ali stood up and paced around the room. "The Americans may be here now, but what happens when they leave? Who stops the terrorists then? Who will be strong against them?" he said, raising his arms, palms up. "I want a child that has no worries. My promotion will bring more money for *our* child, and *our* home. Soon we will make it safer, and I will be able to go home. *Someone* has to fight, and I *choose* to *fight*. This is not just some job," he said, shaking his head. "This should be the duty of all Iraqis! If we had more support, the terrorists would not think they could do whatever they want."

Ali stood stiffly in front of his sobbing wife. He had half a mind to beat her for her comments, but the thought of his unborn child stopped him. He grabbed his brother's cigarettes, which were on the floor next to her, and went out the front door, slamming it behind him before she had a chance to respond.

Ali sat down on a flimsy plastic chair on his brother's front porch. He lit a cigarette and listened to the dead neighborhood. There was no life; everyone was in their homes due to the curfew. At work he was very proud of his job as a protector of people. He hated that he had to come home to this. While he worked his long hours, his heart yearned to go home and to be with his family, but when got home, he was sick of the lack of support and wanted to be around the people who shared his beliefs for a better, safer Iraq. He knew in his heart of hearts that he made a difference every day. *Why could no one else see it? Where was the missing link?* How could he show them, other than going to work every day and doing his best and making the situation better? That's all he could think. After finishing his cigarette, he put it out and stared into the darkening sky. In the end, he decided that was all he could do: go to work and continue on his thankless job that would one day show its fruits, and only he would understand. He wondered if other police officers and soldiers had these same problems. He was sure he was not alone, but those people all came to work every day. Ali walked in the door, now that he had given up on explaining himself. He just wanted to share his possible promotion with someone. He decided to keep work talk at work if he wanted to come home in peace.

Ali went into the guest room and looked at his wife with disappointment. He thought of the child who was soon to come and half-smiled. He could not wait for his arrival.

Ali then lay down on a mattress and tried to fall asleep but found himself tossing and turning because he was still mad. After what seemed an eternity, his wife broke the silence. "I'm sorry."

Ali cringed; he didn't want to hear what was next.

"I guess I never think about the future; I just worry about raising a child alone. I want safety for our child as much as you. It seems that you're very good at your job, and your superiors believe in you. When I hear you talk, I believe in you. I guess it would be far worse if terrorists did what they wanted and our child was raised in fear."

Ali sat up and looked over at his wife, who was staring at him, her legs crossed and makeup halfway wiped up her cheeks. She seemed to be sitting there for some time. He missed her touch. He moved over to her and kissed her.

33. Re-up

Jeremiah was in for a good day; he could feel it when pulled himself out of bed in the morning. First thing he wanted to do was call McKayla. He missed her so much and wished she could be here for this day, more than any other day. Jeremiah decided to sign another contract with the army. He loved his job, he felt like he made a difference, and McKayla was supportive of him. He loved to serve his country and along the way help other people. Above all, he loved the men he worked with and wanted to be there for them. How could he leave them to fend for themselves?

He mourned for Wynn and Duncan, but he knew they made the ultimate sacrifice for America, sacrifices that not even the people of the United States would ever understand. Sure Jeremiah wanted them to understand, but he settled with the fact that they would not, and that is what made the US such a great country: soldiers were willing to give their lives for something people did not realize lingered at their doorsteps. This allowed them to live a happy life, unhindered by the problems people in every country worried about every day. Jeremiah wanted to be there to do his best and more, for a cause only seen by the people who surrounded him.

This morning, they would have his re-enlistment ceremony. He was going to rededicate himself to the United States Army, an organization he had grown to love and trust. He knew it would not be easy. There were always times that he "hated the army," but deep down, he never hated the army. He wanted to lead soldiers and make sure they were ready for whatever came across their path.

Jeremiah put on his cleanest uniform and made sure his boots were in good condition. He checked his weapon to make sure it was clean. He cleaned it every night, but wanted to make sure it was still good to go. He left his room and found himself automatically walking to the room that used to belong to Wynn and Duncan but realized they weren't there before he knocked. He headed up to formation, in a location near the rooms, but afterward they would have to ceremony with the backdrop of the city of Mosul.

After formation, he headed over to the hill where the ceremony would be held and was surprised to see Lt. Colonel DeLuca in attendance. He offered to conduct the ceremony for Jeremiah and four other soldiers who were choosing the army as their career. Two soldiers held up a flag behind them as they swore in as a US soldier yet again. Jeremiah felt like he was on top of the world. He wanted to share it with his family and most of all McKayla.

After lunch, they were given some personal time before heading out on a mission again. Jeremiah decided to take that time to call home. Since he awoke, he had been longing to hear McKayla's voice, and now he wanted to share his day with her.

"Hello?" he heard her on the other end of the line.

"Hey, babe, it's me," Jeremiah said.

He could feel McKayla's excitement when she said, "Hi, babe."

"I miss you," he said immediately.

"Me too," she echoed back.

"I had my ceremony today. It was pretty cool. I will send you the pictures."

"I can't wait to see them," she said, leaving a long pause. "I went to Wynn's memorial service. It was heartbreaking. There was an old, retired general there ..."

"Babe," Jeremiah said, cutting her off. He loved his guys, but he already went to their memorial service here at the base, and well, he didn't know if he could really take much more of that. His saving grace was not thinking of it.

She stopped quickly. "Yeah?"

"Never mind, continue," he said, trying not to sound too insensitive.

"So the general, I guess he is a relative, was discussing how Wynn was always talking about how he wanted to do a good job, and he said that his mission has been accomplished," McKayla said with a crack in her voice. "I couldn't help but cry."

Jeremiah didn't know what to do. He missed his men and felt guilty in some ways for trying to be last off the ramp. He walked away with some bumps and bruises, and two of his best friends didn't walk away at all. He thought Duncan had a chance, but they weren't fast enough, and he lost too much blood.

"Thanks for going, babe," he finally said. "So my re-enlistment papers I signed today, well, I'm going to stay at Fort Lewis." Jeremiah said, trying to change the subject.

"I like that, and then I can be near my family."

"Babe, I love you. I gotta go. I only have a few minutes, and you know, I gotta call my mom."

"I love you; can't wait till you come home." Jeremiah heard the disappointment in her voice; he knew she wanted to talk longer.

"Bye, babe," he said, hanging up the phone. He felt bad. He didn't think she would understand anything he tried to explain to her and found it easier not to talk to her. He dialed his mom.

"Hey, Mom, did you hear the good news?" he said, going back to his excitement of re-enlistment.

"Hi, honey, good to hear your voice. What good news?"

"I just signed my re-enlistment for four more years in the army. I get to stay at Fort Lewis, in the same unit. I get ten thousand dollars too."

"Oh my God," his mom said and paused. He knew she wouldn't be that excited to hear the news. "What does McKayla think?" she said with a hint of annoyance, the most he would hear about the subject.

"She is excited for me."

"Do you have to go back to Iraq?" his mom said immediately, dismissing the answer to her previous question.

"Maybe, maybe Afghanistan," he said without regard to how upset this would make her.

"Afghanistan?" she exclaimed. "Well, if that is what you want, I'm happy for you."

"It is, Mom," he said.

His mom didn't answer, but he could hear muffled talking in the background. When she came back on the line, she said, "Your father wants to talk to you."

Jeremiah was surprised. He had hardly talked to him since he joined the army, little more than the usual pleasantries or the occasional hate mail, as everyone called e-mails that were so negative. He held his breath waiting for his father's ramblings.

"I got it," his father said, indicating that he had picked up a phone in a different room. "Son, what is this, you're going to Afghanistan?" he barked through the phone.

"Whoa, Dad, pump your brakes. That got blown out of proportion really quick. All I did was re-up, and you never know exactly what it entails. Afghanistan is just a possibility. Before you say anything, Dad, I already signed the papers, and this is me ..."

His dad cut him off, "Son ... as much as I hate to say this, I understand. I know what it's like to have soldiers and to be around other soldiers," his father said, breathing deeply. "It's like the most important thing is to take care of each other. You don't have to explain."

Jeremiah sat in shock and nearly dropped the receiver. He couldn't believe what he was hearing and pinched himself to make sure it wasn't a dream.

"Back when I was in the military, I considered extending in 'Nam because I felt bad leaving my soldiers. I'm not saying I like what you're doing. You know I hate this war, but I know where you're coming from. I'm just concerned for you, son. I never wanted you to go through what I went through. All I can say is do your best," Jeremiah's dad said, and he could hear him place the phone down on the counter and walk away.

Jeremiah still didn't believe that just happened.

His mom picked up the phone. "Jeremiah?"

"Mom ... tell Dad ..." Jeremiah couldn't think of the words. "Tell Dad *thank you*."

34. Jihad

It had been several weeks since Abu-Zah'ara lost his freedom, and as his men had said, it had become normal to be imprisoned but not comfortable by all means. The previous night he had integrated into a larger cell with twenty other men. To Abu-Zah'ara's surprise, there were less than a handful of men from his group. Almost everyone had heard of him. It made him wonder how big his group was. He knew it was large but didn't quite know the extent. He knew he was not the only group in town, but he always thought his was the largest. The exact numbers were never known to him, because he didn't ask his men who and how many men they had.

Abu-Zah'ara still pondered what happened that day at the meeting house. What he gathered from his daily talks with his interrogator was that Abu-Sayf and Abu-Ahmed were either captured or killed. He missed the companionship that Abu-Ahmed gave him and the hard work he had done. In other circumstances, Abu-Ahmed would probably be in command of his deeply tied network that ran Mosul and the surrounding areas. Now there was Abu-Zakiriyah, Abu-Aiya, and Towfiq. Towfiq was new to the area and did not know too many people. He could carry out his own missions, but he would run out of money. Abu-Aiya could more or less carry out a mission. He didn't seem to have the ambition to worry about a larger group of people. As for Abu-Zakiriyah, he seemed to want to take care of everything and probably would. This put Abu-Zah'ara at ease.

Abu-Zakiriyah's heart was in the group, and he had dedicated himself to the cause of jihad. In the beginning, he was one of the men who had no training, not even in the military, but that did not stop him. He went out and learned about weapons and how to make bombs. He was a deeply religious man and was always elated when he tried something new and it appeared to work.

Appeared ... Abu-Zah'ara thought to himself. As was the case every day, he had no idea most of the time if it actually worked or what level would measure success. Day in and day out, he was planning attacks, conducting them, losing people, recruiting new ones, and all the while keeping the money and the weapons flowing. Abu-Zah'ara knew that even the news inflated numbers, and there was no way of knowing what was real. He could never tell how much was done or if anything he did ever made that much difference.

Sitting in jail, it seemed completely safe. There was no worry. That upset Abu-Zah'ara; it meant that his attacks were not penetrating fear into the Americans. Occasional explosions would echo into the jail, but the guards were unfazed and just continued about their activities. It was different to be on the receiving end of the mortars, but it didn't faze anyone. Abu-Zah'ara was not scared; he had been shot at on several occasions, but it was irritating to find these people in the same state—fine.

As the day crept on in his cell, Abu-Zah'ara talked with the other inmates, but he became restless as the day continued. He kept waiting for his name to be beckoned to go and talk to his interrogator. He had grown used to talking to her; he knew she knew a lot about him. He didn't admit too much, but he did say he was an *Amir*. He had told her how his group started and how it evolved. He started to talk about the type of attacks they conducted but was careful to leave out specifics. He admitted to knowing some of his men but tried to explain to his interrogator that there was no way to know where they were. They move fast and change locations, especially after someone is arrested.

Dinnertime was getting close, and he was becoming more eager to talk to her. That was his normal routine, but today there was nothing. Maybe they were done talking. *Maybe she is taking a break. I'm sure she will come tomorrow,* he said to himself.

Tomorrow came and went; nothing.

The next day, while he was out in the yard, he saw her walking around outside of the yard. She smiled and waved. He walked up to the fence to talk to her, but she kept walking. He wanted so badly to talk to her. He liked talking about his group. In his jail cell, he didn't like talking too much about his involvement, for fear other Iraqis may turn on him. He might get others to join, but it wasn't worth it. Most didn't seem like they would make good fighters. He didn't think too highly of the few in his cell who were in the group. They were not religious and were only in it for the money. That enraged Abu-Zah'ara; the money was hard to come by and was supposed to help those who worked full time for the *mujahideen* and couldn't hold a job. Abu-Zah'ara still was nice to them; he wasn't about to kick someone out of his group.

Abu-Zah'ara thought about how he came to this crossroads in his life. He knew he was here for religious reasons, but he wasn't sure that was how he started down that road. When he went to the training camp, it seemed like something to do. At the time, he was religious, but not like the others at the training camp. Even after the camp, he felt he should do it because it came easily. When his sister died, it gave him the motivation to begin. During the attacks, everyone talked about the greatness of Allah, and he agreed. If he was doing something wrong, he would not be so successful. He was fighting for Allah, and he had no doubt he was doing the right thing.

Finally, after three days had passed since he'd talked to his interrogator, he finally got called to the little room where his interrogator sat, smoking her cigarettes. Her interpreter sat next to her, with his feet up on a chair, puffing a cigar.

"How are you today?" she asked with a smile on her face.

"Thanks to Allah, I'm good." Abu-Zah'ara said as he took his place in his chair and crossed his legs. Over time, he had become more comfortable and was not as concerned with the straight face he had always portrayed during the first few times he had talked to her.

"So, last time we left off talking about roadside bombs," she said, looking at her file that sat next to her.

"I remember."

"Did you figure out the answers to my questions?"

"I told you, I don't have any more answers."

"Right," she said, rolling her eyes and shooting a glance at her interpreter, "so who is your bomb-maker?"

"It's either Abu-Zakiriyah or Towfiq."

"You don't know which one?"

"They are both skilled in it, but I don't know who is currently making the bombs," he said, folding his arms.

"Towfiq, hmm," she said, pausing momentarily and looking around at her files and notebooks. "I don't believe you have mentioned Towfiq before. What's his full name?" she said with a smile that suggested she knew his full name.

"I don't know his full name. I only met him a few times. Before you ask, I don't know where he lives or sleeps or any of those hundred other questions you have," he said in anticipation of the thirty or so questions she always asked when he mentioned someone new.

"Okay, when is the first time you met him?"

"I don't remember; he just started showing up with Abu-Zakiriyah," he said, annoyed, and turned his head to look out the small window on the door.

"When did he start showing up?"

"About a month ago, or like a month before I decided to come here," he said with a slight laugh.

"Where is he from?" She was incessant with questions.

"I guess Mosul. I never asked."

"Where does he live?"

"I already told you I don't know."

"Where does he make his bombs?"

"That stays between Abu-Zakiriyah and him," he said, smiling. If he even knew, did she really think he would give up something so valuable? He knew she would always try for the information, but he kept that stuff to himself.

"Is Abu-Zakiriyah a good bomb-maker?"

"I believe so."

"Why the new bomb-maker?"

"We don't deny people who want to assist in the fight, especially people with skills and dedication like Towfiq."

"How are Towfiq's bombs different that Abu-Zakiriyah's?"

"The explosion is bigger, but like I said, I never have actually seen the bombs being made. So I can't tell you specifics. I watch them blow up; I'm not concerned with the rest."

"The larger explosion, is it more destructive?" she said, squinting her eyes.

Abu-Zah'ara thought about it. "I'm sure they are, but we don't really look at that."

"Then what do you measure?" she said then put down her notepad on the table. "How do you measure the success of a mission?"

"We don't measure success."

"What do you mean, you don't measure success?"

"I mean we don't."

"Then how do you know how well you're doing?"

"It doesn't matter."

"So you do all of this, and you're saying it doesn't matter? You don't care if you're losing or winning?" she said with a puzzled look on her face.

"You don't get it."

"Then explain it," she said, still very confused.

Abu-Zah'ara uncrossed his legs and crossed them the opposite direction. He leaned back in the chair and folded his arms. He thought about it for a second and then uncrossed his legs and leaned forward, looking directly at her. He wanted to make sure she understood, but it was hard to explain.

"When an attack is conducted, the success or failure is not evaluated."

She cut him off, "We've ..."

He held his hand up to interrupt, something he would not have gotten away with the first couple of weeks they met. "Let me explain. Once the trigger has been pulled and the bullet or rocket or whatever weapons you are using is shot, it is up to Allah what happens. Whether it strikes a person, the vehicle, or whatever the target is, it is totally up to Allah. Allah is the one making the decision if that other person is dying or living. We are fighting for Allah, so the choice he makes is the one that is right. As long as we are fighting, that is what matters."

"That doesn't answer my question," she said, obviously not happy with his answer.

Abu-Zah'ara leaned his elbows on his knees and reached his hands out as if he was trying to hand her the knowledge. "What I'm trying to say is ..." He couldn't get the words right. "The mission is successful as long as the trigger is pulled and the bullet is sent. It is successful if the RPG is shot. The mission is successful as long as you are there to fight; it is up to Allah what happens next. All we have to do is fight."

"Okay," she said, clearly stirring the answer around her brain, "so, you don't think aiming or a person who is a better shot should be taken into consideration?"

"Of course."

"Well, if it is up to Allah, and you are doing the right thing, then any man can go pull the trigger, and Allah will make it hit the person, the vehicle."

"Of course that is not what it's like. It's very difficult for me to explain."

"What you are saying is success is fighting, regardless of the outcome."

"That is our success."

With that, his frail interrogator pulled out a cigarette, lit it, and started puffing. She seemed to form questions and then give up on them, even muttering a few times to her interpreter. After a few minutes, she said, "You're speaking ideologically about your cause."

"Yes."

"Then, in your own personal opinion of your own accomplishments and what you've seen, do you honestly believe you will win this war?"

He turned this question over in his head, as he had been since his capture. He gestured that he needed time to think, holding up a finger. He always knew that no matter the outcome of the attacks, more Americans would appear. They came back—better, faster, and stronger—rarely repeating the same mistake twice. They changed their vehicles and technology to keep up with the group's changing techniques and technology. He looked up at her and said with a straight face, "No." He realized he had to qualify this answer.

"No? If the answer is no, then why do you fight?"

Abu-Zah'ara sat straight and puffed out his chest with pride and said, "Jihad."

"Why do you say no?"

"As I see it, we can blow up a Humvee or a Stryker, but the Americans have ten more to replace that one. You can kill one soldier, and one hundred more can replace him. We can change our methods, but the Americans catch up quickly."

"I don't understand why you're fighting a war that is unwinnable."

"It is jihad; I have to fight. You're occupying my country, and it is my duty as a Muslim to fight jihad. It is the duty of all Muslims to fight jihad. We have to fight, and that is why we fight. This is why we will continue to fight. No matter if we are 'losing' by your standards. We will always fight. It is our duty as Muslims. As long as you occupy our country we will fight jihad."

About the Author

Wilson hails from a long line of storytellers known for their captivating anecdotes of life. A veteran of the Iraq War, Wilson spent more than two years listening to the stories of Iraqis and American soldiers alike. Using lifelong skills, Wilson sketched together a story thought to best explain the war. Wilson enjoys life on the East Coast and has not yet chosen a place to call a permanent home.

Made in the USA
Lexington, KY
09 January 2013